THE
GALLERIST

Michael Levitt is a surgeon and health bureaucrat. He is the author of numerous scientific articles and medical textbook chapters, as well as three medical books for the general public. He is a sought-after public speaker and, in 2003, was awarded the Centenary Medal for services to public education about colorectal cancer.

Michael has been collecting art for many years, has launched art exhibitions and books about art, and has written numerous articles about art and artworks for newspapers, magazines and exhibition catalogues. An exhibition of selected works from the collection he has with his wife Carolyn was held at Ellenbrook Gallery in 2021.

This is Michael's first work of fiction.

THE GALLERIST

Michael Levitt

 FREMANTLE PRESS

'Such is the true purpose of art – not to be a depicter of mini-truths, but an imagiser of the Great Truth.'

Ernest Philpot (1906–1985)

1. WEDNESDAY NOVEMBER 13

Mark Lewis bade the customer farewell and returned to his desk. Alvin Teoh, a barrister working in chambers with one of Mark's established clients, was new to his gallery, and had dropped in a small work by John Passmore that he wanted Mark to sell for him. It was a lovely little painting, Mark thought, acquired by the early-career lawyer at an Eastern States auction three or four years earlier, although its setting – the Port Melbourne docks – was surprising. Passmore had lived and painted mostly from Sydney.

Mark had placed the Passmore on the easel next to his desk. He viewed it with interest and a little uncertainty as he headed to the kitchenette and switched on the kettle. He returned and opened his computer. The major auction houses had just made their spring sale catalogues available online and he was settling in to inspect the available works and projected prices before closing up at his leisure and heading home. It had, until Alvin's arrival, been a quiet Wednesday in his gallery after an uncharacteristically fresh and cloudy November day. The bubbling of the kettle announced the approach of a cup of tea to accompany his much-anticipated scan of the auction's offerings.

Lot 1 on the Sotheby's catalogue was a small portrait by William Dobell, the subject's face painted in a rounded and somewhat comical manner, unflattering yet full of empathy. Mark often wondered who, if not a close friend or relative, ever acquired these portraits. The pool of potential bidders for so many of the works throughout the catalogue was small, but for portraits especially – however well completed – that pool had to be truly tiny.

Unexpectedly, the gallery door opened and a gust of cool air blew in. Mark looked up, part in surprise given the hour, and part in disappointment as the kettle beeped its climax; he politely shut his laptop. Every visitor to his gallery mattered, every potential client warranted his full attention.

He recognised the woman who had entered, not as a client or even as a visitor, but as a local Mount Lawley identity he had often seen along Beaufort Street, shuffling to and fro with her grocery shopping, distinctive in her plain apparel and ever-present beret. She was easily in her sixties, short and plump. Mark, despite never having spoken to her, had generally imagined her to be single and unsophisticated, a harmless soul.

In the woman's arms was what looked like a painting wrapped in brown paper – perhaps two foot by three foot or smaller, if it was in a frame, he estimated reflexively. Mark knew what was coming. It would be a painting from home she hoped she could sell. As much as he loved seeing what people brought in, irrespective of quality or saleability, he never liked disappointing them with the reality of their unremarkable and difficult-to-sell pieces of art; and, imagining his guest to be uncomfortable in, even a little intimidated by, the gallery environment, he was especially unhappy at the prospect of disappointing her.

'Hello, come in, have you got something to show me?' he asked.

'Well I didn't drag this thing here in this breeze just to have a chat!'

He heard a broad Australian accent and no suggestion of any dis-comfort. There was a hint of mischief in her eye as she took off her beret, and Mark returned her smile. This would be fun, whatever he ultimately had to tell her.

'Put the painting on the desk,' he said, 'and tell me about it. I'm Mark Lewis. I recognise you from these parts. Do you live nearby?'

'Pleased to meet you too.' She spoke slowly and deliberately. 'I'm Jan Bilowski. I live in one of the apartments on Field Street, just behind here. I've walked past your gallery many times since you started it, but I've never come inside. To be honest, I hardly have any paintings and I often wonder what you or anyone else sees in the sort of paintings you sell here. If you ever do sell them!'

Mark smiled again. His was a gallery predominantly for the secondary market, older paintings often sold and bought many times before, and he expressed his own strong preference for abstract art in the works that he handled. Many people simply don't like abstract art, but those who did – God bless them – liked what his gallery offered very much.

Jan unwrapped the painting with little flourish or care. She opened the brown paper revealing the back of a cheaply framed masonite board, its portrait orientation evidenced by the frayed hanging wire secured to the frame at its top end and by the placement of the words written beneath the wire. The board was stained by age but had definitely once been white, and on it was painted:

To Katy
Love Charlie
November 1972

'Katy was my sister – Katarina – and this painting was hers. I suppose you could say that Charlie was her boyfriend. Anyway, that was ages ago.' Jan ran her hand lightly over the painted words to the edge of the board, her index finger dwelling on the edge for a moment. 'Katy had a disability from birth – cerebral palsy – and she lived with me for all of her adult life.

'Our parents died when we were both in our early twenties,' she added. 'Katy died last month. She treasured this painting, but I've never liked it at all.' She looked up at Mark. 'I'd like you to sell it for me. It looks like the sort of thing you'd sell.'

Mark turned over the painting and a ripple of shock ran through him. The work was bold, dark, abstract, powerful. It was immediately disturbing in its own right – but more: confusing and alarming because it looked so much like a James Devlin. Mark was not known for his poker face but he'd worked hard to mask his immediate reactions. Remaining composed and giving the appearance of considered thought – especially when confronted with something about which he knew little – was critical to building confidence and, ultimately, trust among clients and artists alike.

Despite his instant sense of recognition, Mark knew it was incredibly unlikely that this was a Devlin, and worryingly possible that this was some sort of scam. After all, the Australian art world had recently been damaged by forgery scams and was literally buzzing at the celebrated Victorian abstract artist's nomination for 2020 Australian of the Year.

Every major gallery in the country was displaying the Devlins in their collections, and Mark was aware that Sotheby's had even been able to extract a major work for their autumn auction. The time was ripe for a scammer to test the market with a fake Devlin.

But Jan wasn't making any effort to present the work to him as a Devlin. If someone had been trying to pass it off as such, the first thing they'd have done would be to ensure that it bore the distinctive red emblem that Devlin had always used as his signature. This painting had no such mark. And the date didn't fit – Devlin's short but intense period of fame came more than a decade later in his hometown of Melbourne. According to Jan's account, this work had been painted in Perth and had quite literally never left the state.

Mark stroked his chin as he studied the painting. 'Well this is very much the sort of piece that I would handle. I am sure you can tell that I like it.'

He felt her looking at him closely. 'You did go rather pale. I thought you might have seen it before.'

'Honestly, I never have.' Mark paused. 'I've just boiled the kettle – would you join me for a cup of tea?'

Jan was happy to do so. Mark made the tea, put some Tim Tams onto a plate and, putting the small Passmore aside, placed the painting on the easel for better viewing.

He sat down opposite her. 'What is the painting called?'

'I don't think it has a name. Katy always called it *Charlie's Painting*.'

'You said he was her boyfriend. Did you ever meet Charlie?'

'No, I didn't. He and Katy were students at the Sir James Mitchell School together. Charlie also had cerebral palsy.'

Mark raised his eyebrows and immediately regretted it, Jan reacting briskly.

'Actually, lots of the students had quite mild disability but still went there. He was always just Charlie to Katy,' she said. 'I never even knew his surname.' Jan took a breath as if to compose herself. 'They were at the school together before it was closed and moved to Coolbinia. Katy was really keen on him and she always said that he was very bright, and that he loved to paint. He gave Katy that painting as a gift when he finished at the school. I've always assumed he and his family moved away from Perth, which was why he never maintained contact. She was devastated when he left, and she hung that painting on her bedroom wall her entire life.'

'How old would he have been?' Mark asked, battling to connect such a sophisticated artwork with Jan's description of the artist.

Jan shrugged. 'I think he was a year older than Katy. This was around the time of her sixteenth birthday, so I suppose he was seventeen when he painted it for her.'

Mark continued to probe Jan for more information, about Charlie, Katy, her own life and her thoughts and preferences about art. Nothing gave Mark more pleasure than learning about the origins of the artworks that he handled, the stories of the people who painted and owned them, the times in which they were created, bought and sold. And Jan seemed pleased to have some company; her family's story of immigration and struggle, and her parents' untimely deaths was imparted with little hesitation.

Mark glanced repeatedly at the painting, its blue tones like those of Perth's summertime sky contrasting with the black at the painting's centre, full of foreboding and sadness. He imagined Katy and Charlie, two teenagers whose lives went in different directions, and the dark hole that separation left in each of their hearts. Had Charlie known he was leaving Katy when he made this painting? Mark looked again. The colours and the depth of emotions it evoked, the urgency of its brushstrokes, were typical of James Devlin. But who was Charlie and how did a mere teenager create this small masterpiece?

Tea and biscuits finished, and the sad story of the Bilowski family told, Mark formulated his response. 'I am happy to try to sell this work for you. For works that are brought into the gallery like this, I take exactly twenty percent of the total sale price, whatever that turns out to be. But honestly, Jan, I have no idea what this painting is worth. I've been obsessively interested in Australian art for over twenty years and I've never heard of any artist whose first name is Charles or Charlie who paints or painted works like these. I'm sorry to say it, but it will probably not be a valuable painting. But I need to find out if he went on to do anything else, if there are any other works of his around, if there is any reason to believe that this might be worth more than one or two hundred dollars.'

Mark saw concentration rather than disappointment on Jan's face.

'Can you leave it with me?' he asked. 'It'll probably be at least a fortnight before I can give you a more accurate price.'

'That's fine with me. There's no hurry.' Mark wrote out the receipt: 'Abstract painting. *Untitled (Charlie's Painting)*. Acrylic on masonite board. 90cm × 60cm. Inscribed verso: *To Katy. Love Charlie. November 1972.*'

2. WEDNESDAY NOVEMBER 13

Long before he opened his gallery, Mark had fantasised about stumbling upon a hidden art treasure. He imagined himself driving down a country road and seeing a handwritten sign – 'Art for sale' – then popping inside an old farmhouse to discover a rare work by Balson or Fairweather, Beckett or Preston, its value and importance unappreciated by its owners. And then figuring out the story that explained how it came to be where it was – the sequence of events, the personal tales of death and departure, the gifting and the purchase, the many layers of human experience that enriched the work.

And, having secured the treasure for sale in his own gallery, Mark fantasised also about the subsequent exchange between him and Patrick O'Beirne, fellow gallerist and mentor, when he would proudly uncover the work at their weekly catch-up. He imagined a multitude of pleasures: surprising Pat, the satisfaction of him confirming that Mark had accurately recognised the work for what it was, hypotheses batted back and forth, and the abiding delight of recounting the unique human story of the discovered painting. Mark was experiencing that fantasy now. Yet, rather than positive anticipation, he felt disquiet. For an hour after Jan left his gallery, Mark stood in front of Charlie's painting. What he felt most acutely was its sense of turmoil. The painting itself was dynamic, profoundly moving and full of mystery. As Pat would say of only the very best works, Charlie's painting was a work of which one would never become tired.

To Mark's eye, the painting was so similar to those of James Devlin – Mark was confident that it would rank very much among his best works: courageous in its execution, evocative and mesmerising in its impact upon the viewer. He continued to look at it, examining its colour scheme and rough brushwork, its energy and its depth.

By Mark's judgement, however, Jan's account of events surrounding the painting's provenance had a ring of authenticity. So, who had really painted this work? Charlie, probably; surely not James Devlin. Or had it been someone altogether more cunning? And, Mark wondered, was he simply overreacting, over-interpreting the work, because of his desire to unearth a rare treasure? This might be nothing more than Charlie's untitled painting, exactly as Jan described it. He needed a second opinion – he needed to consult Pat O'Beirne.

Mark collected the mugs and plates and washed them in the kitchenette. He dried them and put them away, leaving the gallery pristine so that he would be greeted by it in that state the next morning. He returned to his laptop and went to close it down – the image of the Dobell portrait prompting him to stop for a moment and search the catalogue for the Devlin that Sotheby's had listed for auction.

Lot 38: *Paradise* (1982) James Devlin, Acrylic on board, 120cm × 90cm, $30,000–$40,000.

Paradise was larger than Charlie's painting, but the materials were the same, and it also observed a portrait orientation. The blue of the online image, however, was of a deeper tone, the main colour was white rather than black, the dominant features were two geometric shapes painted in a pink hue that was nowhere to be seen in Charlie's painting; and the essential sentiment was lighter, almost joyous, in comparison to Charlie's ominous mood.

But the likeness of the two works was unmistakeable – the rough, dynamic brushstrokes, the sense of urgency and energy, and the power of the impression conveyed. *Paradise* was a strong work, and the price estimate indicated the auction house's confidence in Devlin's burgeoning appeal in the secondary market. But what was the significance, if any, of that generous price estimate for Jan and for Charlie's painting?

Mark picked up the new work, wrapped it again in Jan's brown paper, took it upstairs and placed it against the wall in the gallery's storage area. The painting, and Jan's story, had left him feeling unsettled and he preferred not to leave it on display.

❖❖❖

Mark's townhouse in North Perth was a gallery in its own right. Its walls were covered in paintings of different styles and sizes, different artists and periods, although the vast majority were abstract, originals and generally of no great monetary value. The larger, older and more valuable works that he and Sharon had collected over the years were, by Australian Government decree, on loan to a variety of institutions around Perth, where they would remain until either they were sold, or Australian law was changed.

In Australia, remarkably, some art acquired for the purposes of providing a benefit in retirement could not lawfully be seen and enjoyed by its owners. Years of trying to get through to politicians of all stripes to change this odious legislation had proved futile, other than for the insight it had given Mark into the constrained, unimaginative and fearful lives of Australian taxation officials, politicians and their bureaucrats.

Mark accepted that he would not see his major works again until they were ultimately sold. Still, he and Patrick continued to seek out politicians and journalists in the hope they might see the error and the risk attached to what amounted to state-sponsored censorship of art. The newly appointed Federal Arts Minister was a Western Australian with her offices based in Perth – they would be meeting her in the new year. They continued to hope.

Saddest of all, however, was that Sharon would never see any of their paintings again. She had died about three years ago as a consequence of the side-effects of medication for a particularly aggressive form of arthritis. Sharon had suffered stoically and – Mark gave thanks – only briefly. He felt sure that she would have enjoyed the display of art on his townhouse walls – brightly coloured and sophisticated but unpretentious. Mark remained grateful for what he had in life, but the hole in it left by Sharon's death was always most painful when he returned to his empty home.

Mark sat down and sent Pat a text: *Can we meet at Beaufort instead tomorrow? Have some new things to show you. Check out Sotheby's autumn catalogue. M*

A response immediately: *Will do – see you at 10. P*

3. THURSDAY NOVEMBER 14

Mark's world had disintegrated after Sharon's death. The self-belief and nerve that were so crucial for him, as a surgeon, to embark upon all but the most minor of operations had deserted him and he had lost any sense of the 'thrill of battle' that he had previously found invigorating. Each new patient became a source of anxiety and he knew that he risked making the wrong decisions about when to operate or even which operation to recommend.

Mark had felt the need to stop, and to stop immediately. His roles as surgeon, teacher, mentor and employer were wound up with minimal delay. The sad, irreconcilable fact of Sharon's life insurance payout had enabled him to settle all expenses and debts, step away completely from his thirty-five year–long medical career and reinvent himself as the owner-operator of a small art gallery. The income was modest by comparison, but the outlays were minimal given that he had been able to secure at very little cost a long-term lease of the gallery space.

Establishing Beaufort Gallery had been a lifesaver. He loved the gentle pace and rhythm of this job, the joy of looking at the art he handled, his fascination at the provenance of each and every piece. He loved the artists despite their frequently disorganised behaviour and unrealistic expectations. He loved the clients too, notwithstanding their propensity to indecision, remorse and, occasionally, outright stinginess.

And, as much as anything, he loved that his daughter Olivia had come to work as his second in command. He trusted her opinion about art, about how to deal with clients, her astute judgement of character and her ability to hold the line when it came to dealing with difficult clients. On Thursdays, Mark would open up at nine, Olivia would breeze in, all smiles and full of the latest updates about her household, filled as it was with children and animals, and he would head off for his weekly catch-up with Patrick.

By the time Olivia arrived this Thursday, Mark had replaced Charlie's painting on the easel in the main gallery where he looked at it with undiminished disquiet.

'Ooh! That's new. When did that come in?'

'Yesterday, just as I was about to close. What do you think?'

Mark doubted that Olivia would instantly recognise a Devlin, but he was interested in her reaction to the work itself. Olivia took her time, looked carefully for any signature, assessed the condition of the work, looking for any obvious signs of attempted restoration, and leaned the painting forward to see if there were any clues to its origins and history written on its back. Many times, Mark had rushed to pass comment on a work that Patrick had shown him, a test of sorts as well as an education, only to end up looking foolish for lack of simple inspection. Not so, Olivia.

'Do we know who Charlie is?'

'I don't even know his surname, darling. From what I do know – and that's not an awful lot – he isn't anyone who has figured prominently in Australian art. What do you make of it?'

'Well, it looks like acrylic on ... is that masonite?'

Mark nodded.

'And it looks kind of radical for the early seventies, if that date is correct. As a work, it's got lots of dark energy, a bit tough to look at. Just your kind of thing, Dad.'

The door opened and Patrick entered, with his typically pinched smile and a cheeky glint in his eye.

'Good morning, Olivia, how are you and your tribe?'

Patrick and his wife Helen had become firm friends with the entire Lewis clan, even more so since Sharon's death. Their warmth and their generosity, particularly in assisting with the establishment of the gallery, had been pivotal in rescuing Mark from the spiral of misery and self-doubt that had threatened him and his relationship with his children.

As Olivia delivered her cheerful account of the comings and goings in her own home, Charlie's painting remaining obscured from Pat's line of vision. When Olivia was done, Mark stepped in.

'I've got a couple of things to show you, Pat. Have a look at this one –

it was brought in by a woman who lives locally and who has had it hanging in her home for fifty years.'

Patrick moved around to look at the painting standing on its easel. Like Olivia, he took his time. He also looked at the back of the painting, then stepped away to consider it from a distance. He tilted his head briefly to the side, and grimaced.

'You've got to give me more, Mark.'

'It came in last evening. According to the woman who brought it in, Katy was her sister and Charlie – and that's his only name so far – was Katy's boyfriend. He was about seventeen years old and he painted it for her in nineteen seventy-two.' Mark recounted the entire story, as Jan had told it.

Pat cradled his chin in his right hand and tapped the tip of his nose with his index finger. 'You see, Olivia, your dad thinks this might have been painted by someone altogether more famous.' Patrick had clearly connected Mark's text reference to the spring catalogue to this new work, having noted in particular – as would many Australian gallerists and collectors – the work by James Devlin being offered for sale. 'I'd have called this a Devlin too, Mark. I wonder if her story is really correct. If it is a Devlin, it's a mighty good one and should be worth quite a bit.'

'I've heard of Devlin,' said Olivia, 'but wasn't he an eighties artist?'

'Yes, that's exactly right. It's a mystery, really, because the story behind this work is simple and rings true to me, but the painting looks like a Devlin through and through.'

Patrick approached within centimetres of the painting, as if he could penetrate its depths and discover the truth about it. 'I'm not sure what to think,' he said. 'It hasn't been signed by Devlin.'

Mark then showed them both the small Passmore, replacing Charlie's painting on the easel. As Pat examined it, Mark said to his daughter, 'We're going to head down to the art gallery and I'll be back around midday. If Tony Peterson calls about his Dickerson, tell him I can call him back any time that suits him after then.' Mark had managed to secure a major work in oil, painted in the 1960s by the very popular Australian artist Robert Dickerson for his biggest although by no means most agreeable collector.

'And would you put Charlie's painting back upstairs? I don't want too many people looking at it just yet.'

❖❖❖

Coffee this Thursday was at Frank, the State Gallery café in Northbridge. It was quiet, not a school excursion in sight. Patrick had been silent since leaving Mark's gallery but spoke up as he drank his coffee.

'That Passmore isn't quite right, Mark. I think it needs a bit more work before you can put a price on it. And, as for the other painting, you'll need to do some research. I'd start at the Cerebral Palsy Association and go from there. But you need to tread carefully with James Devlin. He is a successful gallerist and there's no doubt about his ability to pick great new talent. He's a generous supporter of a number of charities and he's an absolute darling of those media lefties. The fact is, Helen and I love his paintings – you probably don't know it, but we bought one of his works for our bloody super fund about twenty years ago.

'But I just don't trust him. I know in my bones that he ramps the prices of some works at auction so that he can inflate the prices he gets in his own gallery.' Pat pulled on the shoulders of his shirt and lifted both sides a little self-consciously, letting in some air to cool him down. 'Don't get me wrong – he's been a great judge of new artists and handles works from all the great Australians. He gets the most for his artists, he doesn't sell bad works, and he doesn't deal in fakes.' He looked around the café, as if checking for someone listening to their conversation. The place was mostly empty. 'But there is something fishy about aspects of his set-up and I would stay well away from him if I was you.'

'OK,' said Mark. 'I had actually thought I might send him an image of Charlie's painting and ask his opinion.'

'Don't do that!' Patrick barked. Then he gave a thin, apologetic smile. 'Figure out as much as you can about the painting and then we can reconsider. You see what you can find out about Charlie and I'll try to find out more about Devlin. You know,' Pat added, 'his career as an artist was only very short – perhaps about four or five years, no more. He left for London in the late eighties and returned to set up his gallery in Melbourne, but he never painted again. He's an enigma, but Helen and I both think he is cunning and slippery, so you need to be careful.'

Patrick's vehemence towards Devlin was a surprise to Mark. Even as a relative novice, he knew that there were many shades of unprofessional and frankly manipulative behaviour in the art industry the world over.

And that Pat and Helen were intermittently aggrieved by the injustice of it whenever they sensed that this had taken place, and forlorn at the damage it did to their industry.

Although Mark had been familiar with Devlin's brief career as an artist, the sudden and mysterious appearance of Charlie's painting cast Devlin's strange story in an even more perplexing light.

'I'd love to see your Devlin one day.' Mark got to his feet. 'Shall we have a look at AGWA's? It was on display last week when I came in.'

On level 1, they found *Constellation* (1984), 100cm squared. The materials, colours and raw energy were identical to Charlie's painting. The central, black, rectangular void of Charlie's painting was emulated in *Constellation* in the form of a similar but larger and less well-defined grey void. The scale of the state gallery's work was larger, and the use of a little pink in the upper aspect suggested a progression from Charlie's painting through *Constellation* to *Paradise*, the work listed for sale at auction later that month.

The two men gazed into the work, each lost in contemplation, their thoughts swirling through its layers. What did it know, this seemingly formless aggregation of acrylic paint on wooden board? Where had it been painted? And what, if anything, connected it to the piece tucked away in Mark's gallery?

4. THURSDAY NOVEMBER 14

The second-floor office above Provenance Gallery overlooked the corner of Johnston and Wellington streets in Melbourne's hip and gritty Collingwood. Old-fashioned, ground-floor, high-street shopping had not yet been replaced by designer brand stores. From his corner window one floor above, James Devlin looked down onto a unique mix of bespoke furniture, clothing, vintage and craft stores. He could see directly into the local barber shop doing a booming trade mostly, he observed, among a veritable invasion of hipsters. On either side of it, two tiny florist shops added dabs of bright colour and ever-changing variety to the streetscape, surrounding him with its bustling, intimate atmosphere.

James Devlin's office was modest in size and austere in its décor. The furniture was in mid-brown wood and the walls were painted off-white. A solitary painting dominated the wall facing his desk – a blaze of yellow on white, hints of darker tones and a few lines of blue paint peering through at the onlooker. One metre squared, it was from his series of mostly monochromatic works of which this one alone remained in his possession.

Decades after its creation, Devlin still found it soothing. Its simplicity and subtlety highlighted for him the unfathomable nature of the attraction that human beings had for fine art. Whether it was admiration at the technical aptitude that allowed depiction of their surroundings with photographic precision; the imagination of the surrealist to distort reality in a dreamlike manner that played with the mind of the viewer; or the ability to convey emotions, even a profound sense of spirituality, through totally abstract form – human beings had been admiring, producing, acquiring and displaying drawings and paintings with pleasure and pride for millennia.

And, not infrequently, paying large sums of money to do so. How often had James Devlin dwelt upon the imponderable strangeness of people spending occasionally obscene amounts on what were nothing more than degradable materials laid upon equally insubstantial surfaces. *Odyssey* – this largely yellow work which had featured in his last ever exhibition – was a perfect example. Just twelve months earlier, a similar work from the same series had been sold by private treaty for over twenty thousand dollars, rich testament to the ability of abstract art to impact upon human emotions. No clearly recognisable shapes or structures. No familiar objects or landscape. Nothing more than dabs and strokes of acrylic paint on a board made of masonite. Yet *Odyssey*, in particular, evoked in Devlin powerful memories and emotions, and calmed him whenever he sat in front of it.

Right now, Devlin was being pulled in many different directions which meant that keeping calm was important. The upcoming round of art auctions would be followed by a major exhibition and sale in his own gallery. This represented a busy and commercially important period of time for James and the staff at Provenance. Numerous pieces in each of the auctions were either from his own collection or belonged to his clients, placed strategically in one or other sale in an effort to raise their profile and elevate their hammer price. A number of other pieces were also of interest to him and to collectors whom he regularly advised as purchasers.

The impact that these auction sales would have on the prices he could subsequently ask at his own exhibition meant that he left as little as possible to chance in his preparation. This year, for the first time, he was selling one of his own works, albeit through a third party, his long-time associate, widely respected plastic surgeon and committed collector, Garth Barrett. James and Garth went back a long way. Their mutual love of art had strengthened the bond between them and had profited each of them handsomely over many years.

As Victorian nominee for Australian of the Year, Devlin was uncomfortable with the spotlight now shining on him. Yet he appreciated the potential benefits – for the causes he so passionately supported as well as his own commercial interests – that could flow from this process.

Devlin had always been studious in portraying outward humility but he was disciplined and privately proactive in fostering his reputation and enhancing his public image. He sipped his macchiato while reviewing the list of engagements and appearances that he had mapped out for the next eight weeks. Speeches for charities, presentations in his honour, visible support for research foundations – he had always managed to support worthy and uncontentious causes and never strayed into political debate. And he had never transgressed in his dealings with employees or acolytes, of whom there had been many.

The spare mobile in his desk's top drawer issued Verdi's 'Triumphal March', telling him that his oldest friend was returning his call.

'Hi Garth. How are you? Just touching base.'

'All good, Harry.'

Harry was James' middle name although he had long since removed it from all official documents. It had been James' nickname as a teenager and Garth had never stopped using it, although only ever in private. In any event, these days, the two men rarely interacted other than in the strictest privacy.

'Just clarifying your interest in the Crooke, Garth, at the Sotheby's auction. It's listed at twenty to twenty-five thousand, but I am sure you'd agree that it's an excellent piece and worth chasing up if you can.'

Ray Crooke was an acclaimed artist whose works consistently did well in the secondary market. His images of Polynesian village life were especially popular and there were many of these in circulation. The specific work coming up for auction was a good size – 45cm × 60cm – and portrayed the inside of a village hut with a woman in traditional dress sitting at a kitchen table, a plate and cup in front of her and the sea and sand visible through the hut's open window. It was, at its heart, an exercise in light, the bulk of the painting being dark, but with the light beaming in through the window of the hut and catching the woman's white blouse with its red floral print. This work was a solid one and deserved to meet the price estimate.

'I think you might take it as far as thirty-five thousand,' suggested Devlin. With the buyer's premium added, this would cost Garth well over forty thousand dollars.

'Got it.'

Devlin knew that Garth understood the part he was playing and that he did not need to inquire further about the origins of the work. Many times, Devlin had helped move works from Garth's collection into someone else's at auction, and at considerable profit. And the profit only compounded for Garth, as a silent partner in Provenance, when those elevated prices were replicated in the post-auction exhibitions and sales at their own gallery featuring works by the artists whose prices they had actively boosted.

'When will you have your exhibition finalised?' asked Garth.

'Not long – about thirty works are already settled and I'll leave the rest until the auctions have been completed. But the Crookes are all in and should do well.' That was the deal, after all. Garth's enthusiastic bidding would ensure a good price for this work at auction, meaning that those in the subsequent exhibition – commendable works though they would undoubtedly be – would likely also justify high prices. And the buoyancy surrounding these works (and others whose prices were also pushed during the auctions) would hopefully create the energy and confidence among visitors to the gallery that would generate excitement – and sales.

It was a successful formula and both Devlin and Barrett shared in the wider spoils. That was their arrangement. Likewise, for the work by Devlin being sold by Sotheby's, Garth Barrett was the listed vendor. No-one would ever doubt that a longstanding collector and trader such as Barrett would have acquired that work fair and square, or that he would now seek to capitalise on the rise and rise of James Devlin by selling it. The truth about its ownership, of course, was a little more complex.

'When the exhibition is finalised, a notice will appear on the gallery newsletter. You'll get the email. How have you and Marnie been?' They chatted for a few minutes, a brief, somewhat wistful exchange. After they'd said goodbye, as Devlin put the phone down, his gaze was drawn across the road to a rowdy group of teenagers emerging from the barber, jostling each other amid playful banter. His thoughts drifted back to a time when contact between Garth and him was also unrestrained and free from apprehension about public scrutiny.

5. FRIDAY NOVEMBER 15

Mark knew the location of the Ability Centre well. He had grown up in the vicinity of what was now referred to as the Yokine Reserve and the surrounding suburb of Coolbinia, but, back then, this organisation had been known as the Centre for Cerebral Palsy and, later, the Sir David Brand Centre and School. Later still it split to become the Sir David Brand School and the Ability Centre. He wasn't entirely sure what he expected to find at Ability Centre, but he was hopeful that there were archives that he could access that might locate and even identify Charlie.

He was greeted at the front office by a woman in her early twenties, whose preoccupation with her mobile phone his arrival interrupted. Her badge identified her as 'Kaylee'. She sat behind a long low desk, a computer screen and keyboard to one side, a telephone to the other. There were several chairs for visitors, the upholstery in good condition, and walls of bare tan-coloured brick, one of which was dominated by a whiteboard covered in posters and flyers advertising the centre's activities and calendar of events.

Mark explained to Kaylee that he owned and operated an art gallery and that he was looking for archival information about a client formerly within the care of cerebral palsy services. Kaylee smiled earnestly and explained that she would need to ask the CEO. She headed off through the door behind her, returning in just a matter of minutes with, Mark presumed, her boss. 'Linda' read the badge. No title, very democratic, thought Mark.

'I'm Linda De Vries,' she said as she offered him a handshake, 'acting CEO at Ability Centre.' The skin of her hand was soft and smooth.

'Kaylee said you were looking for information about a former client. I'm not sure I am in a position to help but come on through to my office and we can have a chat. Do you know when and where this person was under our care?'

Her smile was pleasant if a little reserved. Her accent had a distinct South African lilt and Mark guessed that she was about fifty, although he had always been a bad judge of age. Since Sharon had died, however, he had taken to noting what sort of jewellery women were wearing, especially – he knew he was being ridiculous – whether or not they wore a wedding ring. Linda did not. But she wore a thin, gold necklace with a circular golden pendant that was attractive yet refined. Exactly, he thought, what Sharon would have liked.

The CEO's office looked out over natural bushland adjoining the centre. She offered Mark a seat and she took her own behind an uncluttered wooden desk. Behind her a number of document-laden trays were lined up, conveying both a methodical approach and a substantial workload.

Instinctively, Mark touched the desktop. 'American cherry,' he said.

Linda smiled. 'Veneer only, alas.'

'It's a beautiful surface,' said Mark, absorbing the atmosphere of the room. The wall behind Linda's desk was covered in shelves filled with lever arch files and books. The wall to the left of her desk, opposite the large window, was adorned by a large, framed, black-and-white photograph, featuring (he presumed) clients of the centre, along with their carers, inside a large and bare activity room. Judging by their clothing, it was probably taken in the 1950s. In one way, it was a confronting image of disabled youth in an obviously spartan facility. But it also evoked a clear sense of history and the faces of both staff and clients exuded the unmistakable decency of their collective purpose.

Linda saw the line of Mark's sight. 'I love that photo. I found it in a storeroom shortly after I started working here and had it framed. It's followed me to this office.'

'It's a very powerful image. Things were much more basic then, no doubt,' Mark said, 'but you can almost feel the sincerity of their intent. I find it inspiring.'

Mark sensed a shared aesthetic and sensibility. He took more careful note of her appearance and dress. She was pleasant looking, not as tall as him, and maybe a little overweight, with straight brown, shoulder-length hair. Unexpectedly, he felt self-conscious at the stretching of his shirt over his belly and he shifted in his seat to disguise his midriff.

'You run an art gallery, Kaylee tells me,' Linda said. 'How does that involve this organisation?'

Mark described his gallery, the styles of art it generally displayed, his meeting with Jan Bilowski and the painting she attributed to a former pupil at the Sir James Mitchell School. And that he had committed to provide her with a value for the painting, something that he felt could really only be done by knowing more about the pupil who he only knew as Charlie.

He was conscious that he hadn't disclosed to Linda the unsettling likeness of this painting to the works of James Devlin. And the importance that this fact held to his inquiry at the centre.

'I was hoping there might be some record of a "Charlie" from the late sixties and early seventies and possibly even some archival material of any artwork that might have been produced here.'

There followed a long pause. Mark imagined that he saw a mixture of interest and scepticism in Linda's face. Her brown eyes conveyed intelligence and warmth. He felt strangely disarmed and nervous and, in that instant, he made the decision to be candid.

'What I haven't said is that the work of art closely resembles works by a very well-known Australian artist that were painted maybe ten years after this one seems to have been. The likeness is strong. Yet the story that underpins Charlie's painting is simple and rings true to me.

'I suppose what I am trying to do is to confirm that Charlie even existed, find out what his full name was, figure out if he might still be alive and painting somewhere, and explain why his painting looks so much like something that was produced over a decade later, on the other side of this country.' Mark studied her face, anxious at how much he had just shared.

'If I'm being honest with you,' he said, 'I am inclined to dive into projects and commit energy and time and money to things that a more sensible person would not. I'm just that kind of person, and it isn't necessarily my best feature. So, my belief about Charlie and his painting needs to be qualified by that understanding. But there is something unsettling about all this and I really want to find Charlie. Do you think you can help?'

To his relief, Linda smiled suddenly, a warm and generous smile that provoked a sensation in Mark's chest alerting him to emotions he had not experienced in a long while.

'Well, that is some story,' she said, shaking her head. 'I'll have to dig around to find if and where there are any records of the Sir James Mitchell School. That wasn't ever on this site, and the Sir David Brand School down the road that replaced it is a separate entity altogether.'

Mark's shoulders slumped – had he come to the wrong place?

'But, whatever I am able to do to help, I shall,' Linda added. 'Am I allowed to see the painting?'

6. FRIDAY NOVEMBER 15

Mark returned to his gallery in time to receive Olivia's handover. It had been a good morning with a steady flow of visitors resulting in a strong sale: a delightful small Howard Taylor still life taken by a couple who were new to the gallery. This had been counterbalanced by an exhausting conversation with Tony Peterson, Olivia recounting – not without embellishment – Peterson's description of his current tight financial circumstances nothing more, they agreed, than a transparent and clumsy negotiating strategy.

Olivia had been wise to the ploy and knew the guidelines for this particular negotiation. Tony would be in before close of business to discuss things further with Mark, hoping (no doubt) to reduce the asking price even just a little.

Both Olivia and Mark shook their heads at Peterson's charade both still pleased that the Dickerson, hardly seen since being purchased at its original exhibition and sale in Perth in the 1960s, was about to move to a new home. For Mark, every piece of art bore its own history, the details of its creation, display and ownership all subtly absorbed into the work and reflected back at the next generation of viewers.

After Olivia's departure, Mark checked his mail. Pat had sent through an image of his and Helen's Devlin, entitled *Creation*, also acrylic on masonite, and also from the 1980s. In the preceding twenty-four hours, Mark had been exposed, for the first time in a concerted manner, to numerous images of Devlin's works, and the similarities between them were unmistakable. *Creation* was a furious and frenetic work, the distinct sense of a cathartic event of global scale literally exploding upwards, the dominant white palette conveying to Mark purity or, possibly, God; the characteristic Devlin blue referencing sky and the heavens above. In the upper right corner, the presence of a darker hue presaged, perhaps the cruelty of fate and, conceivably, the evil one day to be confronted by humanity.

Mark envied Pat and Helen's taste and judgement in art. More than twenty years ago, although Devlin was already a notable figure in art circles, they had recognised the scale of his talent and had discerned his potential for investment. And Mark had no doubt that Jan Bilowski had brought him a James Devlin; he just had no idea how she had come by such a little masterpiece, and how (if at all) it was connected to Charlie and Katy.

The afternoon passed quickly. A regular collector popped in, having admired the Dickerson he had spotted in the back of the gallery and interested to see any new arrivals in the gallery. Mark especially liked these sorts of clients – not infrequently, precisely such a casual visit translated into a significant sale. If they didn't have the cash immediately available, or because (sometimes) they didn't wish their partner to know about the acquisition, he readily extended interest-free terms. It secured a sale, helped strengthen an already solid collection and ensured that the work itself entered a new chapter in its personal story.

Just before closing, Mark was planning the New Year exhibition in his gallery of paintings by an artist named Anousheh Gul – a graduate of Curtin University, whose abstract work he thought was exceptional – when Tony Peterson entered the gallery. The man was, Mark had concluded, an acquired taste. Peterson was a well-known businessman of considerable wealth who liked to buy and display art by prominent and fashionable artists. He was prone to ostentation, and insisted upon driving down the prices of his purchases.

But, when all was said and done, Peterson's acquisitions provided support for all levels of the local art industry and his evident faith in art as an investment delivered a positive message to the market. Mark knew that many art cognoscenti viewed Peterson and his collection as crass, even contemptible; how Mark detested that 'money sullies art' brigade, whose envy of the likes of Tony Peterson drove them to dismiss and belittle his entire collection. Without Peterson and that small contingent of consistent collectors, those snobby commentators and self-appointed experts would have no industry within which to parade their arrogance.

For Tony Peterson, who understood the risk of paying large amounts for a painting that was not quite what he thought he had bought, his faith in the gallerist was critical. He had been burned by other purchases from other galleries, but he had made three significant acquisitions from Mark Lewis and had come to trust him. In the case of a Dickerson, this was especially important, as his distinctive style and great commercial appeal lent his art to occasional imitation.

With respect to this work, Mark had no doubt that it was the real thing. The vendor had purchased it from a gallery that had flourished in the 1960s and had been a feature of the Perth art scene until it closed when its owners retired after almost forty years. The piece had been sold at an exhibition exclusively comprising new works by Dickerson at that gallery in 1968 and had been resold by the same gallery to the current owners about a decade later. Although Mark had not been able to locate a catalogue from the original exhibition in which this joyous and radiant painting had been sold, the vendor's account of that purchase, as well as their small but high quality art collection, the apparent age of the work and its deeply authentic nature had made Mark confident of its origins. Pat and Helen, whose opinions Mark invariably sought in these matters, had agreed without hesitation. Perhaps most importantly, communication with the artist's family had confirmed beyond reasonable doubt that this was an original Dickerson.

'It's an absolute beauty, Mark. I've been waiting for something like this for years. I can't wait to hang it at home.'

Mark had known that Peterson was never going to say no to this painting. And buying it by private treaty, away from the auction scene and hidden from public scrutiny, was Peterson's strong preference; he loved to surprise his friends with prestigious acquisitions.

In the end, Peterson did not even quibble about the sale price that was just in excess of $100,000. 'I'll transfer the funds tonight and collect it tomorrow.'

'With your permission, Tony, I'd like to display the painting on my website. There'll be no indication of the price or the buyer, but I'd like to show it off a little if you don't mind.'

'That won't be a problem, Mark. How will you describe it?'

'Oh, I don't know. Something like "Nineteen sixties masterpiece acquired by major Australian collector".'

Mark observed Tony Peterson's self-satisfied smile and knew that he had struck the right note. For now, he had a very happy customer.

7. SATURDAY NOVEMBER 16

Mark awaited Linda's arrival at the gallery with apprehension. He was concerned that she would have found nothing at all to identify Charlie as a resident at Ability Centre, or that there would not be any records that might allow Charlie or any family members to be located. Just as disturbing for Mark, however, was a little bead of dread emanating from his undeniable attraction to Linda and the prospect that this might be reciprocated.

He recognised that his capacity to form a relationship with another woman was impaired, and a complex thing, not something he could comfortably articulate. Having lived with Sharon for thirty years, he recognised the compromises they each had made in maintaining their relationship, the routines that they had constructed and accepted, the things that each tolerated in the other for the greater good, as it had been.

Mark had had an intense but brief relationship in the time since Sharon had died. Jenni had been quite a bit younger than him, bright and outgoing, good company and with many similar interests to Mark. Initially, it had been lots of fun but, within six months of moving into Mark's townhouse, their relationship had descended into mutual resentment. Only in the aftermath of that break-up did Mark realise that this might have been a manifestation of his own issues and that this might, for him, be the likely, even inevitable trajectory of any future relationship.

If his sense that there might be a mutual attraction between him and Linda was correct, he worried they might also take the same destructive pathway. He had experienced deep disillusionment in the process of this recently failed relationship, that only magnified the loneliness he had felt following Sharon's death, and he had no interest in going there again.

Linda was exactly on time, one hour before opening. Charlie's painting was on an easel but not visible from the street; he had hung other works around the gallery with particular purpose. He knew that he was, despite himself, trying to make a good impression, keen to show Linda excellent works of art, to demonstrate his knowledge, to earn her trust and maybe even her affection.

Linda walked in, self-assured and evidently pleased to be visiting the gallery. Her trousers, blouse and long cotton cardigan flattered her full figure. Annoying himself greatly, he observed that Sharon would have approved of her outfit. How he missed Sharon's invariable commentary on what other people were wearing and how their outfits complemented (or detracted from) their appearance. For the duration of their married life, it had driven him crazy – who cared what other people were wearing? – but he now found himself doing it all the time.

'Would you like to pop out for a coffee? We are spoilt for choice around here.'

'That'd be great. But may I have a look around first?'

'Absolutely. You'll never need to twist my arm to talk about paintings.' He took Linda straight to a David Boyd – small, brightly coloured, and essentially figurative.

Mark said, 'To be honest, I find it a little uninspired. But it has a sort of instant visual appeal and the Boyd family have made a monumental contribution to twentieth century art in Australia.' Mark felt that this was a great way to break the ice and begin the tour he had planned. Next was a large work by Donald Laycock, from the early 1970s, intense red with a subtle swirl of colour, exemplifying the colour field era in Australian art. He described his own first purchase of a work of art – as a precocious teenager – by Sydney Ball from the same school, which rocketed to public awareness when, as emerging artists, their works were featured at the 1968 opening of the refurbished National Gallery of Victoria.

'Boyd used thick application of oil to add a textural, sculptural element to his works, a sort of third dimension,' said Mark. 'But the Laycock … for me, this vast, flat, red surface creates a sense of infinite space.'

'I like these,' Linda said. 'I could hang them in my home any time.'

Next Mark showed her a still life by Margaret Olley, its matt surface featuring asparagus on a wooden bench. It depicted a plain and ordinary scene, yet the artist's empathy for her subject – a mere vegetable – was striking. The mood it generated was restrained, even sombre.

'It's beautiful,' Linda said, 'but sad.' She gave him a quick smile. 'How does an artist move you to sadness with asparagus?'

Mark moved on to a favourite from his own collection, a Howard Arkley from his flywire door series. He described Arkley's career-long use of the airbrush, and how he had taken much inspiration from Australia's urban landscapes. 'In the late nineteen seventies, Arkley put together an entire series of paintings inspired by the patterns of wrought iron and aluminium of the flywire doors he observed while walking in suburban Sydney. Initially, they reflected the tight symmetry of a typical flywire door. But towards the end of the series, he broke free of this formality and started to insert these fluid, abstract, psychedelic patterns.'

Mark had never been able to figure out if he loved the painting most because of this visual appeal, because it *was* an Arkley or because of the story that lay at its origins. He could see that Linda was taking it all in, and he was buoyed by her response. 'This one is purely in greys and blacks. But I love the sense of abandon it conveys. I know it's nothing more than a random selection of lines and spray-painted shapes, and colourless at that. In the end, though, Arkley's creativity and imagination cannot be denied. It's like he is reinventing reality.'

'You talk about these artists as if they were all still alive, as if you knew them all,' Linda said.

'To me, it's as if the paintings themselves are telling me these stories. I know they're just oil and acrylic and pen and pencil or even crayon. But they hold so much history and they say so much more than what you might first see.' He rested his hand on the frame of the Arkley as if steadying his own thoughts. Then, conscious of Linda's close attention, he moved on to show her Charlie's painting.

'I suppose we would call this abstract expressionism – there are no recognisable shapes, and there is no attempt to portray a specific object or living form. It probably started early in the twentieth century, courtesy of a Russian artist named Kazimir Malevich and a group known as the Suprematists. But what we now refer to as abstract expressionism became a distinct art movement in New York in the fifties. After the Second World War, Europe was licking its wounds and the new thinking and bold creativity in art shifted from Paris and Berlin to New York. The major artists of that era included Rothko, Pollock, Newman, Krasner, lots of famous names.

'And this is Charlie's painting. It doesn't have a title, at least none that we know of. I know it seems like a disjointed series of crude brushstrokes, like something a child might produce. If the story is true, he was only about seventeen anyway. But to me it speaks of emotion, distress, turmoil – it's as if the artist has felt compelled to put things down in a fervent rush. To me, these drips of paint,' Mark pointed, 'speak to that urgency bordering on chaos.'

Mark ran his hand through his hair, distracted by a mental picture of Charlie at his easel, brush in hand. Then he looked directly at Linda. 'I realise that all of this might sound a bit flaky. And it's difficult for me to be completely impartial about the painting precisely because I look at it as if it was painted by James Devlin.' Together they stood and looked at the painting. 'Devlin is based in Melbourne and his popularity is currently very much on the rise. This seems like almost too good a time for one to suddenly turn up. If this is a Devlin, it is a valuable piece, that's for sure.'

'Since Devlin is alive, why not just ask him?' Linda said. 'Surely he'll remember it – or reject it – immediately?'

Mark turned the painting around to show Linda what had been written on the back. 'If Jan – the lady who brought this in – knew that this was a Devlin, there is no way that she would have chosen to fob it off as a valueless work by an unknown artist. I am convinced that she believes this was given to her sister by an artist called Charlie. She is certain that this painting came into her home along with her sister in the early seventies, ten years before James Devlin started to paint and display his work in Melbourne. And I want to solve this puzzle.'

She returned his gaze, smiling. 'Can we have that coffee now? I think I might've found Charlie.'

8. SATURDAY NOVEMBER 16

As it turned out, records of the Sir James Mitchell School were difficult to access. Linda had instituted a search of the archives held by the State Records Office, but this would take some time and the archivist with whom she had spoken wasn't optimistic she'd find much of direct assistance. They might have lists of class names but, with clients dating back to the nineteen sixties, not many of those pupils – and virtually none of their parents – would still be alive.

'I had more luck at the Sir David Brand School, although not with the names of ex-pupils. One of the teachers who worked at the Sir James Mitchell School, and who moved with the school to the new campus here in Coolbinia, was a keen photographer and he took hundreds of photos of the schools and the old Spastic Centre in Mount Lawley. That photo in my office turns out to have been taken by him.

'He gave many of those photos to the families of the pupils, and gifted the remainder to the new school when he retired in the late eighties. About ten years ago, they scanned the ones that were still in good condition and I had a look through them all and found this.'

Linda showed Mark a reprint of a black-and-white photograph taken, Linda suggested, in one of the original therapy rooms at the school's former Mount Lawley campus. Although the original had faded a little, the picture was clear: a gaunt, dark-haired boy, photographed from behind, his face obscured, was standing in front of an easel, paintbrush in hand with the board positioned in the portrait orientation also mostly obscured. Facing him, in full view of the camera, were other pupils, the closest to the artist being a girl with a pretty smile. The position and pose of these two teenagers was such that it would not be a stretch of the imagination to regard the young artist and his admirer as boyfriend and girlfriend.

'There are no photographic records at the school of the individual clients, so I can't tell you that this is a picture of Charlie and Katy. This photo is dated nineteen seventy-two. But Jan would surely be able to identify her sister if this is Katy.'

Mark nodded his head slowly. 'If that girl is Katy, that boy might be Charlie.'

'Well,' said Linda, 'shall we go and see Jan?'

'I will call her this morning,' said Mark, a current of excitement welling up in him. This puzzle seemed to have developed a hold over him, its solution becoming something hefty as if it somehow offered him redemption, although from what, he didn't know. And Linda, he observed, seemed to have become a significant and willing part of this quest.

❖❖❖

Mark and Linda were impatient to hear Jan's verdict but the gallery remained open on Saturdays until five and predictable operating hours were essential for Mark's clients, both regular and new. He would have to sit it out until closing time. Linda had left but would return. He was waiting for a chance to call Jan and also desperate to speak to Patrick but there was a steady stream of clients and he had to be patient.

A break between visitors just after midday allowed Mark to call Jan. He explained the importance of identifying Charlie – he was not yet prepared to share with her the resemblance between Charlie's painting and the works of James Devlin – if he was to assign a value to her painting. He wanted to check again if she had ever met Charlie and to let her know that he had located a photograph that might be of Charlie, and might also be of Katy. Did she have time to meet?

'I don't want to put you out, Jan. I'd be happy to pop around to your place after the gallery closes if you'd prefer.'

'That would suit me fine. My knee has been playing up and it'd be much better if I can rest it a bit.'

'If you don't mind,' said Mark, 'I would like you to meet the person who located the photograph taken at the James Mitchell School – she is helping me in my search for Charlie.'

'Sure. That's no problem. You know, if the painting isn't worth much, I'd understand it. You seem to be taking this very seriously.'

Mark felt guilty, but he knew that he needed much more information before he could be frank with Jan. 'Please don't worry about me. I love investigating unknown artists and their works. I am doing this as much for me as for you.'

❖❖❖

Mark observed Linda approaching the gallery just before five, an energy in her step that, he felt, conveyed a distinct hint of excitement at the prospect of identifying Katy and, maybe even Charlie. And, quite possibly he hoped, at being in his company.

She opened the gallery door, Mark continuing a discussion with a couple in their early thirties, looking intently at the David Boyd he had showed her only hours earlier.

Mark smiled in her direction and glanced at the easel on which he'd placed a George Haynes landscape, replacing Charlie's painting, but he didn't break step in his account of the small Boyd. Linda moved into the gallery and looked at the other works, casually eavesdropping on Mark's words of encouragement.

'There's no doubt that David Boyd is less critically acclaimed than his brother Arthur. And the prices attached to their works reflect that difference. Arthur Boyd painted on a larger scale and some of his most celebrated works are dark and even confronting. David Boyd adopted a generally more whimsical approach to his works, often using thick and uneven application of paint to add texture. This work is a good example of all of those traits. He's an important Australian artist. It's oil on canvas, so it's made to last. It's appealing to look at. And I think it's a good price.'

Mark left them to look at the painting and walked across to Linda.

'Sorry that I'm holding you up. These two came in around four and I've been boring them senseless ever since!'

'That's no trouble at all. Actually, I think they're trying to catch your attention.'

Mark raised a quick eyebrow and turned to engage again with his customers. 'There's no hurry to make a decision today,' he said. 'I know that it seems like a lot of money, so have a think about it – I am more than happy to hold it for you for a week if that will help you.'

But the first man said that they'd decided to buy it and would like to take it with them; the purchase was completed by credit card, Mark's precis about the artwork and the artist printed off along with the receipt. He wrapped the painting in bubble wrap and brown paper and the couple left just around five fifteen.

Mark and Linda left the gallery a few minutes later, the lights switched off and the alarm activated.

'That seemed like an unexpected choice in painting for them. I'd have imagined they'd be looking for something more contemporary.'

'Yes and no. I think that taste in art is more closely connected to intrinsic human factors than it is to a person's age. Some people don't get abstract art and never will; they need to be able to clearly see what the painting is about. Others can't see any point in photorealism. But you are right – I wouldn't normally expect to sell an early eighties David Boyd to people in their thirties.'

They were heading north, walking around the corner of Beaufort Street onto Walcott Street, through the tiny parking lot that served a few shops set back from the main road. They turned right into Field Street, towards Jan's home.

'What was their story?' asked Linda.

'The one with the beard received a generous sum of money through the estate of his grandmother and wanted to buy something in her memory. Both grew up with art on the walls. I think they wanted something of lasting value in their own home now rather than something that would diminish in worth over time – a sort of heirloom.'

'Was the Boyd a good choice?'

'Well, yes. For sure. I would never sell someone something that didn't meet their brief.' Mark was aware that he sounded a little defensive. 'It might not be to your taste. And it isn't to mine. But they loved its bright colours and its festive energy. I know it will retain its value over time. I hope that they use this purchase as the inspiration to start their own art collection. You never know.'

As they walked down the side lane to Jan's ground-floor apartment Mark concluded out loud, as much to himself as to Linda, 'I am sure his grandmother would have approved.'

❖❖❖

Mark pulled back the flywire door and knocked on the wooden door. He glanced at Linda and caught her eye, pleased that she had appreciated the unspoken reference to their earlier conversation about Howard Arkley. Jan answered the door in dressing gown and slippers.

'Thank you for coming around here for me. My knee's been killing me.'

Mark introduced Linda, and Jan ushered them through into the lounge room, immediately off the entrance area. It was a cramped space of heavy furniture and exposed dark brick, not at all conducive to hanging art.

'It's late for a cup of tea, but would you like one?'

Linda and Mark accepted Jan's offer and she headed off to the nearby kitchen. Linda took out a clear plastic folder containing a copy of the photograph she had found in the archives. Mark took out his own file and laid it on a small round table nearby and looked at Linda, his anticipation building.

Jan shuffled back in with a tray, a pot of tea, some milk and a small plate of biscuits.

'So, what's going on, you two?'

9. TUESDAY NOVEMBER 19

The rising national focus on James Devlin, artist turned art gallerist and generous benefactor, meant that Mark was unsurprised to find one of Devlin's works on display at the Ian Potter Centre in Federation Square. A visit to the Ian Potter was an essential element of every trip Mark made to Melbourne. He was captivated by the breadth of their contemporary Australian collection, taking equal pleasure in reacquainting himself with works he had seen many times before and in seeing, for the first time, works that had been hand-picked by the gallery over decades in recognition of their technical or creative allure or, at times, their propensity to provoke.

He was in Melbourne for the spring sales, a routine he justified to himself as a form of professional development. Seeing artworks in the flesh was always so much more compelling than seeing them online or in a catalogue. And he loved visiting Melbourne since he often stayed with his younger daughter Becky and her husband and their two little children. Becky held a senior managerial role for an Australian clothing chain, and her husband Alan was already a partner in a boutique law firm which had made environmental law its focus.

Wilderness was a striking work. At 150cm × 120cm, it had been Devlin's largest and most ambitious piece. It had been awarded the Wynne Prize for landscape painting in 1985 and had been acquired by the NGV after that exhibition. Its portrait orientation defied the Australian art world's horizontal convention for landscape art, a fact that had added much to its critical appeal. Mark appreciated anew the palette of black and blue and white, the glimpses of pink throughout the work, the raw energy of the brushstrokes and the rectangular shape at the top of the painting that seemed to maintain a precarious hold over all its elements. It was a work of great vigour, evenly maintained across its large surface.

Wilderness was typical of James Devlin but more uplifting and certainly less unsettling than Charlie's painting. Mark stood transfixed and moved. And confused. These were surely all works by the same hand. There could be no other explanation. But if Devlin had not painted Charlie's painting, had Charlie painted them all?

It was with this thought unsettling his mood that, at seven o'clock, Mark entered the Sotheby's auction room to witness the sale of *Paradise*, along with, unbeknownst to him, several other paintings also placed in this auction by James Devlin. Mark found the atmosphere at art auctions strangely calming. Even when bidding to purchase works about which he was passionate, he found that he tended to remain composed and measured, divining the energy surrounding the bidding on each work, sensing the direction bidding would take and the likely endpoint. In an environment when so few variables could be predicted, he often felt paradoxically in control.

This auction included many wonderful works by wonderful artists, and equally many others by artists that were, Mark thought, less so: some overtly decorative, others frankly mass-produced or no longer consistent with contemporary tastes. Mark appreciated that many of these more predictable, comfortable works retained broad appeal among collectors, both new and seasoned. In truth, in his own gallery, he was obliged to handle the full range of works by many well-known artists, and to respect the taste and preferences of his clients.

Lot 29 was a good-sized work by Ray Crooke, yet another of his islander series, attractive but not especially inspiring – formulaic rather than fabulous as Helen O'Beirne would say. Bidding began just below the lower estimate provided by the auction house and proceeded surprisingly briskly towards the upper estimate. The buzz in the audience was audible as two bidders took the work well above the predicted price range. Standing at the back of the room, Mark observed one of them, a tall and elegantly dressed man, perhaps in his early sixties, not actively seeking attention nor hiding from it. He secured the work, the hammer falling ten thousand dollars above the predicted upper limit.

Mark was perplexed. He certainly hadn't felt that a bidding war was imminent for this particular work. Although he appreciated that any painting might exceed the predicted price range where there were two people hellbent on buying it, he hadn't rated this work as anything worthy of such enthusiastic attention. Moreover, the successful bidder oozed class and control, anything but the image of the emotional bidder drawn into a battle to secure a 'must-have' piece of art.

The couple sitting next to Mark, keen auction-goers judging by their diligent recording of the outcome of each lot, although yet to cast a bid themselves, huddled in rapt conversation. As the Crooke was carried away and the next work of art brought on to the stage for display, Mark asked them if they knew who the successful bidder was.

'That's Garth Barrett, the surgeon. He's a regular here – he must have an amazing collection.'

Maybe not, thought Mark. As he waited for *Paradise* to come up for sale, his thoughts turned from the auction to his dinner with Linda on Saturday night, after they'd visited Jan Bilowski.

❖❖❖

He had taken Linda out for early dinner to his favourite pizza restaurant, in South Perth, where tables could not be reserved but you could bring your own alcohol; on the other hand, if you wanted champagne, as he usually did, you needed to bring your own champagne flutes as well. It was a model of excellent food accompanied by the never-ending good cheer of Stephania and Giovanni, the owners.

As usual, by seven on a Saturday night, the restaurant was close to full and the takeaway customers were filling the footpath, jackets and jumpers countering the surprisingly brisk evening.

'I apologise for the scene I caused,' Mark said.

When Jan had seen the photo, she had burst into tears. Shaken by the sudden outpouring of grief at having instantly recognised her sister, Mark moved to hug her and inexplicably found himself sobbing too – for the loss of her lifelong companion, and his own.

'I've dragged you into much more than just the search for a painting, I'm afraid,' said Mark now, pouring them each a glass. 'I'm still holding on to a lot of ...'

'It's been a big afternoon,' Linda said. Then she smiled. 'I think that amounted to some useful therapy for both you and Jan.'

They toasted each other and Mark took a mouthful of his champagne. 'I'm definitely feeling better,' he said. It had indeed been a cathartic experience, many months of loneliness and the struggle, still present after more than three years, to find clear purpose and direction in his life overflowing in the presence of Jan's bare grief and the realisation that they had, in all likelihood, identified Charlie. 'Sharon – my wife – died three years ago and I am still battling to make sense of it all. I was a surgeon, you know, but I felt that I had to quit.' He searched Linda's face for her reaction but couldn't discern one. 'The gallery has been a joy and a saviour. But my emotions remain a law unto themselves. Let's change the subject. Tell me about you, Linda. You seem so much more "together" than me. Please tell me there's something not quite perfect in your story.'

'Oh no,' said Linda. 'There's too much to tell.' But Mark persisted and Linda shared her life story. She'd emigrated from Capetown in 1991 having completed a basic commerce degree and looking to travel. She'd ended up in Sydney where she started in retail on the shop floor of a national company and moved upwards into store management. Ultimately, she took on a national role. She met Eric through work and they'd dated for a year before they were engaged; in another year they were married. When he transferred to the Perth office, she gladly accompanied him.

'Eric and I divorced about ten years ago. Neither of us wanted children, or wanted them more than we wanted our lifestyles. I don't think the two of us ever really connected in a personal or meaningful way. It was all very amicable, even our divorce. Almost mathematical. We divided up the assets and parted company.'

Mark looked intently at Linda, struggling to relate her account of herself to his own observations.

'People ask me all the time if I regret not having children. Surprisingly, I don't think about that so much. What I most regret is the fact that I lived with someone for over ten years without passion, or any real sense of a shared purpose. Looking back at me, how I was back then, I think I just was just going through the motions.'

Then Linda described her feeling of responsibility for her failed marriage, her loneliness and guilt and her sense of failure after their separation. Her only subsequent relationship of any substance had foundered on a series of differences in both likes and dislikes and had left her pessimistic about the merit of any future romantic pursuit.

Mark nodded slowly, surprised and impressed at her candour and moved by her story of unfulfilled expectations. He said, 'I suppose that we all end up in relationships somewhere other than where we'd first imagined; and that hardly anyone gets where they want to in the manner they had initially hoped. I think the most important thing is what we choose to do next.'

'You're right of course.' She smiled. 'What are we going to do next about Charlie? Even Jan could tell we didn't exactly have a clear idea. For what it's worth, though, I agree with you about Charlie's painting. Jan and her story are solid. Her painting was definitely painted by Charlie and it was gifted to Katy as it says, in seventy-two. To me, that seems completely undeniable.'

'But Charlie clearly couldn't have copied James Devlin. And Devlin won't have been inspired by Charlie, let alone have copied his work,' said Mark.

'Chances are that, by some sort of fluke, both artists did similar work separated by two thousand kilometres and about ten years. I can't think of any other explanation?'

'You're probably right,' said Mark. 'If only we knew who Charlie was and what has happened to him, I would be much happier. I'm still struggling with the fact that a work of that depth and intensity was painted by a teenager. The odds are strong that Devlin had nothing at all to do with Charlie's painting, so I can't see any point in raising this with him directly.' Mark popped another slice of pizza onto his plate.

'Jan said she was happy for you to hold onto the painting for as long as you needed to, so there isn't any rush to sort it out.'

'I suppose that's true. I'm off to Melbourne next week and when I get back, I'd like you to meet Pat O'Beirne. I think we need his advice.'

Pizza was predictably delicious. Stephania promised Mark that she would not waste the half-bottle of champagne that he and Linda had not been able to finish, and Mark drove Linda back to her car which she had parked close to his gallery. Any romantic tension that might have surrounded this parting had been defused by Mark's outburst at Jan's home and the fragility of his emotional state that it had exposed. Mark promised to be in touch when he returned from the auctions although he knew already that he would email or phone Linda while he was in Melbourne.

❖❖❖

The excitement of the auction crowd at the appearance of *Paradise* roused Mark from his trance. He was struck by how much more closely the real thing resembled Charlie's painting than did the digital image. It seemed even more arresting now: brighter, lighter, perhaps more joyous. A thrill rose in Mark's chest as the bidding began boldly at the upper end of the predicted range. Bidders on the floor and on two telephones participated in a veritable frenzy. Despite an upper limit predicted to be forty thousand dollars, the price soared over fifty thousand before slowing.

The two buyers on the telephones remained in contention as they approached sixty thousand dollars. Mark imagined the two of them, neither paying attention to the pre-established limit they might have set for themselves, both aware that this was a rare collecting opportunity and a cause for serious bragging rights. In the absence of any price precedent or plain logic, Mark could tell that their bidding would continue until one of them appreciated the folly of their endeavour and stopped. At sixty-two thousand the hammer fell, and the audience applauded the new price record for a work by James Devlin, caught up in the emotion of the moment as much as those who had been competing for the work on the floor and the phones.

Mark was none the wiser about the implications of this result for the value of Charlie's painting. He texted Linda the outcome, along with an image of the work as it was being paraded on the stage. Some seventy lots later, the auction concluded. The evening's events had firmed his resolve to unravel the dilemma surrounding Charlie; for James Devlin, Mark thought, and for anyone who owned his works, it had been an exceptional night.

10. THURSDAY NOVEMBER 21

Thursday midmorning was Mark and Pat's usual meeting time. Pat lived in Perth's southern suburbs and Mark in the north, although neither lived especially far from the serpentine Swan River that defined the boundary between Perth's south and north. Mark especially loved the paved five kilometre-long promenade running along the southern foreshore from the Narrows Bridge to the Causeway, where he and Sharon had frequently walked on weekends, discussing their children and grandchildren, planning their holidays, and taking in the views across the river to the Perth CBD.

Mends Street ran for less than two hundred metres down to the jetty on the southern foreshore from which scores of locals and tourists ferried the short five-minute trip to and from Perth city. Their weekend walks had nearly always ended at their favourite café. Notwithstanding Sharon's unswerving eye for décor and style, the outdated interior of their preferred haunt had never outweighed her strong preference for its coffee.

Mark – and now Pat – had come to love its distinctly uncool ambience as well as the great coffee, and he felt close to Sharon and somehow moored whenever he was there. He and Pat sat just inside to shield themselves from direct sunshine and waited for Linda to join them.

'How were the sales?' asked Pat.

Mark described the two sales that he attended in detail, the atmosphere in the auction rooms and the impressions he had gleaned about the strength of the art market. The national economy remained weak and business confidence shaky in the face of unease at the fiscal direction that the new federal government was taking. Even still, there had been strong demand for excellent works by established artists and the invariable surprises – the unexpected interest in some emerging artists and the surprising lack of interest in some of the more usual 'stars'.

'Do you know of a guy called Garth Barrett?' asked Mark.

'Sure. He's a reasonably well-known collector. He's bought and sold through our auctions over the years, mainly sold, to be honest. Solid works rather than major ones. Probably looking to off-load them away from the main markets in the East. I found him pleasant to deal with – didn't make a fuss about our recommended price ranges, happy to set a realistic reserve price but not interested in just giving away paintings. He's a cosmetic surgeon, I think. Did you meet him there?'

Mark appreciated again how small the pool of serious collectors was across Australia. If Pat knew Barrett, so did most of the established secondary art dealers in all the capital cities, including James Devlin. 'No, I didn't get to meet him. The people sitting next to me knew who he was. It's just that he paid quite a lot for an average Ray Crooke when the general feeling on the night didn't seem to fit with that. I suppose it was just one of those things, but a seasoned collector could easily have spent that much on altogether more interesting works. Do you think he was genuine?'

'Who knows, Mark? It can be a strange game over East – I've told you to keep your eye out for that sort of thing. Did you buy anything?' Pat asked cheekily.

'No, but that couple next to me acquired a lovely little Marie Tuck – a tiny European landscape.' Mark and Pat knew these types well – auction groupies who recognised good works and loved to participate but didn't quite have the means to buy the works they really liked. 'But the highlight for me was the Devlin. It sold really well with multiple bidders. I think the market for his stuff is only going to get stronger.'

Mark reached down and picked up a neatly wrapped painting. 'I've brought in that little Passmore,' he said handing it to Pat. 'I have some concerns about it – there's something about his signature that doesn't look right.' Mark explained that he'd only ever seen Passmore initial or sign in the very lower right corner of his paintings, never in the middle or, as in this case, just to the left of middle. 'Would you have a look at it for me?'

'Leave it with me,' Pat said just as Linda breezed into the café. Mark felt an instant stab of attraction and noticed that she also drew Pat's attention. She smiled and shook Pat's hand while introducing herself, acknowledging Mark by resting her hand briefly on his shoulder. She sat down and coffee was ordered.

'So, where are you two up to?' asked Pat.

'Let me summarise,' said Mark. 'According to Jan Bilowski, Charlie's painting was gifted to her sister, Katy, in nineteen seventy-two. We have a photograph that identifies Katy and might also identify Charlie and as an artist. Personally, I am in no doubt that the painting in my gallery was painted by a teenage client of the Sir James Mitchell School. Jan's story is absolutely solid.'

Coffee arrived as Mark came to his point. 'As much as this work resembles works by James Devlin – honestly, Pat, the likeness is striking – I do not believe that Devlin had anything to do with it at all. He would only have been maybe in his mid-teens when this was painted, and he lived in Victoria. It's Charlie's painting.'

Pat examined the photo of Katy that Linda had unearthed. 'What do you make of all this?' he asked Linda.

Mark saw Linda hesitate, surprised perhaps, that she was being asked for her opinion by Pat O'Beirne on a matter of art. But Mark appreciated a gathering weight around this puzzling scenario, the possibility of a significant and unexpected divergence from accepted truth, about which the opinion of an art outsider might be of particular value. He waited with interest for Linda's response.

'Even as a complete novice,' she said, 'I can see the direct connection between Charlie's painting and images of Devlin's works. I have no idea how, if at all, they are connected, but my intuition is that they are, and that that should be our starting hypothesis. I'm not sure what you think, but we were hoping for some advice and direction.'

Pat blinked at Linda. Mark knew that Pat was a cautious, even sceptical individual and that experience had taught him many hard lessons about the world of art. Pat bit his lower lip and shook his head slowly. 'I'm not exactly sure what to advise,' he told them. 'I agree that Jan's story rings true.' He pulled at his right shirt cuff with his left hand, a nervous action Mark observed.

'I've found out a bit about Devlin which might help,' Pat said. 'He first arrived on the Melbourne art scene in the early eighties and he probably only held about a dozen distinct exhibitions. He was awarded the Wynne Prize along the way with a major work, which is now in the NGV. His works rose in price dramatically and he seemed destined for a stellar – and rewarding – career when he upped and left for London in around nineteen eighty-eight, citing dissatisfaction with the art scene in Australia. He literally gave it all away and went to London.'

Pat told them that Devlin had returned to Melbourne around 1990 or 1991 where he established his own gallery, never painting again but building a stable of excellent up-and-coming artists while also trading successfully in the secondary market. Over time, his business in that market grew substantially and he regularly held exhibitions of older works by highly collectible artists.

'He's done very well for himself.' Pat sipped his coffee, as if debating how to proceed. 'My reservations about him relate to the uncanny way in which he has always been able to time his own sales of all sorts of different artists to correspond to a recent rise in commercial interest in their works. Whenever I see an unexpected spike in the prices of artists whose values I previously thought I understood well, I look for his next exhibition. Mark, you made comment about the Crooke acquired by that surgeon in Melbourne – don't be surprised if Devlin has a Crooke or two in his next gallery exhibition.' He drank the remainder of his coffee in one large swig.

'Whatever else you two do, be careful of James Devlin. He moves in influential circles, he controls his art empire fastidiously, and he is a real contender for Australian of the Year. So, be discrete, and make no claims about anything at all unless you are one hundred percent sure of your facts. If you annoy him, and if he wants to, he can cause you trouble.'

'I don't think I'll be calling him, Pat,' said Mark. 'But how do I progress this? Linda is looking into whether or not she can locate Charlie and whether or not Charlie or his family would be prepared to assist us – privacy legislation makes it quite a sensitive matter.'

Pat tapped lightly on his coffee cup with the teaspoon and said, 'I agree that Charlie's painting is a dead ringer for a James Devlin. But I've seen too many excellent fakes, and too many people have tried to sell me hidden treasures that turned out to be duds for me to get excited straight away. So, while Linda is looking into Charlie, I'd be looking into Devlin even more. No-one's ever understood why he gave it all away, or what he did in London. He's very secretive about his personal life. Maybe his story will provide a link that makes more sense. But, be careful, Mark – Devlin plays for keeps.'

11. THURSDAY NOVEMBER 21

That evening, Mark had early dinner out with Olivia, her husband Hendrick, and their two children. Other families were also taking in the early sitting and the child-friendly menu. While Oscar and Sophie were busy with their colouring-in books, Mark's conversation turned to his search for the origins of Charlie's painting.

'And who exactly is this Linda?' interrupted Olivia, smiling as her father blushed. The table went quiet, even the children pausing to look up at their grandfather suddenly put into the spotlight. 'Since you ask, she is approximately my age, single, attractive and very good company,' said Mark. 'Nothing has happened between us. But we are working together – along with Patrick – to try to locate Charlie and solve this puzzle.' He returned Olivia's gaze with mock defiance. 'She is definitely a "person of interest", if that is what you want to know.'

'Well, I'd love to meet her some time, Dad.' As if pleased with herself for having extracted this admission, Olivia changed the subject. 'I had a good afternoon in the gallery, you know. A doctor and her husband came in around two and bought one of Jo Darbyshire's recent works. You know, the large abstract you'd had hanging in the window last month? They thought they'd missed out because you'd taken it down – it was a nice sale for a Thursday.'

Mark was pleased with news of this sale of the large marine landscape – especially for the artist – and grateful for his daughter's capable cover. He had left the gallery to Olivia all day and joined some old medical friends for a game of golf. Golf was not really one of his favourite activities, but he loved the chat that followed the game, the dark humour of his former colleagues, and the stories of the personalities that populated their workplaces. That much he missed. But the endless calls from anxious patients, on the other hand, the incessant requests to squeeze yet another 'special' case in for an early appointment, the worry about the prospect of an adverse outcome from surgery and the threat of patient complaint despite his best efforts, all reminded him of how much less stressful life was as an art gallerist.

'And James Devlin's gallery sale catalogue arrived today, Dad. Nothing out of the ordinary, really and no new Devlins.'

'Any Ray Crookes?'

Olivia held up her knife and fork, momentarily still. 'Maybe four or five largish works. Why do you ask?'

Mark shook his head. 'It's a long story, darling, can I tell you in the gallery tomorrow?'

'Sure, I'll be in early but I'm leaving around midday. Remember you're coming to us for dinner tomorrow night? Would you like to invite Linda? It's not too early for meeting family is it?'

'In the usual sense, it probably is. But, as it relates to Charlie's painting, we're absolutely hitched for the moment, so it shouldn't be all that strange. And I'd like you two to meet anyway. I'll ask her tonight and let you know.'

When dinner wound up, Mark happily picked up the tab and they went their own ways. On his way home he called Linda to ask her to Olivia and Hendrick's place for dinner. She agreed without hesitation. Asking her to meet his daughter and her family when their relationship was still so unformed must have struck Linda as strange, he thought, but she did not appear deterred. He was comfortable at the atypical, gentle trajectory this new relationship was taking, confident that Linda shared a similar attraction to him and content to wait to see where it would lead them.

12. THURSDAY NOVEMBER 21

Sleep remained an ongoing problem for Mark. Aches and pains related to that afternoon's round of golf compounded his recurring insomnia. Yet the day's exercise, a large glass of wine at dinner and accumulated lack of sleep left him feeling exhausted. Before getting into bed, more in faint hope than realistic expectation of sleep, he selected from his burgeoning library of art books one that he'd been thinking about since he'd been at the Ian Potter in Melbourne and prompted by his conversation with Pat that morning. It was a lavishly illustrated book documenting the history of the Wynne Prize for landscape art, awarded and displayed at the same time every year as the much more famous Archibald Prize for portraiture. He teased himself by working his way from the mid-1960s towards his ultimate objective, the work by James Devlin which had been awarded the 1985 prize and that he had admired in real life just forty-eight hours earlier.

Wilderness was Devlin's most celebrated work. Eyelids heavy despite the anticipation, Mark turned the page to reveal the 1985 winner, seeing it once again with a more acute awareness and a fresh perspective. The central black elements, the shades of blue and the gestural strokes of white, all of which generated a sense of energetic motion, as well as the hints of pink, were typical of Devlin's paintings; the portrait orientation along with the impression created by the urgent application of paint were absolutely characteristic. Devlin had maintained control of this energy across the entire work, evidence of his growing assuredness at that time and of the compelling vision that had driven this work, infusing it with a penetrating clarity. Mark was mesmerised by the work, at the very point of losing consciousness.

With the deepest sense of peace, he emerged into cool, dry air. There was sparse, olive-coloured vegetation on flat, dark earth; bright blue sky above with white clouds edged in pink suggesting that sunset was not far off. Mark looked around him, wondering where he was and where he should go. The earth beneath his bare feet felt cool and smooth, not at all hot and dusty, as it appeared. He knew that he needed to find Sharon and he walked towards a group of trees. There was no wind and no sound; he felt totally calm, hampered only by some discomfort in his hips.

Beyond the trees he saw a group of people enjoying a picnic. Olivia and Linda were there, as was Jan. There were children playing with a ball, which seemed very light as they bounced it and hit it high into the air. Becky was the youngest and she was having a great time. Linda came towards him and asked, 'Where is Charlie?'

'I don't know. I haven't found him.'

'Pat has gone to look for him,' she said.

Mark had completely forgotten about Charlie and hadn't been looking for him at all. And now he remembered that he couldn't find Sharon either. A deep foreboding overcame him. Then the children started to scream – dark clouds were forming overhead and there was confusion and panic among the adults. The temperature dropped and Mark started to shiver. Everyone had abandoned him, and he was completely alone. Where was Sharon? He couldn't see her anywhere and shouted her name. From the side, Garth Barrett, dressed in a smart business suit, appeared and swung a punch that struck his belly.

Mark woke with a jolt. For a few moments, the shock of being punched and the alarm at not being able to find Sharon remained real; even as he regained full consciousness, the confusion and distress of his dream stayed with him. As did the chill of not being under the bed covers. He needed to speak to Sharon. He wanted to tell her about everything, about the girls and their children, about Charlie and his painting, about Barrett and Devlin – and about Linda.

The book lay open on Mark's abdomen and he stared hard into Devlin's *Wilderness*, willing himself to re-enter his dream, but he couldn't get back inside it again. He gazed up at the ceiling and steadied his breathing. Unable to comprehend the confused threads of his feelings, he got out of bed and went to make himself a hot drink. As he walked to the kitchen, the CBD's tallest buildings were clearly visible through the windows, lit brightly against the night sky. Mark felt they were close enough to touch but, like the meaning of his dream, frustratingly out of reach.

13. FRIDAY NOVEMBER 22

Without doubt, Olivia and Rebecca featured in Mark's happiest thoughts. How he wished Becky could spend more time in Perth. He couldn't wait until summer when the whole clan would gather in a rented beach house somewhere in the south-west corner of Western Australia for ten days of family holiday time. This was a tradition pre-dating Sharon's death and one that they continued without undue nostalgia, primarily because it was and always had been such fun. Finding the right house each year was now Mark's challenge, and he had to start early and work hard to find places that might match Sharon's previous consummate choices. This summer's house had long been secured and he was planning on spending some time during the day, if time permitted, looking for next summer's destination.

This Friday morning in the gallery was a quiet one and provided Mark the opportunity to bring Olivia up to speed with the Melbourne auction and the developments surrounding Charlie's painting. Olivia also recalled Pat's earlier comments about auction ramping.

'Do you think Garth Barrett is somehow connected to James Devlin?' she asked.

'I have no idea. They're probably about the same age, and the art world is small, so they will undoubtedly know each other quite well. If Barrett has traded through Pat and Helen, he'll have traded through Devlin's gallery for sure. I can see how pushing up the price for that painting plays into Devlin's hands, with the works that he has on offer in his own gallery. But how Barrett might benefit from paying too much for it, I don't know. If he was to sell it any time in the next few years, he would undoubtedly make a loss.'

'What if Barrett and Devlin are business associates? What if they both benefit from pushing up the prices in Devlin's gallery? Maybe they've known each other a long time, and this is what they've always done?'

That didn't seem like too much of a stretch of the imagination. Mark appreciated only too well how vulnerable a new art gallery business could be, and how tempting it might have been even for Devlin to manipulate the market, at least during those early years of his own gallery when cashflow was low and his reputation as a gallerist yet to be established. But surely a busy and reputable surgeon like Barrett didn't need to risk involvement in something quite so tenuous; and now that he was so well established, surely Devlin didn't need to risk his own reputation? And, if this was an unholy alliance of sorts, why would Barrett make himself so visible at the auction? He could quite legitimately have bid by phone and they'd have been none the wiser – why expose the possibility of a commercial interest if it wasn't necessary?

'If we could establish a connection between James Devlin and Garth Barrett, that would be consistent with the impression we have that Barrett was ramping the price, presumably for their mutual benefit,' Olivia said.

'I don't know. Other than as gallerist and collector, I don't see any particular connection. And there's just too much risk for Barrett. I agree that it doesn't feel right, but I don't know how to take it further.'

'You know, we were all in England around the same time Devlin was too. You were doing your specialist training at the Royal Free, weren't you? Maybe Barrett trained in England and might have met Devlin there.'

'Sure, but, as I recall, I was working quite long hours in London. Any spare time, your mum had us all heading off into the countryside to see different places and not into town to look at galleries. How would Barrett and Devlin have crossed paths, assuming Barrett even went to England?'

'We can find out about Barrett, I'm sure. I bet he has a website. I'm on to it!'

Before leaving at midday, Olivia produced a small dossier on Garth Barrett. Indeed, he had trained in London after obtaining his Australian surgical fellowship, working first in East London's Homerton Hospital as a plastic surgery registrar, and then as senior registrar in plastic and reconstructive surgery at the nearby but altogether more famous St Bartholomew's Hospital. He had returned to Melbourne, taking up a consultant post at the Royal Melbourne Hospital in July 1990.

'He was a pretty good all-rounder,' Olivia said. 'Barrett's family lived in the outer suburbs of Melbourne and none of his immediate family were professional people. He came from a working-class background, won a sporting scholarship to Melbourne Grammar for year eleven, and went on to be dux. He played top-level amateur football throughout his medical school studies. I expect he only stopped playing footy when he began to actively pursue his career as a surgeon.'

'All this is on his website? Who puts that sort of stuff on a website?'

'Actually, most of that's from an article about him in a *Weekend Australian* magazine published five years ago. He's a high-profile kind of guy, Dad: college committees, hospital boards, sporting club roles, you name it.'

In many ways, this sounded unremarkable to Mark. He had studied with the same sorts of multi-talented, sporting and academic superstars, people who could quite legitimately have made careers for themselves in music, sports or business. Medicine seemed to attract these over-achievers; once they had qualified and found themselves more or less committed to a life in the profession, becoming a surgeon – with its added reputation and income, and the presumption of a wonderful lifestyle – was a logical step for many of them.

What didn't quite fit was that Barrett claimed to have been a collector of art literally from the year he returned to Australia. Mark knew only too well that, back in 1990, Barrett would have been distracted by building his practice, by an excess of on-call duties as his senior colleagues handed unwanted work over to him as the newly appointed surgeon, and by a family at a demanding stage of life. Judging by the details on his website, he had married before going to London and one, possibly two of his three children had been born over there. There didn't seem to be a logical basis – either in terms of his upbringing or his work schedule – that underpinned this prompt and sustained involvement in art collecting and investment.

'I doubt he grew up in a home with lots of art on the walls,' Mark muttered, more to himself than to Olivia. 'Does the article explain how he got into art?'

Indeed, Olivia went on to explain, he claimed to have always had an interest in art and this had been, according to the same article, brought to life while he was in London, with its galleries and museums. Mark shook his head and wondered how, as a busy surgical trainee, Barrett had ever found the time.

14. FRIDAY NOVEMBER 22

Linda and Mark stepped out of the car outside Olivia and Hendrik's home. Here in Maylands, the river shore was dotted with open spaces and parks where families picnicked on weekends. Friday evening at dusk, however, the foreshore was empty, a solitary canoeist on the water paddling his way upstream, the river surface ruffled by the last efforts of the sea breeze. Mark had insisted on collecting Linda from her apartment in East Perth – he was a little anxious to see how things would play out when he dropped her home later that night.

At the same time, he could also appreciate the adolescent thrill attached to the pas de deux that was now taking place with Linda. And he was, he recognised, genuinely unsure of himself or what would eventuate.

The evening went smoothly. Olivia was bubbly and gracious, Hendrik quiet and competent, the children providing plenty of distraction and occasional hilarity, more than sufficient to overcome the initial awkwardness of welcoming a new guest to the family group. The atmosphere was relaxed, especially after the children went to bed, aided by being read two favourite books and serenaded with a selection of tuneless songs by their grandfather.

Olivia was interested to learn about Linda, and Linda was engaged by the warmth and affection that filled the numerous intersecting conversations. When they left the dinner table to enjoy a hot drink and some chocolates in the lounge room, Linda was drawn to a wall covered in framed family photographs. One in particular took her by surprise – a ten-year-old team photograph of Hendrik's premiership-winning rugby team.

'Is that you?' Linda asked, pointing at one young man.

'Absolutely. I haven't changed a bit,' he grinned, patting his abdomen ruefully. 'We had a good team that year.'

'I knew that team,' said Linda. 'My ex-husband was a keen rugby player and your halfback, Jonty something or other, was a very good friend of his from work.'

'Jonty Simmonds, you're right.'

'They were both South Africans, of course,' Linda said. 'We used to spend a lot of time with Jonty and his girlfriend, actually with a series of them.'

'That sounds like Jonty,' Hendrik said.

'I watched a few games over the years – I probably saw you play!'

By this stage, Mark and Olivia were listening to the exchange, smiling at the unlikelihood of this connection.

Suddenly, Olivia said, 'Do you think Devlin might have played football with Barrett? Do you think that's how they knew each other, from high school?'

'How do you know either of them actually played sport?' Hendrik asked, well aware of the speculation surrounding Devlin and Barrett from Olivia's debriefings.

'Barrett did for sure. He was a top amateur footy player,' said Mark. 'Aussie Rules,' he added by way of clarification. 'But I'm not sure about Devlin. He's about the same age as Barrett and he looks sort of athletic, he might've played some sport. But, even if he did, I doubt the two of them ever played at the same level. I don't even know where Devlin grew up!' Mark exhaled in exasperation. 'His website is so scanty. Why is there so little we know about him? Are his parents still alive? Does he have any siblings? How did he get involved in fine art? He protects himself so fiercely from the media. It's ridiculous!'

'Maybe not, Dad. How much personal detail do you have on your website? And if it wasn't for that newspaper article about Barrett, we'd know relatively little about him either.'

Mark nodded in grudging agreement.

'Why don't we assume that these two did play football together at school or even at university?' Linda said. 'We know where Barrett grew up and we can find out where he went to school and where he played his early football. People will remember him; if Devlin was there, they'll remember him as well.'

'That should be easy,' Olivia offered. 'I can look up Melbourne Grammar and Melbourne University records. I'll bet there are old yearbooks that will say who played in which teams.'

'Has anyone thought of just asking Devlin directly, about the painting at least?' Hendrik asked.

'Sweetheart,' said Olivia, 'if Devlin and Barrett are colluding to push up the prices of paintings he is selling through his gallery, that is big news, and not something to even suggest without proof. The last thing Dad wants to do is upset one of Australia's most respected gallery operators. And the painting ….' Olivia hesitated. 'That painting is mixed up in this, somehow. We just don't yet know how.'

'When we solve the mystery,' Mark said, 'we'll be able to tell Devlin all about it. He'll probably shake his head and laugh at us. But I have to know everything I can before I involve him.'

'Or Barrett,' said Olivia. 'It's just us for now.'

❖❖❖

'That was a lovely night,' Linda said. 'Your family is completely delightful.'

Mark smiled, yet to turn on the car engine. 'Thank you, they are truly beautiful.' He turned to face Linda and took a deep breath. 'This won't be a surprise to you, but I am not quite in the right … place at the moment.' He smiled at her again, tension and anxiety rising rapidly. 'I know I am getting too involved in this James Devlin thing. And – you saw me at Jan's place – I'm about as out of shape emotionally speaking as I could possibly be for someone thinking about starting up a relationship. With you, of course, but I mean about any relationship.'

'It was definitely good for you to get all that out of your system, Mark. But it doesn't mean that you're a total emotional wreck.'

'Thanks. I really did feel better after that … meltdown.' He closed his eyes for a moment before going on. 'You are so lovely, you really are. I mean, if I wasn't completely comfortable about you, I'd never have wanted to introduce you to Olivia and the family; I'd never have introduced you to Pat.'

'Well, I'm glad you're comfortable about me. Although that's not the most flattering description I've ever received. If it's any additional comfort to you, you don't seem unhinged to me.' She shifted slightly in her seat to face him. 'And I think you're a great guy. You're interesting to talk to, you're fun to be with. I get that you're passionate about this painting; I get that you're still grieving for Sharon. I've really been enjoying the time we've been spending together.'

There was a long pause. Mark looked at Linda directly and she returned his gaze. 'I have an issue with starting up another relationship,' he repeated. 'That's kind of obvious, I know. Do you think you can put up with this strange arrangement for a little bit longer? I love spending time with you but I'm not quite … not quite ready …'

Linda took hold of Mark's forearm with both hands. 'That's fine, Mark. Let's not ruin something that might work out very well by forcing things at the wrong moment. I'm enjoying myself, I'm enjoying your company and I'm more than happy to let things play out. OK?'

'Thank you. That's … perfect.' Mark started the engine and began to edge out onto the road. 'Do you have any spare leave at the moment?' he asked. 'Tonight's conversation has given me the strangest plan. I really like your idea about following Garth Barrett back to school to see if that leads us to Devlin. I'm certain those two are connected.'

15. TUESDAY NOVEMBER 26

Mark was sitting at his gallery desk, sipping his morning coffee as he re-read the email from Olivia. She had found no record of James Devlin attending Melbourne Grammar School and he'd been a student at Monash, not Melbourne University. Even at Monash, she could find no evidence that he'd played football or any other sport. The phone rang.

'I've had a look at that little Passmore for you.'

It was Pat. Mark was keen to hear about Alvin Teoh's work. 'What do you think?'

'Neither Helen nor I think it looks like a Passmore. The palette isn't right, and the subject matter doesn't really fit. It's entitled *Port Phillip Bay* and Passmore painted lots of waterfront scenes and people bathing. But he only ever visited Melbourne once in his entire life, for about a week, and I don't think he ever painted a Melbourne scene.'

As always, Mark was bewildered at how Pat knew what he did about Australian art and artists. Mark liked the painting and had initially imagined it would be of some value and of great interest, precisely because of the unusual locale it depicted. He had hoped that Pat would find the link between this work and John Passmore.

'It gets a whole lot worse, I'm afraid.' Pat was on a roll. 'As you spotted, it is initialled "J.P." in Passmore's style, but, as you said, when Passmore did sign or initial his works, he invariably did so in the very lower right of his paintings. Not plonked in the middle at the lower edge.

'I estimate that it's in a seventies frame. That doesn't mean that it was necessarily painted in the seventies, but I took it out of the frame and the frame actually covers about two centimetres of painting all around. That's about an additional ten to fifteen percent of painted surface.'

Mark was trying to digest the information. Who would cover a significant amount of the painted surface? If it was a painting by anyone of repute, that would instantly reduce its value. This was not what Mark had expected and he wondered how he was going to explain the doubt about authorship to its owner.

'The bit exposed by the frame has been varnished but the bit covered by the frame has not. I looked at the painted initials under fluorescent light and that paint is not found anywhere else on the work. But there is a tiny drop of that same paint on the frame just where the initials have been placed.'

'I think I get it,' Mark said, although he didn't really get it at all. 'What is going on?'

Mark could hear the wry smile in Pat's tone. 'I don't know when this lovely little work was painted, Mark, but I think it was probably framed in the seventies. I've no idea why they chose to cover so much of the painting, but there are some holes caused by nails in each of the corners so they were probably trying to cover them up. It's obvious that the initials were added later in a style intended to resemble Passmore's. And then the exposed painting surface was covered in varnish, all part of the same subterfuge, to create the impression that the initials were part of the original.'

'So, it's not a Passmore?'

'No, in my opinion, it isn't. It doesn't look like a Passmore. The placement of the initials is wrong for a Passmore. Not only did he not sign all his own paintings, he was never driven by commercial interests and it is inconceivable – to me at least – that he would have later initialled any work to claim it as his own. It's just not his.'

'So, you're saying it's a forgery?'

'The painting's not really a forgery. I think it's a nice painting that, at some point, someone thought they could pass off as being painted by a much more famous artist. I'd say that the initials have been added later on, in an effort to add value. It's a pretty little picture. But it isn't what your client thinks he bought.'

'Why would anyone choose to pretend it's a Passmore when it's of a Melbourne scene? And if they had done any homework, surely they'd have placed the initials in the right lower corner. How did they think they'd get away with this?'

'Mark, they did get away with it. They fooled the auction house that sold it to your client and they might have fooled previous auction houses or galleries. Who knows how many times this lovely little pretender has changed hands over the years?'

This was strange new ground for Mark. Pat had told him many stories about fakes and forgeries in Australian art, but he'd always imagined that the auction houses would be the place where these were filtered out, not traded on. 'What should I advise Alvin?' Mark asked.

'He'll need to take it up with the people he bought it from. But I wouldn't hold my breath, Mark. They'll tell him anything they like. That the title of the painting might have been added by a subsequent owner who thought it looked like Port Phillip Bay. Or that lots of artists add their initials to their paintings much later on. Or that one owner simply chose to varnish the work. I'm telling you, they won't be easy to shift.'

Mark was not looking forward to his conversation with Alvin Teoh. He made arrangements with Pat to have the deconstructed painting photographed and the technical findings documented. He would collect the work and documentation when he and Pat next caught up. Then he told Pat he was heading back to Melbourne in search of a connection between Devlin and Barrett, although he did not mention the fact that Linda was accompanying him. Mark was uncomfortable enough about his hopes and uncertainties about his relationship with Linda without creating a public impression that, as yet, held no real substance.

'Just be careful, Mark. You're working on all sorts of assumptions and theories that might be wrong. And between Devlin and Barrett, they have both the inclination and the means to make you pay if you get this wrong.'

16. FRIDAY NOVEMBER 29

They had flown out of Perth on a Thursday evening, getting into Tulla-marine late and collecting their rental car before heading straight to the serviced apartments in Ferntree Gully, east of Melbourne. Linda had ascertained that Garth Barrett's older brother, Doug, owned and operated a large car-repair business on property acquired in the days before Melbourne's massive urban sprawl overwhelmed this previously sleepy outer suburb. Barrett's Repairs was a well-respected enterprise and, according to its website, gained considerable custom from car rental businesses and local citizens throughout the eastern suburbs of Melbourne.

The apartment block was literally next door to Barrett's garage. It offered comfortable accommodation and the suite Mark booked had two bedrooms. They arrived after midnight local time and each went straight to sleep. Mark was conscious they were creating the impression that they were formally in a relationship when they were not, but he had no doubt that it was the tantalising state of their relationship, as much as their ongoing investigation into the origins of Charlie's painting, that had encouraged them each to commit the time and the expense on such a speculative mission. It was if their search for Garth Barrett and the origins of Charlie's painting had become part of a strange courting ritual.

After they got up in the morning, a little fatigued by the three-hour change in time zone, they set out on foot, directly past Barrett's Repairs. Mark had broken down their first challenge to that of finding out where the Barrett boys had gone to school. They figured that, wherever Doug had gone to school, Garth was likely to have done so as well. And that this school might hold the records of their student enrolments or even their junior football teams.

They had agreed that making inquiries in person was less likely to arouse suspicion than making a 'cold call' to Doug Barrett from interstate. Catching Doug at work on that day – assuming that he hadn't retired – was more problematic, as was trying to recognise him on the basis of the images of him that they had extracted from the internet. There was also the issue of what they would ask him. Mark was pleased to hand over the primary responsibility for that to Linda who had been happy to volunteer.

Linda and Mark walked as close to the front window of the Barrett's Repair office they considered to be advisable, but there was no immediate sign of anyone resembling Doug Barrett. Around the side of the building, however, workers were on the job. One tall man, with a weathered face and wearing soiled overalls, approached them.

'Can I help you?' he asked. His overalls bore the Barrett's Repairs logo on the breast pocket and the name 'Doug'. They had their man.

'We're just in Ferntree Gully for the day,' said Linda, 'and wondered if you knew the place well enough to recommend somewhere for coffee or a nice spot for lunch.'

'I sure can.' Doug proceeded to recommend just two places – one for coffee back up the Burwood Highway and a picturesque spot for lunch in the nearby Wally Tew Reserve.

'Have you been in Ferntree Gully a long time?' asked Linda.

'More or less my whole life. I grew up in Upwey but I've worked and lived in Ferntree Gully for over half my life.'

'Did you go to school in Upwey? Were their schools here back then?'

Doug smiled at Linda's accent. 'You're not a local, that's easy to tell. Yes, I went to Upwey Primary School, and Upwey High. Up to year ten. Then I did my apprenticeship in Ferntree Gully and … well that's a long story.'

Linda thanked him and they set off to have that coffee and to plan their next move.

❖❖❖

It was the last full week of the academic year which accounted, Mark imagined, for the more than usually unruly atmosphere at Upwey High School. They found the reception office attended by a woman wearing large-lensed spectacles which conferred upon her a serious, bookish appearance.

Their strategy, developed over what had been, thanks to Doug's advice, a very nice coffee accompanied by a fresh and tasty pastry, was to ask direct questions, Linda taking the lead.

'I'm looking for some information about the surgeon, Garth Barrett, who attended this school, I think, in the nineteen sixties or seventies. Do you keep any records of the students who've gone through here?'

'We do indeed. May I ask who I am speaking to?'

Mark and Linda introduced themselves. As they'd rehearsed over morning coffee, Linda said. 'We're freelance journalists and we're preparing an article about James Devlin, the well-known art gallerist ahead of the Australian of the Year announcements. We've struggled to find out much about him, but we've been told that he and Garth Barrett were schoolmates in the seventies. We wondered if James Devlin had also been a student here.'

The receptionist gave them a courteous smile, seemingly happy to oblige. 'I've read about Mr Devlin in the newspapers. We do keep a record of our prominent graduates.' Returning to her screen, she said, 'Dr Barrett and both of his brothers were students at Upwey High. Dr Barrett is certainly certainly one of our more illustrious graduates. He attended this school ...' the receptionist now scrolling through documents on her computer screen '... from nineteen seventy to seventy-three. He won a scholarship to Melbourne Grammar for his final year of secondary school and went on to study medicine ... at the University of Melbourne ... and is a plastic and reconstructive surgeon ... at Royal Melbourne Hospital, I think.'

She looked up, pleased to have been able to locate the essential facts with so little delay.

Mark spoke up. 'Do you have any record of James Devlin? You might know him as being famous in the art world here.' He heard the tension in his own voice, and Linda shot him a glance. He could feel her rebuke and hoped he hadn't foiled her plan. He glanced back with an apologetic shrug of his shoulders.

'No, we don't have any record of James Devlin here around that time.' Her eyes returned to the screen. 'We had a Gary Devlin here in the late seventies and Amanda Devlin – I think maybe siblings – around the same time. Devlins again in the early eighties – Gavin, Trenton and Julie; Mark and Christopher in the late eighties and early nineties – looks like there have been a whole lot of Devlins around here over the years.' She smiled and looked up. 'Does that help?'

'Thank you,' said Linda. 'Was there a football ground around here? A local team Garth Barrett might have played for?'

'Yes indeed – and there still is. The Bushrangers have been going strong in this region for years. They had their eightieth anniversary last year. I'd guess that most of the local boys have played with them at some stage of their lives, so Dr Barrett might well have played for them too. Some of the older men still playing are into their forties. They started a women's team here about three years ago and that's also going strong.'

'Do you know where their home ground is? Do they have a clubroom or something like that? There might be great old photos from the early days – maybe even some of Garth Barrett?' Mark was trying to sound enthusiastic – that James Devlin hadn't gone to school here wasn't necessarily the end of the line for this inquiry, although the odds of him having played football with Barrett had diminished sharply.

'You're right here.' She smiled broadly. 'The Upwey Tecoma Bush-rangers have their home base just behind my office on the recreation reserve. There's a really nice new clubroom there which was built for last year's celebrations. Although it's not the footy season, you might find Glen Derricks there. He's the club secretary and historian, and he's often in there pottering about.' Her eyes narrowed as if, all of a sudden, she had become suspicious of them and anxious she had been too forthcoming. 'Will there be anything else?'

Linda answered. 'No, but thank you for your help. It doesn't look as if James Devlin ever attended this school after all. We're sorry to have taken up your time. Let's see if we can track down … is it Glen?'

The receptionist repeated the name of the club secretary and, keen not to arouse any more misgivings, Linda and Mark left the school office to look for the Bushrangers' clubrooms.

Outside, Mark turned to Linda. 'Do you think she bought that story?'

'Who knows?' said Linda. 'But there is still a dim little light on at the end of our tunnel. Let's see if there's anyone in the clubrooms.'

17. FRIDAY NOVEMBER 29

The Bushrangers' clubhouse sat close to the main playing field, perhaps fifty metres from the recently restored picket fence that marked the boundary of the oval. It was a new building, with a central administrative area, a modest kiosk, and a change room on either side. There was no sign of activity on the field or in the reception area, with a handwritten sign attached to the inside of its glass door that read:

Upwey Tecoma Bushrangers FC
New members welcome
Next season senior training commences
Sunday February 8 at 5.00pm
Inquiries: Glen Derricks

Mark rang the number that was listed beneath Glen Derricks' name and left a short message on the voicemail service. After a pleasantly mild morning, the skies were turning dark and the temperature was dropping rather quickly.

Melbourne! thought Mark. Within minutes it was raining. The pair scurried back to their hotel room and were shaking out their raincoats when Glen Derricks returned their call. He had a broad Australian accent and seemed eager to assist in any inquiry about the Bushrangers or the people who'd played for them. Although he had no clear recollection of Garth Barrett, he was familiar with Barrett's reputation around the club as 'a terrific footballer and a fine young man'. But did he recall someone by the name of James Devlin having played around that time?

'The art gallery man and charity guy? I've heard about him – and we've had quite a few Devlins playing for us over the years – but I don't think he ever played for the Rangers. To be honest, Garth was quite a few years older than me so I didn't really follow him myself. And I didn't start keeping records of our player lists until about the mid-nineties. I think Garth played juniors here in the sixties and seventies. As far as I know, no-one at the club's ever said anything about James Devlin – did he come from around here?'

Mark said that he didn't know where Devlin had come from, but that he thought that he and Barrett were old friends; he conceded that he was really only acting on a bit of a hunch. 'But if you've got no records before nineteen ninety, we're probably at a dead end.'

'Well that's not entirely true,' Glen said. 'We've got literally hundreds of photos of teams and players going back into the nineteen forties. We went through them all for our eightieth, and I got some of the older local families to help try and name as many of the players in those photos as possible. Some we mounted for a display for the actual celebration, but they've all been scanned and stored. If you can be bothered looking through them, I'd be happy to let you in. Do you think you'd recognise him as a teenager?'

Mark's ability to recognise a youthful Devlin was, he surmised, the least of his problems. They had a photo of Devlin published in the *Age* that had been taken at one of his exhibitions in 1984, so they had an idea what he looked like in his twenties. But there didn't, after all, appear to be solid evidence of any link between Devlin and this football club, let alone between Devlin and Barrett as teenagers or in their early adult years. And who even knew where Devlin had been brought up? Yet, wherever he had, there would be many people who had been his schoolmates, friends, teachers; and some of them must know something about him. Even finding something concrete that ruled out a link between the two men as teenagers would be something.

'Thank you, Glen, for your help – my partner and I –' Mark turned to Linda apologetically – 'would love to have a look through those photos.'

'Are you free this afternoon? Tomorrow is a cricket day here and the place will be packed. I don't like the office being open when there are crowds of people in and out.'

'This afternoon is perfect, what time suits?'

❖❖❖

Having agreed upon two thirty pm at the clubhouse, Mark and Linda packed up their rental car, checked out and headed off to try out the restaurant at the Wally Tew Reserve that Doug Barrett had recommended. The rain continued throughout the afternoon forming a mist that obscured the view from the restaurant but which made Mark feel that they were perched on top of a cloud.

Mark said, 'There's a painting in the Art Gallery of South Australia by the surrealist artist James Gleeson. It's called *The Message Arrives.* It's a large painting of a sort of dystopian landscape with a swirling cloud in the centre and not a human figure or a recognisable structure in sight; I feel we're sitting in that painting right now.'

Linda shook her head and smiled. 'I think you must remember every painting you've ever seen.'

'It's a strange thing. It's as if paintings are a sort of language that I understand. They're like stories to me that, once I've heard them, I don't forget them. They leave an indelible impression or they convey a particular meaning that makes me recall the image in detail, like each brushstroke is part of the overall story. It's not that I'm consciously urging myself to remember those details, it's more that they sort of form part of my own life experience.'

The salads and fresh bread they'd ordered arrived.

'I'm envious of the extra dimension that art gives you,' Linda said. 'Is it something you learned or is it more ... instinctive?'

'I think art is like music or wine or even books. The more you immerse yourself in looking at – or listening or tasting or reading – the more you come to appreciate its subtleties and joys. It's not that everyone's tastes in art will be the same, however much time they spend looking at it.' Mark looked directly into Linda's eyes, a serious and searching gaze. 'Not everyone will be moved by the same paintings and not everyone will hear the same stories. The words contained in those brushstrokes and surface markings will be different for different people. But to me, it's as if the artist is trying to tell me something, like a message directed specifically at me. And once I've grasped that message, I never seem to forget it.'

They each tucked into their meals with gusto. Playing at detectives had given them a healthy appetite. When he was done, Mark set down his fork. 'I know this is a strange question, but are you looking for anything specific in a new partner?'

Linda set down her cutlery too. 'I wouldn't really say that I am actively looking for a partner, if I'm honest. I admit that I do get lonely on my own and that I end up missing out on going out to dinner or going to live shows. Travelling alone is also more difficult. I especially hate doing all those things on my own. But I also quite enjoy my own company, so I really haven't felt desperate to find another man.' She gave him an appraising look. 'I'm still open to the idea, Mark. Obviously. It's just that I'm a little sensitised to the prospect that I'll find myself in another relationship wondering if I'm just going through the same motions I did with Eric. How about you? What are you looking for?'

'It's a little like that for me too, although, right now frankly, I don't always like my own company,' Mark gave her a crooked smile. 'But I am also frightened that I'll end up in a new relationship and find myself rehashing old issues and repeating old ways of behaving. It's not something I feel comfortable talking about – I know that must seem like I'm holding back from you. Let's just say that there are inevitably areas of asymmetry in any relationship, where one person's wishes are significantly different to the other's. It's hard for me to … describe, but I know that for me it led to resentment and withdrawal and avoidance.' Mark drummed his fingers lightly on the table, feeling self-conscious. 'I think that must be true to some extent, of every relationship, ever. How could two people ever really be so alike in their interests and outlook? Honestly, of late, I've had this recurring sinking feeling that any relationship I enter will be doomed to reach the same unhappy destination.'

'I get that, Mark. But have you thought of any possible solution? I mean, I'm no therapist, but you did spend thirty fulfilling years with one woman who, I presume, didn't share identical likes and preferences with you, and that worked out OK. Surely it is still at least conceivable that you could find that sort of happiness with someone else?'

Mark wiped his mouth with his serviette as if he could hide his most private thoughts behind it. After thirty years together, his life with Sharon had assumed patterns and routines into which he had grown comfortable. Yet he knew that he didn't want to recreate those routines with Linda.

'I seem to have lost confidence that I can. Honestly, if I could explain it to you any better, I would.'

'In the meantime,' said Linda, 'we have a gallerist to find. Let's go see what we can find out from Glen.'

18. FRIDAY NOVEMBER 29

A surprisingly warm sun shone through the clouds over the Upwey Reserve. Only one other vehicle occupied the carpark, which was situated directly behind the administration building. Trees had been planted around its perimeter, but the fresh bitumen surface created a matt expanse that brought to Mark's mind the scorching surface of a Rothko masterpiece.

The rear door was open and Glen Derricks met them as they entered. He was dressed in shorts, T-shirt and sandals despite the rainy weather. He greeted them with a generous smile and introduced himself with a handshake first to Linda, then to Mark, ushering them into an office with a view over the playing fields. He had already brought the historical images up onto the computer screen and had positioned two chairs for their viewing.

'For the anniversary, I arranged them chronologically,' Glen said. 'Mostly, we knew which teams were from which years, but that was a lot easier for the last thirty years and not so easy before the eighties. The period of time you'll be interested in – when Garth Barrett was playing for the Rangers – will be about nineteen sixty-four to seventy-three. We know that he didn't play for us after that season, when he moved to Melbourne. Mostly, we have photos but not so many names of players. I got lots of locals to assist us in identifying the players, and the Barrett family were a big help.

'I'll start you in seventy-three and you can work backwards – my apologies if the dates are not as accurate as you'd have liked. I'll be around the place if you need me – sing out or phone me. I hope you find your man!'

When Glen had left them, Mark said, 'This really is a wild goose chase, isn't it?'

'Probably. But we're here now,' Linda said. She brought up the image of James Devlin taken at the exhibition opening back in 1984 on her phone. He was a handsome young man, almost pretty, looking slightly to the left of the photographer, with an apologetic smile. 'What have we got to lose?'

'I'm not even sure I'll recognise Barrett, let alone Devlin,' Mark said.

Glen's digital filing system turned out to be simple and user-friendly.

Mark clicked on the 1973 file, the last year Barrett had attended the local school, and the likeliest year to include his image, if not Devlin's. A series of pictures of different teams and individuals appeared, mostly formal team shots, with occasional action photos of generally poorer quality.

Impatient to find something of use, Mark clicked on the first image, a group of players holding a trophy aloft. They appeared to be a senior team, judging by the occasional beard. Linda placed her hand over his, stopping him from manipulating the mouse.

'Let's be systematic, OK?'

She took control of the mouse and quickly discovered that, by hovering the cursor over a photograph, a descriptor appeared, making it easy to see which team (seniors, reserves, under-eighteens and so on) was captured in that image; by right-clicking on the image, a list of names of the people in the photographs appeared by row, from right to left. She located the under-sixteens team photo, Garth Barrett's age group in 1973.

And there he was, a youthful facsimile of the current Barrett, seated in the centre of the front row alongside an adult, no doubt their coach. All the boys had their arms folded across their chests. There were boys of a wide variety of heights and degrees of physical development, some lean or even muscular, others chubby and 'soft'; some evidently athletic and others seemingly making up the numbers.

Linda leaned closer, scanning the faces, then pointing excitedly at the screen. 'Is that him?'

The teenager had blond hair, longer than any of the other boys, creating the impression he was either fashionable or rebellious, or both. He stood behind and several players to the right of Garth Barrett.

Mark right-clicked to reveal the list of names of the players. Garth Barrett was listed as 'Graham Brian "Garth" Barrett (centre half-forward, captain)', and the blond-haired teenager was also clearly listed: 'James Harold Devlin (right wing)'.

'Bloody hell!' Mark said, taken aback by the ease and the unlikeliness of their discovery. 'I'm not sure I can believe it.'

'We need a copy of that photograph and the player list, if Glen will let us have it,' Linda said. 'And we need to find out where James Devlin went to school. There'll be lots of people who remember him from his school days. Although I'm still not sure any of this helps us figure out anything to do with Charlie's painting.'

At that moment Glen stuck his head around the door. 'How's it going?'

'We've found them,' said Mark, trying to sound matter-of-fact. 'James Devlin really did play alongside Garth Barrett – have a look at this.'

It didn't take a second glance for Glen to agree that the under-sixteens' right winger was the same person pictured in the *Age*. 'Well, I'll be. I wish I'd known that before our eightieth celebrations.'

Glen obliged their request for a copy of the photograph and the player list. 'Can I ask why you are so keen on looking for James Devlin?'

Mark provided the same account that he had earlier in the day. In the course of the article they were preparing for publication, he and Linda had stumbled on to the fact that Devlin might have been a friend of Garth Barrett's and that they might be able to find out more about Devlin through this connection.

'It was a long shot, Glen, but I think it has paid off. There is so much about James Devlin's early life that will be of real interest to Victorian readers.'

Glen shook his head. He was bemused by the explanation and had the look of a man who doubted he would ever really understand 'city folk'. 'Well, good luck. I'm glad I could help.'

They shook Glen's hand and departed, the photocopy securely in Linda's file. They remained silent until they were in the car and safely on the Burwood Highway back to Melbourne.

'You know,' said Linda, 'Glen Derricks is going to be in contact with James Devlin within days. Forget about Charlie's painting for a moment, but if you and Pat are right about the relationship between Barrett and Devlin, the news that some people are investigating their association will make Devlin pretty nervous. Even if there's nothing to that association, at the very least he won't be happy that we've been snooping around.'

'You're right,' said Mark. 'The minute he knows what we've been looking for, he'll want to know why. I don't think Glen was all that convinced by our story. It's hard to imagine James Devlin will be either.'

'Oh well,' said Linda, 'we'll have to cross that bridge when we come to it.'

Mark glanced at her. 'But your hunch about the football connection was awesome,' he said and Linda grinned, clearly pleased with herself.

Traffic into Port Melbourne was predictably slow late on a Friday afternoon, but unlike the traffic, conversation flowed. The five o'clock news prompted discussions about politics and their respective viewpoints; Mark noted that Linda did not seem concerned to impress or agree with him although she was, like him, not possessed of intensely passionate, partisan opinions.

'I have become progressively more suspicious of ideologies,' Linda said. 'It's not that I don't see many things as clearly right or clearly wrong. It's just that I don't see that the answer to every issue that confronts society can be found in a manifesto written by one individual living at one point of human existence.'

Mark nodded. He had also become tired of political parties constantly referring to 'true believers'. He, too, had noted with despair the manner in which politics had been hijacked by individuals professing to be the holders of their political party's truths, their polarised views taking precedence over those who saw the human condition more as a continuum. He sided with those who admitted uncertainty, and sought contemporary and human solutions.

'I've definitely come to a different view of the universe these last few years,' said Mark. 'Watching Sharon's illness and her death, I was overwhelmed by the sense that this was all … unfathomable. It couldn't be explained – I mean, I knew what was happening, but there was no compelling sense of why. Why Sharon? Why at this point in her life? Or in ours?'

Outside, the buildings were becoming taller and the streets more crowded. Melbourne was closing in on them as Mark hurried to express himself.

'Amazingly, I reached a point where I didn't feel anger or resentment so much as I came to appreciate the truth that I was not in control of these events. That I wasn't even supposed to be able to control them. That life and the universe had their own trajectories.'

'That sounds as if you became a bit detached from everything. Like you were watching events from a distance.'

'Sort of. But I wasn't indifferent to it all. It was more that I realised that I didn't necessarily have the "right" to understand everything. And so I was able to stop railing against the frustration of not being able to do so. These days, I actively choose to be humbled by life's sheer uncertainty.' He caught Linda's eye and smiled.

'That all sounds kind of spiritual,' said Linda.

'Well, I wouldn't say I suddenly discovered God or anything. But there's a lot of what's happened lately that is … mysterious, let's say.'

'Embracing mystery? Sounds like the theme of this trip.'

Mark laughed. Their GPS device issued its final instructions as they turned on to Nott Street. They had arrived.

19. FRIDAY NOVEMBER 29

Showered and dressed afresh, Linda and Mark walked to Becky and Alan's home, taking the gifts he had brought with him for his grandchildren and Linda stopping briefly at a bottle shop to select a bottle of Devil's Lair chardonnay. They arrived in time to see the children straight out of their baths and very much ready for bed.

Isabelle, all of four, was thrilled to see her grandfather to tell him all about her current thoughts and activities, and excited to be able to show off to another adult, especially a lady. Georgia was a bundle of smiles, not quite one, and happy to be held by the visitors.

The night passed quickly. The story of Charlie's painting, the discovery of a link between James Devlin and Garth Barrett, and the sense this was all in some way connected was greeted with wonder by Alan, but with some scepticism by Becky.

'Why not just ask James Devlin if he recognises the painting? Maybe he has the answer and all your investigating will have been unnecessary.'

Like Olivia, Becky also had a strong eye for art. But, unlike her sister, Becky was unmoved by its provenance; her appreciation was sophisticated but unsentimental. Mark explained his sense – his belief – that the painting in his gallery really was painted by a teenager with mild cerebral palsy. And his equally strongly held belief that the painting belonging to Jan Bilowski so resembled the works of James Devlin that he was no longer sure whether Devlin was the artist he purported to have been.

Up until that point, neither Linda nor Mark had openly articulated that thought. Mark caught Linda's eye, reassured as she nodded her affirmation.

'What I don't understand,' Becky said, 'is why you are spending so much time investigating James Devlin. Why not find out who Charlie was and what happened to him?'

'That makes perfectly good sense,' said Linda. 'And we are trying to find out more about Charlie; it's just that we don't know what his full name is and many of the people connected with the Sir James Mitchell School back then have died or disappeared. Even if he is still alive, it's not going to be easy to locate him, but if he's dead, we'll have even less chance.'

There was a brief, sober silence before Becky asked, 'What are you two up to tomorrow?' She, Alan and the girls had an all-day commitment made well before this surprise visit.

'We're driving out to the Bendigo Art Gallery and then flying back home on the seven o'clock flight. Just a very quick trip this time.' Mark was already anticipating Becky's return trip to Perth for the summer holidays. By 9.30 the hosts were fading, so Linda and Mark bade their farewells and headed out along the beachfront promenade.

'That was a nice night,' Linda said. 'Your family is so lovely.'

'I think that's as much to do with you as it is to do with us.' Mark hesitated, unsure how he should take the conversation further in this direction. 'You must know that I think that you are totally gorgeous. And if I was in anywhere near the right state of mind, I would probably have ... well ... already made a fool of myself.' He knew that might not have come out well. 'And probably ruined everything. But, if I'm honest about it, I have been thinking about ... that sort of thing, more or less from the moment we first met.'

They walked on past Nott Street, heading towards the port. The *Spirit of Tasmania* had left the dock for its overnight journey south, leaving the jetty still and sparsely lit.

'I like you too, Mark. I am glad that you haven't ... tried something that you might have regretted. But surely you can see that me just being here with you this weekend is, well, a sign that I'm not fretting that you might or might not? I mean, what do you think Becky and Alan imagine we're doing together?'

Mark was relieved to see a smile in her eyes. 'OK. I know. I really do like you very much. But I am having a bit of an issue with relationships at the moment.' He knew that wasn't the whole truth. 'Well, specifically with sex in relationships.' He panicked. 'I *can* have sex. I mean, I *like* having sex.'

'What is your issue with sex, then?' Linda said, caught somewhere between amusement and solicitous therapist.

'In general – and I get it that this makes perfectly good sense, and that it's completely normal, and …' Mark struggled to express himself. 'One partner in every relationship is always going to be more interested in having sex than the other one.' He looked up into the dark night sky and the high clouds drifting across, praying for either assistance or salvation. 'These days, sex seems to have become the starting point of every new relationship, well before people get to know each other. And the partner less interested in sex inevitably … let's say … overplays their enthusiasm for it, for fear of ruining the chances of the relationship being a lasting one.

'But down the track, you know, there's just no hiding that lack of enthusiasm forever. There really isn't. And sex becomes a chore and something that she – or he – resents. And when that resentment becomes apparent to both of them, sex becomes something lonely and dispiriting.' Mark stopped to look at her. 'I have really wanted just to be in your company and get to know you. But I am desperate not to go down exactly *that* path with you and end up one of us resentful and the other one lonely, instead of both of us happy.'

'Which one have you been, Mark: lonely or resentful?'

'I think sex, and all my confusing thoughts about it, have contributed to the loneliest experiences of my life. I mean, I've been … at times … unbelievably lonely since Sharon died, but then I started a new relationship and, before long, I found myself having sex with an openly reluctant and resentful partner. It was altogether the worst thing imaginable. Depressing, humiliating. And I just do not want to end up there ever again.'

'It's absolutely not that I'm some sort of sex fiend,' Mark added defensively, 'or that I'm looking for … gymnastics.' He thought he heard Linda stifle a laugh. 'The point is,' Mark said carefully, 'that I don't ever want to have to apologise for just wanting to have sex. Do you know what I mean?'

'I think I get it. Sex was a bit of a battleground for Eric and me too. Maybe it is for lots of couples. The bit that was worst, though, was that I became indifferent. I couldn't find the motivation to change what we were doing. I just couldn't be bothered.'

The red and green guide lights flashed out in Port Phillip Bay, set against the black water and inky sky.

'I've never spoken openly about sex, actually,' said Linda, staring out at them. 'Not with Eric, not with girlfriends, not really with anyone. Maybe the truth of the matter is, I don't really like having sex. I don't think I could honestly say that having sex has ever given me distinct physical pleasure. But that doesn't mean that sex hasn't been fun – or at least sometimes funny. Sex for me is sort of like eating coriander.'

'Coriander?' said Mark, startled.

'On its own, I really don't like coriander at all. So, for future reference, I definitely don't like Thai food. But when coriander is disguised by other food that I really do like, and food that specifically goes well with coriander, I enjoy the meal.'

Mark laughed. 'OK, I get your point,' he said. 'I appreciate you being so honest. But do you understand what I'm trying to say? If it's going to work for me, it has to be on the basis of being completely open. And, if being open – about everything – means that it *isn't* going to work, then we both have to accept that. And not torture the relationship to the point of resentment.' He paused. 'I wonder what food most describes what sex is like for me?'

'Maybe grandma's famous beef and liver pie?' Linda said. 'You know, the one that you had to battle your way through but then make a huge fuss over. You certainly don't seem to have been enjoying it much, that's for sure.'

Together, they began to walk again. The noise of cars on Beach Street merged with the sound of the waves lapping on the sure.

'No. Fresh ciabatta loaf. That's it for me,' Mark said suddenly, grinning. 'As much as I love eating it with butter and a delicious topping, I rarely even get to slice the loaf, let alone butter it, before I've consumed it all in a mad rush. It has literally gone before I can savour the moment. I'm left wondering with more than a little regret why I didn't take more time, slice it and butter it, actually enjoy it …'

They had stopped alongside the First World War memorial close to the wharf. They silently searched each other's eyes.

'I wonder what we are having for breakfast?' asked Linda, taking his hand and leading him back to the apartment.

20. SATURDAY NOVEMBER 30

As they left Melbourne proper and entered Hume, the flat, bare landscape crisscrossed by towering power lines cut an arid, somewhat dispiriting scene. Neither of them had previously been to Bendigo and, as they drove, they compared the travel notes of their lives. Mark felt relaxed, any anxieties about the beginning of intimacy between them allayed by the night before. He noticed in particular the way the skin of Linda's forehead was exposed by using her sunglasses as a headband, and how smooth it was. For him, the previous night's experience had offered as much relief as pleasure and had been unashamedly swift. For Linda, he hoped, it had been gentle and unhurried and, as she had reassured him, satisfying.

Entering the south-west corner of the Macedon Ranges, the scenery changed – rolling, tree-topped hills, green tinges still evident in the pastures, and cattle grazing in the paddocks. Cloud cover appeared from nowhere, surprisingly grey and reminiscent of a Devlin painting, and the temperature dropped as the highway took them up through more densely wooded territory.

Old farmsteads, some with dilapidated sheds, marked the landscape; graveyards of decomposing motor vehicles stood alongside several of the homesteads, memorials to more prosperous times. An hour later they reached the outskirts of Bendigo, then drove on into the town centre, where a profusion of modest, single-storey residences of different ages and styles sprawled across the flat terrain, and numerous old-style motels dotted the road toward their gallery destination. As they approached View Street, Mark was taken aback at the sight of Sacred Heart Cathedral, a massive Gothic edifice. Like the motels they had just passed, the grand cathedral spoke clearly of an earlier time and of the conventions of previous generations.

The gallery itself was even older than the cathedral – and, as he told Linda, one of Australia's oldest regional galleries. It had its regular standing exhibitions of European and colonial period Australian art, as well as a program of guest speakers and children's workshops, but Mark rather thought the gallery had mounted a display of its major works from the 1980s specifically to be able to include their James Devlin.

They strolled downhill together to enter through an archway in its bare brick façade and Mark purchased their entrance tickets. The exhibition was artfully curated and the explanatory text was full of historical and biographical material about the artists represented. Mark was drawn especially to works by familiar artists. An impressive diptych – *Hillside at Night* – a colour etching and dry point on paper by David Rankin, appealed for its dark and foreboding minimalism; *Metropolis #13* was a wonderful example of Robert Jacks' work at the height of his powers of geometric abstraction; *Painting Two*, also oil on canvas, by Peter Booth, displayed Booth's talent for abstraction, ample evidence of the range of his oeuvre.

There were great figurative works from the 80s on show as well such as *Yes, No*, a typical John Brack painting featuring a myriad of pencils. There were also striking works of human figures, most notably Howard Arkley's *Zappo Head 1987*. Arkley had produced a series of these haunted, mask-like images which he described as self-portraits drawn from the mirror after several days of intense amphetamine use. Arkley had died of a heroin overdose twelve years later, aged forty-eight.

Devlin's work, *Harmony*, was also on display, the same size as Charlie's painting and made of the same materials. The characteristic red insignia of Devlin's works, absent from Charlie's painting, was there in the lower right corner of the painting. The work was thoughtfully framed and was accompanied by a critique of the work, and a brief biography of Devlin.

Harmony was predominantly white and blue, conjuring the Australian summertime sky as did so many of Devlin's works. It had a strong, dynamic flow to it, commencing in its lower left corner as disorderly brushstrokes in blue and white running across the surface, side to side and then rising upwards as a thick core of white cloud, overlaying some stripes of blue paint, and dissipating in the upper aspect of the board into a dreamy skyline of pinkish clouds over blue.

Mark, however, felt that this was somehow less coherent than Charlie's painting. Although it exhibited many of the features of Devlin's other works, it was somehow less satisfying and less moving. Linda stood beside him, looking at it closely.

'There's nothing harmonious about this painting,' she said.

'I agree – it's more of a dynamic and energetic painting. Did you read the blurb? There's incredibly little biographical detail. It doesn't make any reference to him being a Victorian and they don't even list his year of birth.' Mark shook his head slowly as they moved on to complete the exhibition.

They browsed briefly in the gallery shop and Linda purchased a copy of the exhibition catalogue for Mark as a souvenir of their visit – and of the 'official' start of their relationship.

After lunch, they set off for the airport. Linda did the driving and Mark settled in to read through the catalogue. Sun beat strongly through the front windscreen. A full page had been dedicated to the image of *Harmony*, and Mark dwelt on it once again. The warmth, the weekend's emotions and the beer he'd had at lunch crept up on him and he felt himself surrounded by cloud, as if he was ascending quickly, against gravity. He felt the warmth as he rose up, closer to the sun. A wave of anxiety rolled over him, unsure of when or how his ascent would come to an end, where he was heading and who would be there. The white cloud suddenly cleared, and he could see that he was now well above it, patches of blue sky and grey-pink cloud all around. He felt light, weightless.

Among the clouds, Sharon approached him. 'Has the message arrived?' she asked.

'What message? I wasn't expecting a message.'

'A message from the girls, of course. They had something to tell me.' Her voice was not hers, but whose was it?

'We were with Becky last night and she didn't give us any message,' Linda said, appearing in the conversation.

When Mark turned back, Sharon had gone.

'I was supposed to deliver a message from the girls,' he told Linda, distressed. 'I've lost it somewhere.'

'It was a message from God,' said Linda, but Mark had already started to descend, a rapid, frightening fall through warm, white cloud, a pain in his neck jolting him to a sudden stop.

'Are you alright?' asked Linda.

'I must have fallen asleep. I was … dreaming.' He struggled upright still trying to separate dream from reality. The catalogue lay on the car floor in front of him. 'It was connected to the painting I was looking at in the catalogue.' He sighed and shook his head. 'You were in there, and Sharon. The girls. It was all a bit weird but I don't think it meant anything in particular.'

'Seems like there's a lot of stuff going on in that brain of yours right now,' said Linda.

Mark took a long swig from his water bottle and leaned forward to pick the catalogue up off the floor. There was an almost biblical aspect to *Harmony*, he thought, like a depiction of Jacob's dream in the Old Testament, of an ascent to heaven. And now, as they descended the Macedon Ranges, a panoramic view of Melbourne caught in the strong afternoon sun appeared before them, the vista befitting such grand contemplation.

'OK, mastermind,' Mark said to Linda, 'how are we going to track down Charlie?'

21. MONDAY DECEMBER 2

Less than forty-eight hours before his important pre-Christmas sale, James Devlin was disquieted and tense. He had just finished a call from Glen Derricks asking him to reconnect with his old football club and describing in detail the worrying interest being shown in him – and Garth Barrett – by a couple claiming to be journalists. He wondered if that was the reason for his message from Garth asking to meet with him in person, something the pair rarely did these days.

Barrett owned a house on the Mornington Peninsula. They had arranged to meet there in Mount Martha at eight pm. Over the years, they had done this a few times only, and neither of them felt comfortable having to do so. They were each so recognisable around Melbourne, and with someone using Barrett as a means to locate Devlin so close to the exhibition and sale that depended in part for its success upon their secretive association, they both felt the need to meet well away from potentially prying eyes.

Garth Barrett needed to be told what he had learned and Garth's advice would be useful. For now, Devlin had no option but to wait until the evening. So he parked his negative thoughts, summoned his second coffee for the day from his PA, and went over his plans for the following night's exhibition opening.

22. MONDAY DECEMBER 2

By midmorning in Perth, Linda had caught up on the emails and issues that had arisen during her brief absence. She enjoyed leading the team at the Centre and felt that she had earned their respect and trust. She was keen to apply for the permanent position about which she was feeling more confident, her self-esteem currently on an uncommon high.

The awkwardness she had anticipated with Mark after their Melbourne trip had not eventuated. Rather, they both felt somehow lighter and more relaxed in each other's company. Although their timetables and commitments would inevitably diverge, she sensed no undue neediness or possessiveness from Mark. Their entire interaction on Saturday had been unforced and enjoyable, their separation after their return to Perth warm, their Sunday apart comfortable and their conversation on Sunday evening undemanding. It all felt good and they had arranged to catch up for dinner later that evening.

She closed her office door, a signal to the office staff that she wanted a little time to herself, and she examined the report she had just received from the State Records Office. There was, as she had been warned, very little information available and no photographic records at all. Other than lists of pupils in attendance for the period of her search, there was nothing of use. Of considerable help, Linda thought, was that there were only two Charles or Charlies who had attended the Sir James Mitchell School in 1972: Charles Noble and Charles Templeman.

Charles Noble had been a pupil in year ten in 1972, making him fifteen at the time of the photograph – he was unlikely to be the tall pupil at his easel with Katy Bilowski watching on adoringly. Charles Templeman, however, had been in year twelve in that year and seemed a good fit for their search. She sent an email to the principal at the Sir David Brand

School asking about availability of pupil records from the Sir James Mitchell School in 1972 and left it at that. She wasn't hopeful.

From what Linda could see, Charles Templeman had completed his education in 1972, his name not appearing in class lists from 1973 and beyond. His departure would have been a plausible reason to have given his girlfriend a gift. Linda decided to make the assumption that Charles Templeman was their Charlie; an internet search for Charles/Charlie Templeman was unrewarding.

Did Charlie Templeman have any siblings? Maybe they would be traceable. Public access to Births, Deaths and Marriages was available online but only for births at least one century earlier. Frustratingly, digitised records of the *West Australian* on the National Library of Australia website only went up to December 31, 1954, meaning that any siblings born after Charlie would not be in those records.

In any event, Linda's search of the birth notices in December 1954 alone, day by day, was not only unrewarding but overwhelmingly time-consuming. Charlie might not have had any siblings she thought, a little gloomily. This approach seemed hopeless.

Linda pushed her chair away from her desk and pondered her options. Because Charles Templeman's name first appeared in class lists from 1964, when he would possibly have been in year four, Charlie must have attended some other school before commencing at the Sir James Mitchell School; a quick online search identified Subiaco Primary School in Bagot Road which would possibly have been where he had first gone. As it turned out, the very helpful school receptionist who answered Linda's call made it clear that they held no records of class lists and no archival photographs that might identify Charlie or any potential siblings. Likewise, the Subiaco Museum held no such details and simply referred Linda to the National Library site; she was back where she had started.

Who else might hold some record of Charlie's early existence? How else might she reach back in time, to find some element, however flimsy, that might link him to the present?

Linda sent Mark an SMS: *What time are we catching up? I think we're getting closer.*

23. MONDAY DECEMBER 2

James Devlin tried to calm himself as the early evening traffic crawled along Melbourne's M3. It had been over a decade since he had visited Garth Barrett in Mount Martha. He hadn't trusted himself to remember the directions so he used Google Maps and accepted its advice regarding all aspects of the route to be followed. He now wished he'd taken a chance on his memory.

Driving his VW Golf, Devlin felt reassuringly invisible. Having not been able to afford expensive cars until his gallery had established itself in his forties, he had never developed a taste for them. But despite feeling secluded and cocooned, he appreciated an incoming tide of anxiety, the rare meeting with Garth a measure of the delicate situation in which they now found themselves. He imagined that Garth was likely also somewhere on the way to Mount Martha, probably also feeling anxious and on edge.

Virtually becalmed on the motorway, Devlin felt trapped by the towering concrete walls atop concrete embankments that ran alongside long stretches of the M3. He had worked hard to obscure the relationship he had with Garth and exposure of that relationship ran the serious risk of damaging both of their reputations. But, for Devlin, it was the fact that this inquiry had established his teenage connection to Garth that made him especially uneasy.

As 7.30 closed in and the traffic began to flow again, James found his claustrophobia easing. He felt he now had the space to put things in clearer perspective and to consider his options – and to listen to what Garth had to say; together, they would figure it out.

Still following instructions, he took the M11 turn-off heading west and then south again towards Portsea. The dropping sun caught rolling pastures and vineyards to his left – the first real glimpse of a rural landscape – in a soft light, the cloud cover clearing. The GPS directions now became more frequent, passing through the incongruously suburban landscape of Mount Martha and, for the first time, revealing the ocean. The sudden sight of water, combined with an unexpected descent towards it, caught James Devlin by surprise. He had to turn sharply into Pacific Terrace and, on his left, recognised the short but steep driveway of the Barretts' holiday home. It was just past eight o'clock.

Barrett opened the front door just as Devlin rang the bell.

'Hello, Harry, how are you? I'm sorry to drag you out here – I am a bit worried about things.'

They entered Garth's home through a high-ceilinged hallway, Devlin noting a small Arthur Boyd and a David Aspden ink drawing on the walls, both of which he had helped Garth secure. They ascended a staircase and entered an expansive kitchen and family room that overlooked the ocean through full-length windows. Devlin spotted a Roland Wakelin oil and a work in crayon by Sid Nolan; every square centimetre of wall space was occupied by fine Australian art. The view over the ocean was breathtaking in the fading light; it was, Devlin recalled, even more spectacular in full daylight.

The house was empty save for the two old friends who sat at the kitchen table, each with a mid-strength beer.

'My brother called me yesterday,' Barrett said. 'He had dinner with friends on Saturday night who recounted to him a strange approach to their daughter – who works at the local high school – last Friday morning by a couple of people asking about me. And also about you. She thought Doug would be interested to know how far and wide his brother's fame had spread. But the thing is that, just before then, also on Friday morning, a couple had also been at Doug's workshop asking for directions about coffee and asking if he was a local.'

Devlin sipped his beer, trying to align Garth's story with what Glen Derricks had already told him. Barrett continued.

'Doug was pretty sure the couple were fishing for information – he wasn't sure what about – but it started with questions about him and they then went on to ask where he had gone to school. They sound like the same couple who ended up at the school.'

Devlin considered his friend. They had both done well out of their partnership, but of late he had sensed that Garth was beginning to think about easing back on trading in art. He was close to retirement, increasingly distracted by his growing brood of grandchildren and understandably more risk-averse than in his youth. Devlin had planned on their arrangement continuing for just a little longer but appreciated that it might already have run its race.

'So, the friend's daughter recalled the man's name. Mark Lewis.'

Devlin shrugged, unmoved. Barrett continued, 'They said they were journalists but when I searched this man – Mark Lewis – I came up with this.' Barrett showed Devlin his phone where he had downloaded the Beaufort Gallery website. 'I hate to say it, but I'm fairly certain this is the guy who was asking about us.'

Devlin remained very still, assimilating this new information, dread rising in his chest. Then he said, 'I have some information of my own.'

Barrett raised his eyebrows.

'After they went to the school,' Devlin said, 'that couple made their way to the Bushrangers home ground and tracked down a photograph of you – and me – from the year we won the under-sixteens' grand final. A club tragic rang me this morning to ask me about becoming a member of a sort of Bushrangers alumnus. Putting that aside, this couple was specifically looking to find me and had gone about that by linking me to you.' Even to his own ears, Devlin's tone sounded shrill. 'He told the guy they were journalists and were writing an article about me. I don't know how they made the football connection, but if this guy is a gallerist that is worrying.'

The two men looked at each other. Barrett sighed and said, 'And making up a story to disguise himself tells me he knows something more.'

'Or thinks he knows something more,' added Devlin. 'Most likely, he thinks he's figured out our bidding arrangements. I've not heard about his gallery before. What do you know?'

Barrett summarised what he had found out so far – that Mark Lewis was a small-time art gallerist from Perth, that the gallery had commenced about two years earlier, occasionally represented some new local artists but concentrated mainly on the secondary market, with a readily detectable emphasis upon abstract works.

In addition, Barrett continued, a simple search had found that Mark Lewis had previously been a reasonably well-respected surgeon practising until a few years ago, a member of a number of local surgical groups and committees in his time and, based upon his patient feedback profile, a popular doctor but still with the occasional disgruntled customer voicing their opinion online.

'To be honest, Harry, I haven't ever come across him. A different craft group, a different profile, I suppose.'

'And the woman? Is that his wife or partner?'

'No idea, Harry. That's as much as I know.'

Devlin watched his friend thinking: his surgeon's brain considering the information, assessing the risks and preparing his next move.

'You know that I don't like anyone fishing about,' said Barrett, 'whether it's just about me or about our connections. But what really worries me is that he is looking for connections from the past.'

Devlin added what he barely dared to say. 'And why from Perth? What does that mean?'

'Do you think he has stumbled on an old painting? Or maybe a forgery?'

'Possibly. But why would one of my paintings make him think of our connection? Anyway, I have a complete record of all my paintings, Garth. If there is a painting at the heart of this ... inquiry ... I'd know immediately if it was a fake or not. But, so far at least, there haven't been any forgeries of my work.'

The two men pondered their options. They could simply wait and see what developed; quite possibly, there was little or no substance to Lewis' inquiries.

'It's tricky,' said Barrett. 'If we overreact, we might end up exposing our connection unnecessarily.'

'"First do no harm".' Devlin permitted himself a rueful smile. 'But my gut is telling me that we have a real problem. At the very least, we need to find out more about Lewis and his gallery. Maybe there is a painting?'

Inaction had never been in Devlin's repertoire. He could at least counter by finding out what he could about Lewis and by getting Lewis off his back.

Devlin flicked through Beaufort Gallery's website as they compared notes about Perth's somewhat provincial art-investment scene. A handful of wealthy businesspeople mostly trading outside the local auction environment, and a somewhat larger circle of professionals – doctors and lawyers mainly – accumulating collections of varying scale and depth trading inside that scene. In essence, just two auction houses in town, with an emphasis on Western Australian artists.

Both men had, over the years, taken advantage of the Western Australian art market, buying quality works by Western Australian artists in the East and sending them to one or other Perth-based auction house for occasionally healthy profit. And it worked both ways for them, Western Australian collectors often preferring to sell their major pieces by non–Western Australian artists on the East coast, imagining that this would attract higher prices, notwithstanding the higher seller's premium, let alone the ease of bidding by telephone.

Their musings about the Perth art scene conjured a clearer plan of action in Devlin's mind. 'This chap Lewis will have a mentor, and I'd bet anything that it is Pat O'Beirne. I suspect Lewis was a collector in his surgical years and, judging by the works on his website, he's much more likely to have collected through O'Beirne. They definitely have that feel to them.'

Garth drained his beer as Devlin summed up.

'If we assume that Lewis knows O'Beirne well and, given that he has only recently entered the market as a dealer, it's also safe to assume that Lewis will have discussed any suspicions he has about our relationship with O'Beirne. And I'd bet that he'd also discuss any contentious paintings that come his way with O'Beirne. Unless, of course, they are in competition with each other.'

'No, Harry. Lewis is likely to have been a trusting collector – you know that medicos are typically in that vein.' Barrett smiled at Devlin. 'You know Pat O'Beirne better than I do – but he is as honest as the day is long. I'd describe my dealings with him as a little frosty but always fair. I honestly don't think we can get to Lewis through O'Beirne. We should assume that the two are somehow in on this together, at least until we know more.'

Devlin nodded. But he knew he could not simply do nothing. There was too much at stake.

They formulated a plan, which would be enacted without delay, and agreed that they would try to minimise the need for further face-to-face meetings. And they wished each other good luck for the following evening's exhibition opening.

They set out for Melbourne about fifteen minutes apart, each deep in thought about the past. Devlin knew that Barrett would now start preparing to exit their longstanding business arrangement. But his primary focus was on Mark Lewis. If it came to it, he knew he would destroy the man rather than be exposed.

24. MONDAY DECEMBER 2

Linda parked alongside Hyde Park and followed the house numbers until she located Mark's. There was a gate opening into a laneway of sorts, and an intercom, but she couldn't see the house to which this connected. There were Federation-era houses either side and the veranda on one side was guarded by a statuesque Afghan hound that raised its head, contemptuously, sizing her up with cool indifference. Linda rang the bell.

A light went on from the intercom.

'Push the gate and come on up the path,' said Mark's voice.

The path continued between two brick walls belonging to the houses on either side before opening into a small courtyard and a few steps leading up to a large wooden door. The size of the house obscured from the roadside was a surprise. As she stepped up towards it, the front door opened, and Mark greeted her with a gentle kiss on the lips. 'Come on in!'

They ascended the stairs to the main living area. 'Your home is beautiful. You're so close to the park and the city, and you can see the CBD from here,' she said, surprised.

'All credit for the design rests with Sharon,' he replied. 'Not being able to enjoy the home she created was just one of the many tragedies of her death.'

'You seem very happy to be here despite those memories,' said Linda, although Mark sensed a hint of a question within it.

'I can't change what's happened,' Mark explained, 'but this house is definitely one good thing that has happened to me.'

'Tell me about all these paintings then.'

Mark obliged, work by work, describing the art, the artists and the history of each acquisition. He dwelt upon a lovely impressionist image of boys fishing off rocks, painted in around 1970 by a little-known artist apparently still alive somewhere in Australia, pointing out the visible bits of the newspaper on which it had been painted. 'The artist was too poor to afford even a wooden board,' said Mark, 'but the urge to express himself was clearly irresistible. It makes me think about Charlie. I remember this painting hanging in my parents' house here in Perth, but it disappeared after they sold that house and I later discovered it cowering in a cupboard under the stairs of their beach house. I rescued it, reframed it and have hung it ever since. It is probably my favourite painting in this house.'

Mark brought the art tour to an end and Linda drove them to Leederville. She parked behind the restaurant and they walked around the fish market to the Kailis restaurant entrance on Oxford Street. It was a warm early summer evening but there was a steady south-westerly breeze still blowing, cooling the air but unsettling the mood. Parrots were making an immense racket in the trees and it was a relief to get out of the wind and away from the noise.

The restaurant remained a landmark on the Perth dining scene, in large part because of its enduring connection to the Kailis family, one of a remarkable handful of Greek immigrant families from the tiny island of Kastellorizo that settled in Perth in the early twentieth century. Mark loved, in particular, their fried snapper and chips. He had reserved a booth and they settled in to discuss Linda's findings.

'So, this information is not for wide dissemination, especially not until we can track down the people involved. But, between us for now, I am pretty sure our Charlie was a pupil at the Sir James Mitchell school named Charles Kevin Templeman. He started his education there in nineteen sixty-four and left – graduated really – in late seventy-two.'

'I've never heard of Charles or Charlie Templeman in relation to art,' said Mark. 'I wonder what happened to him.'

'I've searched the death register as well and I even looked on the Find A Grave website but there's no mention of him. I can't find out if he had any siblings and his parents would both be about ninety by now if they're still alive. I've asked the current school principal about him but, other than that, I'm at a bit of a dead end, to be honest. How else can we trace his origins?'

They paused while a waitress with a distinctly French accent took their orders.

Then Mark said, 'Let's think about what we do know. I think we can agree that Charlie's painting was created at the time that this Charles Templeman was a client of the David Brand Centre. Maybe he had only mild disability, making it possible that he is the pupil seen at the canvas in the photograph with Katy Bilowski. This is all in keeping with the assumption that the date on Charlie's painting is correct and that Charlie is the artist and not James Devlin. As much as it looks like it is by Devlin. And Charlie seems to have disappeared, at least off the Western Australian radar.'

'It feels like we are back at the beginning,' said Linda. 'Charlie did not morph into James Devlin, they could hardly be less alike. If there is a connection between Charlie's painting and James Devlin, we need to have a theory or theories and test them out. Otherwise, you will probably have to show Devlin that image.'

'I think we need to share this stuff with Pat. We need his advice.'

Their food and wine arrived, Linda enjoying her grilled barramundi no less than Mark his fried fish and chips. Mark resolved to set up a meeting with Pat and they were finished within an hour. 'I'd love you to stay the night,' Mark said.

'I packed a bag just in case.'

25. TUESDAY DECEMBER 3

Many people owed James Devlin favours. Not – with very few exceptions – because he held something over them, but because he had always been such a generous supporter of both talented or otherwise earnest individuals. Rarely did he permit himself the lenience of dealing cruelly with people, however irritating or inept they might be. It had been a successful formula and, as it turned out, a brilliant cover for the other side of his business life.

He had taken note of Mark Lewis' website, paying attention to works that were for sale and, in particular, recent major sales. He had also noted that the site was obviously updated frequently, making the site more interesting and creating a clear sense of a well-tended business. He was impressed by this sort of attention to detail, and he appreciated that Lewis was unlikely to be a reckless individual who would set off in pursuit of his and Garth's shared past for no particular purpose.

What had caught his eye was the recent sale of a magnificent Robert Dickerson oil, clearly an early work of the highest quality, even on the basis of the digital image on the website. It contained several human figures in an evidently celebratory pose and had the depth of colour and powerful empathy for its characters that typified Dickerson's early works. Devlin estimated that this was from the mid to late 1960s and knew that it would have attracted a six-figure sum. He had searched his own meticulously kept records for all sales of Dickerson works going back well over twenty years and had not seen this work. The absence of any other information on the website about the painting was of added interest – there was nothing to indicate where it had first been exhibited although it was reasonable to assume that it had been acquired in Perth or at least held there for a long time.

Given the general anxiety among collectors about the provenance of valuable works of art, he could easily imagine a major collector having reservations about such an acquisition. Australian art had been subject to a number of scandals surrounding efforts by individuals embedded within the art industry to profit from the sale of forgeries of prominent artists such as Whiteley, Blackman and Dickerson. Dickerson's stylised human figures lent themselves to emulation by profiteers, but this work, Devlin could tell, was undeniably the real thing.

One of Devlin's pet hates was the peddling of fake art. Now would be an opportune moment for an article by a prominent journalist about this unhappy trend as an avenue to attack and distract Mark Lewis.

James Devlin picked up his phone and dialled. Catherine Deehan was senior art editor at the *Age*. 'Good morning, James. I hope you're not worried that I won't be at the opening tonight – I wouldn't miss covering it for anything. And you always serve such delicious champagne.'

'No! Not at all. I know you'll be there tonight. It's a great exhibition ... and I'm also looking forward to a glass of Veuve. Actually, I'm ringing to see if you might consider writing another piece about forgery. I can't give you many specifics, but I've recently become aware of another rash of forgeries around the place, and you know how I feel about the damage this does to our industry.'

'Who are they forging this time?'

'You know I won't tell you, Catherine. The moment I mention a particular artist, I'll have dealers and collectors who hold their works calling me from all around the country screaming blue bloody murder. But it involves the usual targets, there are no surprises. The only difference is that the quality of these more recent forgeries is altogether more sophisticated and the challenge for authentication is becoming really hard.'

'I'm not sure there's a particularly good story in all that, James. Isn't there anything else you can give me?'

'I am happy for you to quote me as your source, and I can tell you that this problem is not confined to Melbourne and Sydney. This is becoming an Australia-wide phenomenon and all collectors and dealers are at risk.' Devlin paused. 'You know this is a bit of a crusade for me. I'd really appreciate your support, and this message needs to get out sooner rather than later.'

Devlin knew that the journalist would understand the deal he was proposing, the not-so-subtle threat that his support and confidence were too valuable to put at risk by refusing to write this article. She posed a few more questions looking for something that might provide a little more detail, but Devlin was firm in resisting. He was confident that, even though Catherine had always preferred writing stories about the world of art – stories were so much less work, and so much more likely to be read by the general public – art forgery was one issue she didn't mind addressing from time to time. Many readers garnered a salacious thrill reading stories about wealthy Australians getting fooled by forgeries; and Devlin had given her all the information she needed for a brief article, which would, no doubt, be embellished with established facts she had at her fingertips, the names of those artists whose works had previously been forged, as well as the names of the forgers who had been previously found out. An easy piece after all.

Devlin concluded the call and sat for at his desk for a moment, gazing at *Odyssey* hanging in front of him with its swirling, soothing yellow tones. Then he made his next call.

Brad Collins was a private investigator whose path Devlin had crossed many years earlier when Collins was still a police detective. Devlin's persistent and passionate fundraising support for Brad's disabled daughter had almost single-handedly covered the cost of the home improvements that had allowed Collins and his wife to take on their daughter's care at home. It had changed the course of her life and that of his whole family. Collins was profoundly grateful to Devlin, who he regarded as a selfless man and mentor, and he had provided ready assistance to Devlin as a private investigator in the past.

'Nice to hear from you, Mr Devlin,' said Collins, with evident pleasure. 'Congratulations on your nomination. Very well deserved. How can I help?'

'Thanks, Brad. I hope you're all doing well. Actually, I'm after a bit of assistance, if possible. There is a colleague – another art gallery operator – in Perth who has been making inquiry about me, some of which seems quite inappropriate and intrusive. This chap even flew across to Melbourne to pursue the matter. I'm not exactly sure what it is all about, but he also made inquiry about one of my most important clients and neither of us feels comfortable about it.'

Devlin felt Collins listening intently.

'It is even possible that there is a forgery of one of my paintings involved. You might well hear something in the newspapers soon about a whole new wave of art fraud.' Devlin adjusted some paper on his desk and tapped it with his pen. 'What I'd like is for you – or a trusted colleague – to find out as much as you reasonably and discretely can about this man, his gallery, his routines, his business associates, his life partner. I'm keen to know if he has a painting of mine or one that looks like mine – I'm trying to figure out why he is so interested in me and how I can … discourage him.'

The arrangement would be that Collins would be Devlin's sole point of contact and that all expenses would be reimbursed and his fee paid without delay. Collins knew Devlin to be a man of his word and he accepted the assignment without hesitation; the deadline for information was one week.

Devlin was satisfied and relieved with his morning's work. And he still had all afternoon to review the hang and the running sheet for the evening's exhibition opening. He was excited about the information he might receive about Lewis and quietly confident that the individual who had recently purchased that Dickerson from Lewis' gallery would soon be raising concerns about the veracity of his acquisition. James Devlin was always most comfortable on the front foot, happier in offence rather than defence – his life and livelihood had been built upon this approach.

26. THURSDAY DECEMBER 5

Monitoring Mark Lewis' exit from his house was proving a little more challenging than expected for Richard Barclay, an experienced Perth-based private investigator and well known to Brad Collins in Melbourne. Most private investigators maintained networks of trusted fellow-PIs across the country, sharing the required information and fees rather than wasting time and clients' money by travelling to do the work themselves.

From Barclay's point of view, this assignment was a simple matter of gathering information about the movements and associates of Mark Lewis, about the operations of his art gallery, and (if it was possible) obtaining an image of a particular work of art whose existence, let alone exact appearance, was unknown. Possible likenesses of the work in question had been emailed through to him by Collins without identifying the artist, but Barclay felt confident that he would recognise at first glance any work as evidently unstructured and unappealing as the ones he had been sent; he wondered about the sanity of those who paid large sums for this sort of thing. Although he also wondered who the original artist might be, he understood that he was being intentionally kept in the dark and he respected that the confidentiality of the artist needed to be respected.

The laneway behind Lewis' residence, into which his car would reverse as he exited for work, was easy to watch, but it was not so easy to predict which way he might turn – south down the lane towards the city, or up the lane heading north, and then either west or east. Barclay couldn't park in the lane so he opted to watch from Glendower Street, to the south.

Barclay gave himself until ten am to wait; if Lewis hadn't emerged by then he would pay the gallery a visit. Barclay felt confident that he could pass himself off as a potential albeit inexperienced art buyer. But the simple act of following Lewis became momentarily more complicated when Lewis emerged from his garage around nine forty-five and headed north up the lane, on foot. Barclay hopped out of his car and locked it, guessing that Lewis would be heading up Fitzgerald Street in the direction of his gallery.

This prediction proved correct, the PI having taken note of Lewis' checked short-sleeved shirt and navy trousers and seeing them at some distance heading north, as predicted, along the footpath. He much preferred the anonymity of sitting in a car to working on foot; if the person he was trailing suddenly caught a taxi, took a bus or simply got a lift, he was pretty much defeated. He picked up the pace to close the gap and, at length, saw Lewis turn west on Angove Street; Barclay was familiar with the area and a coffee shop seemed Lewis' likely destination.

Barclay strode up Angove Street on its northern side where numerous coffee shops and restaurants were lined up one after the other. He was heading slowly but purposefully for the furthest café, looking carefully into each one for Lewis' checked shirt. He spotted it easily in The Old Laundry café, also noting another man sitting with Lewis and plenty of empty tables within. He walked past the café, turned first right and immediately right again heading back down to Fitzgerald and around the block, ascending Angove Street once again. This time, he entered The Old Laundry purposefully and sat diagonally opposite Lewis and his companion, positioning his mobile phone to face them directly; he fired off a number of photos remotely, settled back and waited to see what would happen. He noticed the men exchange a wrapped parcel, a painting for sure, thought Barclay, which Lewis placed on the seat next to him. It seemed small and certainly smaller than the size of painting he'd been told to look out for. But his interest was piqued.

He noted the arrival of a woman joining Lewis and the other man, all oblivious to his close scrutiny. More photos were silently obtained in rapid succession. Barclay had been provided with a brief list, including images, of the 'personae dramatis', and he recognised Pat O'Beirne immediately. In all likelihood, judging by her age, the as yet unidentified brunette was the woman listed as Lewis' partner. Orders for coffee were taken in quick succession from both tables.

He observed the group of three leaning in for many minutes, as if in a hushed conversation.

Just as their coffees arrived, Barclay heard a phone ring, saw Lewis answer it and observed an instant tension in his body. Lewis turned away from the other two but Barclay could see the others were now both alert to a problem linked to the phone call. Then Lewis returned to the group, placing the phone in the middle of the table, presumably on speakerphone. They huddled around the phone – Lewis appeared to be explaining to the others what had transpired. He looked angry.

There was another short exchange between the group of three. The man Barclay presumed was O'Beirne picked up his phone and appeared to be preparing to make a call or search online, as the others continued their conversation. Having found what he was looking for, O'Beirne read from his phone as the others listened.

For a few more minutes O'Beirne held court, the other two appearing to hang off every word and the phone still positioned in the centre of the table. At one point, Lewis went pale and, shortly after, picked up the phone, spoke a few more words and hung up. He stood up abruptly, gathered up his wrapped painting and the group dispersed. Having arrived on foot, Barclay was unable to continue to follow any one of them; he watched Lewis enter the woman's vehicle and drive off while O'Beirne left in the other direction altogether, presumably heading to his own car. Barclay finished his coffee and headed back to Glendower Street to collect his car. The gallery would be his next destination.

27. THURSDAY DECEMBER 5

'That man is a total pig!' Olivia was filled with fury when Mark returned to the gallery. Tony Peterson had barged into the gallery before nine am and had demanded to speak to her father. 'He was so rude and insulting. About you, Dad. He's convinced you've sold him an expensive fake. He wants his money back. He wants the money back for every painting you've ever sold him. He was aggressive, swearing. He's going to go to the media. He really is on the warpath. Ohh! I hate that man!'

Mark detested the way some customers felt they could behave, but he could not abide them treating Olivia badly. He had not invited her into the business to have her excoriated by ill-tempered clients.

That bastard, he thought. He could have his money back any time, just as long as he never did business with him again. Lewis had spent many hours researching this work and assuring himself of its origins. Pat had agreed it was by Dickerson's hand and he had showed it to Dickerson's family who were also happy to say that it was his. Mark had explained all of this to Peterson.

'Did you find the article that triggered all this?'

'Yes, Dad, it's in the *Age*. It quotes Devlin.' She looked up at her father. 'Is he some sort of Dickerson expert on top of everything else?'

'According to Pat, Devlin's an outspoken critic of fakes and forgeries and anyone that peddles them. This is also a pet topic for the *Age* – they exposed that guy Peter Gant ten years ago.'

Olivia was re-reading the article she'd downloaded after her phone call to her father. 'There's references here to recent history – Whiteley, Blackman, Tucker and Dickerson – but nothing specific about any artists right now.'

'Pat said he hasn't heard a word about this. It's news to him.'

'Dad. Did Pat think it had anything to do with your trip to Melbourne?'

Mark sighed heavily. 'He does. I put the sale of the Dickerson on the website – with Tony's permission – and Pat is pretty sure Devlin will have used that fact and his connections to try to trigger exactly this response. He said he was probably just throwing mud to see if it would stick.'

'It's not just mud, Dad. Devlin is sending us a message. He's telling us that he can make things very uncomfortable for us.'

Mark felt a deep unease at what might happen to his business if the media became involved – he knew that they would happily run with a story about a potential forgery, devastate the gallery along the way, and not give a damn about the truth, not even if the painting was subsequently proven to be an original. They'd be only too happy to fire Tony Peterson's bullets for him. Despicable, shallow, selfish, lazy, he thought to himself.

Mark went off to make a cup of tea before calling the wounded buyer. No doubt, Peterson had already shown off his fabulous new painting to some of his friends and was now imagining their reactions to news about fake Dickersons circulating around the country. Even the suggestion that he might have bought a fake would be too humiliating for him to bear. A volatile character at the best of times, Mark knew that Peterson would be dreaming up his most piercing revenge.

Mark checked the email correspondence he had conducted with the artist's family one more time. How he wished he had a concrete record of the exhibition at which this work had first appeared. Sadly, the gallery that had represented Dickerson in those early days had long closed, the dealer had died, and newspaper records of the exhibition simply made no mention of this specific painting. According to Roger Clifton, the vendor, the painting had first been exhibited and sold at the very well-regarded Raymond Bell Gallery in the late 1960s, from where Roger and his wife had also acquired it when it was resold about ten years later. There had been no written record or catalogue of the original exhibition, but the gallery's word was widely considered to be unimpeachable, and there had been no doubt in anyone's mind that this was the original work, signed and dated '1967'.

Mark phoned Tony Peterson, not sure how he would deal with him. By and large, however, throughout both his medical and gallerist careers, he had found that escalating a dispute, even when he felt sure such anger and aggression was warranted, rarely aided its resolution. In that frame of mind, and conscious that Olivia was listening, he started as calmly as he could manage. 'Tony, it's Mark Lewis. Olivia has spoken to me and I'm calling to see if I can figure out what has happened.'

'I've been dudded, that's what has happened. You've sold me a fake, and an expensive fake at that. Actually, you've made a first-class fool of me, and I am fucking furious with you.'

Lewis closed his eyes and shook his head at Peterson's foul mouth. 'Tony, I've double-checked my correspondence with the artist's family, and they were quite clear that they believed that this painting was by the hand of Robert Dickerson. It's not just my opinion. I've taken it as high as I can go.'

But Peterson was of no mind to listen to logic. 'I don't think you're in touch with what's happening around the country, Lewis. You obviously haven't read the newspapers. There are high quality forgeries all around the country and you just don't know what's going on. I knew I shouldn't have made such a major purchase from such a small gallery. Honestly,' he now separated each word for emphasis, 'you don't know what you're doing.' Returning to his usual tempo, he said, 'I want my money back immediately. Don't think you're going to weasel your way out of this one.'

'Tony, I am happy to refund you your money but not until I see that painting back in my gallery in exactly the same condition that it left the gallery.' Mark's plans to be calm and considered were beginning to fray at the edges. 'And you needn't be concerned for a single minute that you'll ever be dudded by me or my gallery again, Tony, because I wouldn't sell you a poster print let alone the bubble wrap it came in.' Olivia raised her eyebrows but Mark looked away as he finished off, his voice now loud and shrill. 'You're the one who has no idea what he's doing, you foul-mouthed bully!' And Mark hung up, only momentarily gratified. Then he looked at his daughter.

'I'm not sure that was necessarily the best approach,' Olivia said, 'given the threats he made about going to the media. But he definitely deserved it.' She stopped, cup of tea midair. 'And how on earth are you going to pay Tony back? We paid the Cliftons as soon as he paid us.'

She was right: he'd made his point to Tony Peterson but at what price?

28. THURSDAY DECEMBER 5

Repaying Tony Peterson would be an issue for Mark, for sure. But, before he could give that matter any thought, at precisely that moment, the gallery door opened and a man entered, smiled and asked if he could look around. He was slim but strongly built, with short greying hair, dressed conservatively. He was on his own, and not quite the usual demographic for a late Thursday morning at Beaufort Gallery. That was something Mark loved about this work – the varied mix of people who came in among whom, he never knew, might be the next purchase.

Olivia stood up to greet the visitor, introduced herself and asked if he would like any information about the paintings on display, or about paintings in general. Mark detected a wariness in his daughter's approach to the customer. Perhaps the morning had rattled her more than she cared to show.

'Thanks, I'm just happy having a look.' The visitor smiled disarmingly, scanning the gallery, Mark thought, as if he'd lost his wallet and was now looking for it.

'I'm going to make myself a fresh cup of tea,' said Mark to them both. 'Would either of you like one?'

'Thanks, Dad,' replied Olivia, 'I'd love one.'

'That would be very nice, thank you,' said the visitor.

❖❖❖

The three of them chatted over tea and biscuits. The visitor gave his name as Robert Jones and described himself as a retired police officer who lived south of the river but who had just begun looking at property around Perth for his nephew who was planning to move from Brisbane.

He had been looking in nearby Maylands and Inglewood and had stopped on Beaufort Street intending to have a coffee when he was distracted by the gallery and decided to pop in. He conceded that he was entirely unfamiliar with the world of art.

Mark provided Jones with brief personal biographies and a potted history of the gallery, while Olivia remained quiet. Mark spoke to him about some of the paintings hanging in the gallery although he didn't seem to have a purchase in mind and wasn't responsive to Mark's enthusiasm. Jones thanked them both for their hospitality, said he would return if he decided to make a purchase and disappeared into the midday warmth.

'What was he all about?' Olivia said.

'What do you mean?'

'He wasn't interested in any paintings, that's for sure. He made me uncomfortable.'

'I didn't pick up on that.'

'Dad, you're hopeless at that sort of thing. Mum would've picked him out in a flash! It was the way he carried himself. Couldn't you feel it? It was like he was an immediate physical threat. He's ex-police. I bet he's a private investigator. He was here to find out about you, Dad, not about any paintings.' Olivia exhaled in frustration. 'It's a shame Linda wasn't here. She'd have figured him out.'

'What would a PI be doing here?'

'Finding stuff out for James Devlin! Dad – you've been poking about in his affairs and he is poking you right back. Maybe that article in the *Age* wasn't just a coincidence.'

Mark looked blankly at his daughter, his shoulders slumped.

'I don't know, Dad. Devlin might have been onto our website, seen your blurb about the Dickerson and somehow got the *Age* to run a complete Dorothy Dixer. I'm not saying that Devlin knows who Tony Peterson is, but he will know what type of person might be in the market for a big Dickerson and he certainly knows how sensitive every collector is these days about fakes and forgeries. Maybe that guy is working for Devlin.'

Mark felt hollow. This was not at all what he had imagined when he moved into the gallery business. To be honest, until Jan Bilowski had brought Charlie's painting into his gallery, there had been calm and stability in his life – and a little loneliness too.

'OK, Olivia. Let's assume you're right. Pat and Linda also thought the newspaper article might not have been a coincidence. If that guy is going to be watching us, I'd like to warn Linda – do you think she'll think I'm crazy?'

Olivia smiled. 'Dad. She must already know that you're not completely sane.' She raised her eyebrows, her face full of affection for her father. 'But maybe let me speak to her, since it's me who thinks these events are all connected.'

Mark dialled Linda, intending to hand her over to Olivia, but the call went through to voicemail. Mark hated receiving voicemails – and didn't imagine he was the only one who felt that way – so he hung up and typed out a text.

Olivia is OK. A very strange day here. Call whenever you can. xx

29. THURSDAY DECEMBER 5

Ray Clarke had been a journalist for over thirty years, an arts journalist for twenty-five of those, and now senior arts editor at the *West Australian* for a decade. Jonathan Bolton had experienced first-hand his boss' insistence upon thorough fact-checking and grammatical precision, characteristics that had both irritated and inspired an entire generation of journalists under his guidance. Bolton couldn't deny the excitement he sensed at the prospect of covering the potentially significant art forgery scandal that had been handed to him just half an hour earlier.

The *West's* new chief editor, Jayne Lee, who had been in the job for barely two months, had first brought the story to Clarke as a matter of urgency. An irate Tony Peterson – who Clarke said he knew to be a successful businessman and a significant local art collector – had contacted the chief, calling upon their shared background in a major real estate firm, Peterson as a key business partner, Lee formerly an upwardly mobile head of marketing and public relations.

Bolton was trying to pull together the facts of the case with Clarke's guidance. Bolton summarised. 'Peterson says that he placed his trust in the gallery – belonging to a guy called Mark Lewis – but that there was no documentation of the original exhibition or purchase, only of a subsequent purchase of the same work through the same gallery. He quoted Melbourne-based gallerist James Devlin from today's *Age* that there's a new wave of high-quality fakes, including fake Dickersons. He was fully angry.'

Clarke frowned. 'That might not be the precise phrase we include in the article, Jonathan. Now, I know Peterson, and everyone knows Devlin, but I've not heard of Mark Lewis. Sounds like he's a small dealer so that could make it interesting. But running a story like this can ruin any gallery, even if there is no proof of forgery, so I want as much information as you can get. Have you got an image of the painting?'

Bolton explained that it was on Mark Lewis' website as he accessed the site and the image on his mobile phone and showed it to Clarke. Clarke brought up the website on his desktop to gain a better view of the painting. Bolton knew that Clarke was an experienced arts reporter and was familiar with many of the artists whose works and exhibitions the *West* covered.

'That Dickerson looks OK to me. I need you to speak to Mark Lewis, Jonathan. He will be able to explain the provenance of the painting and why he believes that it is genuine. I'd be surprised if he doesn't already know that Tony Peterson is unhappy, so even how Lewis reacts to our approach might give us a clue as to what has happened. But we need to find out as much as we can before we run any story about this painting. Go speak to Lewis now.'

Jonathan Bolton was keen to expose the presumed forgery and concerned that he and the *West* would lose first bite at this story if he delayed. But Clarke was impossible to get past and Bolton had no choice but to follow his instructions. He rang the gallery and was greeted by a friendly, female voice.

'Beaufort Gallery. Olivia speaking. How can I help you?'

The gallery representative's response to Bolton's inquiry sounded well prepared. 'Mr Lewis is aware of Mr Peterson's concerns about the authenticity of the painting, but the gallery is confident that it is indeed a work by Robert Dickerson. Is there any way that I can help you?'

'I was hoping that I could discuss this with Mr Lewis in person. Would that be possible?'

'Of course. Mr Lewis will be happy to meet with you – but you will need to bring photo identification and you must appreciate that Mr Peterson remains the owner of the painting in question and that the painting remains in his possession for the present moment.'

'That's great. Can I see him today, perhaps?'

'Mr Lewis will be in the gallery until five today and would be able to meet with you at any time until then.'

They settled on a time, leaving Bolton excited by the looming contest between defiant gallerist and scorned collector. He debriefed with his boss and set off for the gallery.

30. THURSDAY DECEMBER 5

In the gallery, Mark was busying himself with the arrangements for Anousheh Gul's January exhibition, a welcome distraction from the morning's disruptions. In his opinion, she was a real talent with a unique artistic voice. He was excited to be holding her first solo exhibition but probably more pleased that, following a long conversation with Pat, he now had an agreed strategy to contend with any fallout from Tony Peterson's tantrum.

Pat's had been a steadying influence – he knew the people at the *West* and had assured Mark that they would research their material carefully before publishing anything. The opportunity to explain the process by which the authenticity of this painting – of any painting, for that matter – had been established through this interview was a huge relief.

Linda had also phoned in to the gallery to check on Olivia, and to touch base with Mark following on from their earlier conversation at the café, before Olivia's phone call had interrupted proceedings. 'I feel bad that I didn't have the presence of mind to look at earlier photos at the football club. We might have learned more about how long Devlin had been in that part of Melbourne.'

'It was both of us, Linda. Pat is right, of course, we should have checked further back. It was a lost opportunity, that's for sure. But we were so excited just to have discovered Devlin in that first photo, and I was anxious that Glen Derricks was going to start asking more difficult questions, I just wanted to get out of there.'

'I'm still on Charlie's trail' said Linda. 'I heard back from the principal and there's more to learn about Charlie Templeman. Apparently, he didn't join the school until year four. He'd struggled to cope in the state school system because he was socially awkward and a little withdrawn and he'd been prone to aggressive outbursts. I think it was probably because of these behavioural difficulties as much as anything else that his parents sought the assistance of the Sir James Mitchell School.'

Reading from the information provided by the principal, Linda told Mark that Charles Kevin Templeman had been born on October 26, 1955. His parents were listed as John and Laura Templeman and were living in the inner-western suburb of Daglish in 1964 but had moved to the northern suburb of Wanneroo by 1972.

'That must have been a long commute back in those days,' said Mark.

'It still is now. John was recorded as "Branch Manager, R&I Bank" and Laura as "Shop Assistant, Aherns". I've searched them both, but I haven't found anything of any help at all. But I have arranged to meet Father Bryan Norris at Subiaco Cathedral tomorrow morning.' That had been another idea of Pat's from their morning conversation – if the Templeman family had been Catholic, he'd said, they would very likely have had Charlie baptised. And Pat assured them that churches kept fastidious records of baptisms. He suggested they start in the Subiaco area, close to where the Templemans had lived at that time, and Linda had chosen its oldest and largest church as the logical first port of call.

'That's potentially very helpful. Great work. But I wonder why there's nothing to find about any of them?' asked Mark. 'Good luck with that meeting,' he added, knowing that he would never have thought to look into baptism records.

'I'm going to pop back into the gallery around five,' said Linda. 'You've been threatening to cook me dinner for a while and tonight seems like a good time to test you out. Is that OK?'

'With pleasure. I'll stock up on Asian vegetables on my way home,' said Mark.

❖❖❖

By the time Jonathan Bolton entered the gallery, Mark felt that some inner calm had returned. Olivia greeted the journalist and Mark guided him into the back area where he had set up a table and chairs for their meeting. He closed the door, made his customary offer of a cup of tea, which Bolton declined, and asked: 'How can I help you?'

Bolton described exactly what had happened that day – his own conversation with Peterson, his review of the article in the *Age*, his brief evaluation of James Devlin, and his instructions from Ray Clarke. 'Can you prove that the painting Mr Peterson bought from you is not a forgery?'

'That's a good question and the short answer is no.' Mark had fully expected the surprised expression on the journalist's face that this prompted. 'But, unless a painting is created under your immediate supervision, literally so you can see the artist painting it until completion, and you take possession of it immediately upon its completion, absolutely no-one can ever be certain that any painting is truly by that artist. Even at the original exhibition of this painting here in Perth back in nineteen sixty-eight, when the artist was likely in attendance at the exhibition opening, and there were maybe twenty works of art all being sold as his, even then, only that artist could absolutely know that he had painted them all, with no other assistance. The gallery at that time naturally took Dickerson's word that these were his own works; I have no doubt that they were.

'Even if we were to ask the artist fifty years after the event, if that was his work, he might only be able to guess. Or he might no longer like the work and might wish to disassociate himself from it. Catalogues produced by the gallery at the time of the exhibition can be of great value, too, especially if an image of the work in question is reproduced in that catalogue. These days, the vast majority of works for sale across the country are visible online, leaving a more or less permanent record of what happened. Not so in nineteen sixty-eight, alas.'

Mark explained the rest of the puzzle – the absence of any record of a catalogue, the documents of second sale from 1978 but their absence from the original sale in 1968, the opinion of a senior and trusted dealer, the opinion of the artist's family. The next step would be to obtain highly specialised testing of the painting – special imaging and chemical testing of the materials used – to indicate if this was more or less likely to be an original Dickerson. 'But testing is inordinately expensive and, in any event, the likelihood of this being an original – and a very good one at that – is exceptionally high.'

Bolton had been taking copious notes, although he was, with Mark's permission, also recording the conversation. 'So, does this apply to every painting that you sell here too?'

'That's exactly right. There is some element of doubt about almost every painting ever bought and sold – mostly, that doubt is infinitesimally small. Occasionally, like this one, more work needs to be done to alleviate doubt. And, from time to time, doubt cannot be confidently eliminated and that can be really awkward because you suspect it's an original, but you just cannot build a strong enough case.' As in the case of Charlie's painting, thought Mark.

'Rarely,' he added, 'some paintings are proven to be forgeries. Wrong style, wrong materials, wrong documentation, wrong provenance.' Now his mind flashed to the small Passmore that Pat had returned in the morning and which was now wrapped up in the storeroom above them. It was a perfect example. But there was too much still unknown about it to go wading into that swamp right now, and not with a journalist, of all people. 'Those are the ones that today's article was talking about. Not something like Tony Peterson's painting. I wager that even James Devlin would call this particular work an original if he saw it and saw the artist's family's confident assessment.'

Bolton leaned forward and continued to pepper Mark with questions, about Dickerson, about Australian art, forgeries in art, the gallery itself and how Mark had come to own and operate it. Mark could tell that the journalist was engaged by their conversation.

'What do *you* make of the article in the *Age*?' asked Bolton finally.

Mark's undisciplined outburst on the phone with Tony Peterson was not going to be repeated. 'I am a small player in a small market,' he said, 'so I cannot lay claim to having my finger on the pulse of the art scene in this country. James Devlin is a big player in a much bigger market. But I am not aware of any sudden influx of suspect works, by any of the artists mentioned in the article, and I've checked with the people I know and trust here in Perth and they haven't heard anything like that either.'

'So why the article? And let's face it, Devlin is an authoritative voice.'

'Who knows – his connections in the art world are deeper and broader than mine. His really is a big name. But Devlin makes no specific mention of Dickerson and certainly not of this work. To be honest, the article doesn't share any practically useful detail at all.'

Bolton looked a little deflated.

'I still think there is a good story in this for you, Jonathan, if you want to run with it. The artist's family would need to consent, but they would be as enthusiastic as anyone about an article that helped dispel the myths about forgeries and helped expose the fakes that undoubtedly exist.' He outlined what an article like this might cover and he suggested that, once he had calmed down, Tony Peterson might actually appreciate the coverage, as a counter to any implied doubt arising from the *Age* article.

Bolton left shortly after four, Mark walking him around the gallery with potted accounts of a few of the works on display before showing him out the front door.

'How did that go?' asked Olivia as soon as the door closed.

'He seems very nice.'

'Does that mean he is going to write something or not?'

'I really don't know. But Jonathan Bolton is not the decision-maker at the *West*. And I can't call the shots at the *West* the way James Devlin can at the *Age*. We'll just have to wait and see.'

31. FRIDAY DECEMBER 6

Early on Friday morning, Linda reversed out of Mark's garage and headed south along Fitzgerald Street and then east to Salvado Road in Subiaco. Having observed her arrival with Mark Lewis the previous evening, Richard Barclay followed at a discreet distance. It was just after seven when she turned left into the small car park alongside St Joseph's church and easily found an empty parking bay. Barclay circled round and found a paid parking spot in the nearby hospital car park that offered him a clear view of Linda's parked car.

Linda had called the church the previous afternoon and had asked to meet with Father Bryan Norris; she didn't fancy trying to explain her search for information about the Templeman family over the phone. The parish secretary had put her on hold and had, after just a minute or two, returned to the conversation stating that Father Bryan would be able to meet her the next morning after mass.

'Mass starts at seven. He will meet you straight after. His schedule over the next few weeks is very busy.'

It was clear to Linda that the priest was inviting – perhaps pressing – her to attend mass. This was not something about which she was entirely comfortable. But she appreciated that she was going to be asking a favour of him and that he was at liberty to set her a small test of her own commitment to her task. And he was, quite possibly, reaching out to a fellow human being, the precise outcome of which could not ever be confidently predicted.

Linda entered the church through the main door. The service had already commenced, Father Norris, she presumed, speaking into a microphone from the pulpit, his voice measured and even, echoing a little in the mostly empty church. There was a tiny crowd in attendance, possibly fifteen people in all, mostly sitting at the front of what was a daunting space. The church's spacious feel was the result of its high ceilings which were, like its walls, painted in off-white and cream. Its internal columns and arches were a dove grey, the effect of these pale colours being to allow the limited morning sunlight entering through a series of modestly sized stained-glass windows on its east side, and to cast a hazy, warm light throughout. Linda moved to the left and sat towards the back, feeling awkward but not unwelcome in the peaceful space.

The prayers themselves comprised words that were familiar to her but for which she felt no real personal connection. Even so, she was soothed by the priest's resonant voice as well as the generous sentiments his words expressed. At one point, the parishioners turned to greet each other and shake each other's hands. The person closest to Linda turned, extended her hand, and said, sincerely, 'Peace be with you.'

Linda automatically took her hand. 'And with you,' she said, a little startled but moved by this contact with a stranger.

Within minutes of this gentle flurry of camaraderie, Father Norris drew the mass to its conclusion. The parishioners quietly left through the main door and Linda moved towards the front of the church, the priest acknowledging her approach, his eyes smiling. He was tall and lithe, athletic, she thought.

'You must be Linda,' he said. 'Welcome to St Joseph's. It's a warm morning isn't it? Why don't we go to my office, it's a little cooler in there.'

Linda followed Father Norris across a small courtyard to his office on the ground floor of an older double-storey brick-and-tile building alongside the church. In his office they sat down in comfortable armchairs, away from the priest's neat desk. There was an old bookcase along one wall imbuing the entire room with a scholarly atmosphere accompanied by the appealing scent of old leather.

'How did you find the service?' the priest asked.

'It was very pleasant, thank you. I found it peaceful and unpretentious.'

'And how can I be of assistance to you?'

Linda explained the story of her search – and Mark's – for Charlie Templeman. She explained the central part played by Charlie's painting and the connection it had with the Sir James Mitchell School through Katy Bilowski and her sister Jan. She told him that it was Charlie's apparent disappearance, and that of his parents, that had most confounded them, despite their best efforts. It was a long shot, but they knew that the Templeman family had lived in the Subiaco area and they were looking for any more information – anything at all – that might lead them in a more productive direction.

'We wondered if your church kept records of children baptised here. We don't even know that Charlie was baptised, let alone that he was baptised here. All we've got is Charlie's date of birth. And we don't know if he had any siblings, older or younger, or if they were baptised. But, if he did have any siblings, identifying them might help us locate Charlie.'

The priest thought for a while, the office bathed in quiet, somehow sheltered from the noise of the traffic only metres away.

'We have records of every baptism conducted at this church, dating back well over a century. Of course, they are private records belonging to the church and I could not allow you direct access to them. But we are able to look through them and I'd be happy to share what we have about any baptisms in this family.'

He paused again, as if he was formulating a question in his mind, but, when he spoke, it was just to make a statement. 'If you give me Charlie Templeman's date of birth, we will see what our records reveal. I will call you as soon as I have anything to report.' Linda felt reassured by his tone. Perhaps, she imagined, he could also appreciate that there was more to her search than simply locating the current whereabouts of just one individual.

❖❖❖

Mark walked to breakfast and coffee at Sayers Sister, his mood and appetite buoyed by Linda's visit. Hyde Park rewarded him with views of a pair of black swans stewarding their brood of tiny cygnets, half a dozen ibis wading in the lake in search of food, and maybe a dozen other species of waterbird. The jacarandas were past their best, but, caught by the bright morning light, the lilac carpet of fallen flowers beneath them created a glorious and unnatural glow.

He breathed in, and felt deep gratitude for his evolving relationship with Linda, who had already embarked upon a full day's work. It was a small moment of peace for Mark before heading in to the gallery and the uncertainty that faced him there on many fronts – Devlin, Peterson, the *West* and, of course, Charlie. But as it turned out, Mark's day was unproductive and uneventful. He went in search of information about James Devlin's early life but found the internet impenetrable and unhelpful. There was no word from any quarter about the Dickerson. He spoke to Alvin Teoh to tell him of the concerns he had about his small painting, to advise him how best to approach the auction house from whom he had purchased it to ask for a refund, and to do his best to reassure him that this was a rare and atypical event. Alas, Mark thought, this was precisely the sort of experience that might curtail the developing collector's appetite for investing in art.

Visitors to the gallery were few, and Mark spent some time in the upstairs storeroom selecting different works to display for the weekend. He brought Charlie's painting downstairs and set it up discreetly at the back of the gallery for a while; his line of vision was drawn again into the central, black, rectangular void that anchored the entire painting. It was like gazing into the night sky, he thought, stars glittering in the inky darkness, as mysterious and inaccessible as the outer reaches of space. He loved looking at this painting regardless of the confusion in his life that it had spurred; it had, at the very least, led him to Linda.

Just the same, he felt uneasy about the work, and ever less comfortable about it being discovered before it had been properly attributed. With journalists likely to be coming back at some stage, he decided that the time had come to get it well out of the way upstairs. He photographed the painting in good light before wrapping it securely and putting it back upstairs.

Then he returned to his laptop to search local secondary schools in the Upwey area, considering which ones had been in operation in the early 1970s. He wasn't sure that he would be able to extract any useful information as he doubted any school would publish information about class lists, present or past, on their websites. He'd probably have to request a search of the equivalent Victorian archives. It was going to be impossible to identify and quiz Devlin's classmates if he couldn't locate where he'd gone to school.

And he realised that he would soon have to advise Jan Bilowski that he had not been able to attribute any specific value to Charlie's painting. He had become attached to the painting and couldn't bear the thought that it would be sold to anyone who did not appreciate, as he did, its provenance and power. He had formulated the idea of a contract that would allow him to buy the painting from Jan while still providing her with an assurance that she would benefit if, for any reason, it could later be shown to be of greater value. He would have to double-check with Pat and Linda, but he knew he had to offer Jan some resolution before too much longer.

32. FRIDAY DECEMBER 6

James Devlin was keen to complete his duties at Monash University, where he was being honoured for his generosity and his community work. He had on innumerable occasions used his influence among art collectors and critics, politicians and entrepreneurs, to garner financial support for worthy causes. He rewarded them with access to his knowledge, insights and predictions about the world of Australian art, and he elevated fundraising events by including impressive displays of fine art or by donating works for auction. Monash had, in his honour, named a newly refurbished lecture theatre in the Menzies Building within the Arts precinct of the university's Clayton campus. He had received the email he was expecting from Brad Collins just as the ceremony started. Brad had been discreet in his cover note, but the sense was that there was little of note found in Perth; nevertheless, Devlin's unease at Mark Lewis' pointed line of inquiry would not let up and he was anxious to get to the attached report.

The newly completed lecture theatre was smartly appointed and equipped with the latest technology. The university – which held a magnificent collection of twentieth and early twenty-first century Australian fine art – had placed its sole artwork by James Devlin prominently in the revamped lecture theatre. Although slightly to his left, he was afforded an unimpeded view of his painting as he sat in the front row, a painting he remembered well, having thought deeply at the time about its title, *Abyss*.

Devlin's vision was drawn again to the central triangle of sky blue, a soothing oasis surrounded by chaotic brushstrokes that emanated a disturbing energy. A series of parallel white lines to the left of the blue triangle created the impression of stairs heading down to it, urging the viewer to descend into its offer of a calming refuge. Infrequent among Devlin's works was the use of red, appearing on the right side of the painting like blood at a crime scene. There was, on the other hand, the rising cloud of white paint, so characteristic of Devlin's works, in the upper half of the painting, contaminated in this work by streaks of black, and bordered on its right side by a column of dirty brown, like smoke issuing from a bushfire.

It was a troubling work for Devlin, even now. He was grateful for the honour bestowed on him by Monash University, and proud of – and still committed to – his community work. But he felt a deep heaviness as the painting hovered in the periphery of his thoughts, and it was with a sense of relief that he made his retreat after he had delivered his brief speech and the formalities had ended. He caught an Uber and opened Collins' report.

It was longer and more detailed than he had expected. Collins' colleague had included a lot of material gleaned from public domain sources as well as from personal inquiry. The impression surrounding Lewis was that of an earnest individual, a modest but successful surgical career, a happy family, a tragic loss, and an unpretentious gallery. Lewis was evidently closely connected to Pat O'Beirne, as Devlin had suspected, following on from over two decades during which Lewis had been primarily a collector.

There was a description of Lewis' daughter who worked in the gallery, and her family – and nothing to raise any alarm. No obvious sign in the gallery of any works resembling his own, and no reference in discussion to anything similar. And there was a description of the third party, Linda De Vries, who had been with Lewis in Victoria and who was evidently the current woman in his life, presently acting CEO at the Ability Centre for cerebral palsy.

A small depth charge exploded inside James Devlin. His pulse racing, he searched the Centre's website and noted its purpose, history and location. He extended his search, frantic as he retraced his memory, piecing things together, the course of events leading inexorably to one conclusion. He drew in a sharp breath, feeling a mixture of paralysis, anxiety and fear. Ideas, memories and thoughts collided uncontrollably in his brain, unfiltered, disorganised and useless to him. He searched for something to jolt himself into a more effective reaction. But he could not. He felt defeated, exposed, unworthy, despicable. This could not be a coincidence; his unease about Lewis' inquiries was justified. He could not fathom how this had occurred – he literally could not think straight. He closed his eyes, witness to the bleakest of imaginings, powerless to suppress the darkest of thoughts – shame and grief, humiliation, loss and regret.

By the time the Uber reached North Fitzroy, James Devlin had regained some semblance of composure. Although he had been meticulous in collating and recording all works attributable to him, his inescapable conclusion was that Mark Lewis had stumbled upon a painting that had escaped that process. Lewis had almost certainly recognised the style of the work, but the provenance wouldn't have matched up and the work was probably not signed. Any interest they'd been showing in Garth Barrett had been entirely as a means to find out more about him.

Devlin supposed that Pat O'Beirne had been engaged early on to verify Lewis' misgivings about the painting. That they hadn't approached Devlin directly probably reflected their suspicions about the work and about their reservations concerning Devlin.

If it came to it, Devlin knew that he could simply deny the work was his, and could dispute the provenance, whatever that might be. But if Lewis and his little team of detectives kept pursuing it, Devlin's denials might count for nothing.

How he wished he could set this issue aside once and for all, to be free of the remorse and the threat of public recrimination. Now it seemed as if it was all suddenly descending upon him, at a time destined to maximise his fall from grace. From public acclaim. From respect.

Yet he was still only surmising – catastrophising perhaps. He needed to be sure that there really was a painting, a missing Devlin; and, if there was, he needed to take possession of it. What would his next move be? And what risks were attached to such a decision?

The Uber pulled up outside his home. He thanked the driver and got out. In this matter, he knew, he was on his own. There was no-one whose advice he could seek. It was already clear to him that Garth had lost the desire to continue their business relationship and, in any event, Garth would be deeply disturbed – his response possibly unpredictable – if he found out what Devlin had learned today. And James Devlin knew that, more than ever, he needed ice calm and a considered plan. As he had in the past, he would once again have to rely on his own intuition to emerge from this unscathed.

33. FRIDAY DECEMBER 6

Linda arrived at work around eight fifteen to be confronted by an air-conditioning failure that, on this scorching day, threatened to cause chaos and complaint across her site. It never ceased to amaze Linda how difficult it was to obtain expert advice and technical assistance for this vital facility in a city with such a predictably hot and dry climate; and the hotter it was, the harder to obtain that help it always seemed to be.

She had arranged to pop into the gallery after work and to head back with Mark to his place after that. They were going to Olivia's for dinner and she was looking forward to catching up with the family. Linda enjoyed the company of all of Mark's family, and she felt that Olivia, Becky and their children had embraced her with genuine warmth. For Linda, it was as if she had, literally overnight, slotted into a new, more complex and colourful life, and she was enjoying every minute of it.

She also recognised that she had been preoccupied and less effective at work this week, her relationship with Mark and her involvement in the search for Charlie rendering her day job somehow less engaging. She spent most of the day glued to her chair, fielding questions from staff about the air-con and in furious and repeated communication with the people who might be able to get it working reliably.

It was not until after four o'clock that the day's central problem had been brought under control with any sense of stability or certainty. She was now the last person still at work, and she had lost the appetite for embarking upon any of the day's numerous other tasks that she had been obliged to leave untouched.

The ringtone of Linda's mobile phone startled her, and she reached for it, happily anticipating that it was Mark, but the incoming landline number was not immediately familiar.

'Linda de Vries speaking.'

'Hello, Linda, it's Father Norris.'

Linda was surprised and a little excited to be hearing from him so soon.

'Thank you for getting back to me so soon. Did you find anything?'

'I did indeed.'

'Was Charlie baptised at your church?' Linda said, unable to match his steady tone.

'That was a quite a hunch of yours. Our Charlie was baptised here on February twenty, nineteen fifty-six. Like you, we also have his date of birth as October twenty-six, nineteen fifty-five.'

Linda thought she detected a protective instinct that the priest was extending towards this unknown individual, an instinct that she and Mark had come to share. And she could sense the measured way in which he released the information, happy to share it, but obliging her to make the next inquiry; a life spent listening and responding to others, she felt, in appreciation of the importance of silence as a prelude to honesty and self-reflection.

'Were you able to identify any siblings?'

'We have a brother, John Harold Templeman, who was baptised at St Joseph's on August three, nineteen fifty-seven, and who was born on June ten in the same year. Named after his father, I would imagine.' Linda scribbled down the details as Father Bryan continued. 'But no others that I can find in the five years either before Charlie or after John junior, at least not here at St Joseph's. It is entirely possible that there are other siblings who were baptised at other churches around Perth, depending upon where the family was living at the time.'

Linda's heart sank. She had already searched for John Templeman while looking for Charlie's father. There was nowhere new to go with that name. And the prospect of examining church records around town in search of some other sibling who probably did not even exist struck Linda as a forlorn endeavour.

'I hope this information leads you to Charlie. If you find him, or John, please let them know that they were baptised here at St Joseph's. And that they'd be welcome here any time.'

'Thank you, Father Bryan. If I track either of them down, I shall definitely let them know. And thank you for your help … and for being so kind.' She paused, unable in the moment to fully express herself, and disappointed at being no closer to locating Charlie.

'You are also always welcome here anytime. God bless you, Linda.'

It was still well before five but, she persuaded herself, time to leave for the week. Before she did, Linda googled John Templeman once again. Then John Templeman junior. Nothing on either account that was of any assistance. Then she googled James Devlin and clicked on the Wikipedia site, knowing already it had little to say about his early life. Other than having been born in Melbourne, and having studied arts at Monash, it was thin on even basic details – no date of birth, nothing about his parents or any siblings, stubbornly silent on his childhood and school years.

The websites of various galleries, including Melbourne's NGV, carried the most limited of biographies and CVs but none provided any detailed information that preceded the commencement of his career as an artist. He had no Facebook page and Devlin's gallery Facebook page had only the scantiest information about the man himself, most of it drawing attention to his nomination as Victoria's Australian of the Year.

Frustrated, Linda lamely googled 'James Devlin date of birth'. She was greeted with a previously unseen but typically brief biography, a photo of the artist, his place of birth listed as 'Australia' and his date of birth as June 10, 1957. That date was instantly familiar, her brain humming in an effort to complete the connection. Then her heart jumped. She reached for the notes she had scribbled from her conversation with Father Bryan. John junior, whose whereabouts she had also not been able to determine, shared exactly the same birthday as James Devlin.

Linda put her hands to her chest, closed her eyes, tried to contain her thoughts and control her heart rate. The pieces suddenly seemed to fit together. She printed off the screen page, in the end so easily located. It contained such seemingly inconsequential information, yet it was so disturbing in its implication and, if that implication was true, so critical in explaining Charlie's painting.

❖❖❖

There was a restrained mood in the gallery. Mark was seated facing the front door, Pat to his right and Helen to his left, her back to the door, the three of them in deep discussion. Mark spotted Linda approaching the gallery and, as he did, his serious, anxious expression melted. Linda let herself in and Mark greeted her with a hug.

'Are you OK?' Linda asked.

'I'm not really too sure.' Mark swivelled, holding Linda's hand, and introducing her to Helen. 'Linda, this is Helen O'Beirne, who was the very first person to introduce me to the world of collecting art. Helen, this is Linda De Vries, who I have heartlessly embroiled in the search for Charlie and his painting.'

'I'm not sure heartless is quite the right description, Mark,' Helen said. 'I have heard plenty about you, Linda, and it has all been good.' The two women shook hands, Mark confident that they would instantly appreciate their shared inclination towards both positivity and candour.

'What's going on?' asked Linda. She spotted Charlie's painting once again on display on an easel. Linda hadn't seen it in a while and she was, for the first time, taken aback by its strength, its pitch-black heart and the loosely controlled chaos that surrounded it. Her attention on this occasion was drawn to a series of parallel brushstrokes in the lower right quadrant of the painting, like a flight of steps, that she hadn't previously appreciated.

'The *West* has decided to run an article on Tony Peterson's painting in their weekend edition,' Mark told her. 'The senior arts editor rang me this afternoon to give me advance notice. It sounds as if they are going for the story side of things – Is this a forgery? Has this man been misled? Can you trust an art dealer? – that sort of angle.'

'He rang you to tell you that?' asked Linda.

'The senior editor isn't happy about it,' said Pat. 'His new boss knows Peterson and insisted upon an article. The article won't openly state that it's a forgery, but it will spread a lot of dirt and that could spell trouble for Mark.'

'I called Pat and Helen as soon as the *West* rang me,' Mark said. 'I'm trying to figure out what I should do.'

Linda took in the new information. She appreciated that this might be seriously damaging to Mark's reputation. But she was also bursting to tell them what she had found. 'I've got some news of my own – about Charlie's painting – if this isn't the wrong time to talk about it?'

Instantly, the three gallerists gave Linda their attention as she presented Mark with the print-off.

'You know we've been searching everywhere about James Devlin but there isn't a lot to read about his origins. Not anywhere,' she said.

Mark looked with bemusement at the short list of facts Linda had just handed him.

Linda described her encounter with Father Norris at St Joseph's Church, catching Pat's eye in acknowledgement of his advice in this regard. She described the priest's follow-up call and the link between his scanty information and her unexpected internet find.

'Charlie had a brother, John Templeman junior,' Linda said. 'And according to the baptism records and this internet site, John junior and James Devlin share exactly the same birthdate.' She paused to let this simple fact sink in. 'Day, month and year.'

None of the three new recipients of that information uttered a sound.

'This is what I think,' Linda said. 'James Devlin was born John Templeman junior right here in Perth. But it was Charlie who was the artist in the family. They left Perth for Melbourne probably soon after Charlie finished at the Sir James Mitchell School. Maybe they all changed their names and started new lives. Someone – probably James – saw the potential in Charlie's paintings and decided to cash in and present himself as the artist.'

'So, what happened to Charlie?' Helen said.

'I don't know, but I believe he painted this work,' Linda said, pointing to the small masterpiece on the easel, 'and I think that he might have painted them all.'

'Maybe his family recognised the potential for Charlie's art to be commercially successful. But they needed a more publicly presentable figure to pose as the artist to make it succeed,' said Mark, sounding excited. 'It's possible that James Devlin has masqueraded as the artist more or less his whole adult life.'

'I've never trusted that man,' said Helen.

At that moment Patrick rose from his chair and walked the few paces to Charlie's painting, studying it more intently than ever.

'This work and Devlin's oeuvre are all by the same hand,' he said. 'The provenance of this work is solid, making Charlie the artist. Those identical birthdates will not be a coincidence.' He pushed his hands into his pockets as if the answers might be found there. 'James Devlin is Charlie's brother but, as Linda says, Charlie is the artist. The absence of Devlin's typical red insignia simply highlights the fact that this work, probably like no other, escaped the family's net.'

'It doesn't all quite fit, though. Why did Devlin – I mean, Charlie – suddenly stop painting?' asked Mark.

'Maybe he became ill?' said Pat. 'Maybe he died? Either way, the supply of paintings stopped. Devlin knew that he couldn't paint like his brother and couldn't sustain the subterfuge. So, he headed off to London, hid from the Australian art scene, feigned disillusionment with being an artist but thought that he could still make a living as a gallerist.'

'And he was right,' Mark said.

'And when he was in London,' said Linda, 'he caught up with his old footy mate, Garth Barrett, hatched a business plan where they would ramp up prices for art, and then proved to be a very successful gallerist.'

'And a great judge of art, old and new,' added Mark. 'He's also been very generous with his time, his support for other artists, his donations to good causes. He hasn't kept it all to himself.'

Pat shook his head. 'Why do you think Barrett would want to get involved in that scam? He was destined for an excellent career and income. Surely he wasn't so close to Devlin to warrant that risk?'

'I bet that Barrett also knew the paintings weren't by Devlin,' said Helen. 'They've ripped so many people off with their ramping, never forget that. There've been as many potential collectors turned off art when they realise they've paid too much for a painting as there've been collectors who've benefited from Devlin's investment advice. I'm not as impressed with him as you all seem to be.'

'That's true,' said Pat. 'Distorting and manipulating the market is a seriously bad thing. It's a blight on the art world. Regardless of his generosity. And I'm still sure that he has contributed somehow to this terrible business with Tony Peterson. But fooling the art world for thirty years about being something you are not, that is … way out there.'

Pat returned to his seat. 'When you think about it, he must have been maybe just twenty-five years of age when all this was happening. Yet he – or maybe someone very close to him – knew that Charlie's work was good.'

'And,' said Helen, 'we still don't know what happened to Charlie.'

34. FRIDAY DECEMBER 6

Mark settled into the passenger seat as Linda reversed and headed into Friday evening traffic. It was after six and they would have to go directly to Olivia and Hendrick's. They started to speak simultaneously.

'You first,' Mark insisted.

Linda smiled. 'Do you plan to tell Olivia about the birthdate?'

'Not tonight. Pat was really firm about keeping this information close for now, and I couldn't accept his help with this newspaper nightmare and ignore his advice about Charlie's painting.'

There had been no mistaking the strength of Pat's feelings about the need for confidentiality. 'This information is potentially explosive,' he'd stated with more force than Mark had ever heard from him. 'I have no doubt that all this fits together, but it does hinge on a common birthdate that might, conceivably, be pure coincidence and that might be plain wrong. Right now, we cannot share this information with anyone at all.' Pat had looked at each of them sternly. 'Let's think about it overnight and get together again tomorrow.'

'Do you think you'll get any sleep tonight?' asked Linda. The four of them had settled on plan of action in response to the impending article in Saturday's *West*. The gallery would be open, and it would be business as usual. They had agreed upon plans for Mark to prepare a clear and unapologetic script aimed at customers – new and old – concerned about the authenticity of works for sale or those previously acquired. And a robust defence of the provenance of Tony Peterson's painting. Mark would also compose an email to Robert Dickerson's family, explaining the sequence of events and advising them of the impending newspaper article. It would be a difficult task and he was unsure how the family would respond; in reality, he was advising them out of courtesy about events over which he had no real control, and he hoped that they would see it as such.

Pat would write a more scholarly piece about fakes and forgeries in Australian art which would be uploaded to the Beaufort Gallery website. He and Helen would join Mark and Linda in the gallery from its opening to provide moral support.

'They are such good people,' said Linda. 'How did you get to know them?'

'I met Helen first and it was her passion for particular works of art that gelled with me and set me on this strange path.' Mark described his journey from growing up in a household with lots of contemporary art on its walls, to a holiday on Queensland's Sunshine Coast with Sharon and the girls many years later, when Olivia wasn't even ten years old. The three 'girls' had gone off shopping and he had wandered the main street of Noosa, stumbled upon an art gallery and had his interest in the notion of art as an investment pricked by a gallerist-cum-salesman. He had always been grateful to that man for rekindling his lifelong passion for art.

'But I really had no idea what I was doing, and the first person I was directed to for proper advice was Helen O'Beirne. She listened to what I had to say and told me to go away and look at art, books and galleries, figure out what was good and what was not, what was fabulous and what was formulaic, and to come back when I had sorted myself out!'

Mark had been impatient to get on with the project and he had challenged Helen there and then by asking how many books he would have to read and how many paintings he would have to study to know as much as she already did. Helen had held him in a cool stare, sizing him up, and had agreed to assemble some investment-quality works for him to assess. Not without some hesitation, Mark had placed his trust in Helen and started his collection with two of the works Helen had shown him on that occasion.

Thereafter, Helen and Pat had nudged and directed him towards acquiring art of investment quality, and away from other works they believed were not. They had always given him unfettered access to their advice and expertise, even occasionally assisting him to acquire works from other gallerists, and regularly advising him against acquiring works from their own auctions which they believed were not appropriate for his evolving collection. Over time, Mark had developed the sort of appreciation of art-as-investment that Helen had wanted for him way back at the start. More importantly, he had developed a deep trust for Helen and Pat's advice, and had gleaned from them a view of a sort of 'art ecosystem', where works of art pass from one owner to another, often only after many years, decades or even generations, and where all elements of that ecosystem – artists, private gallerists, auction houses, major institutions and collectors of all stripes – play their part and, at times, take their cut.

Linda listened as they eased their way through the heavy traffic on Guildford Road, aiming for Peninsula Road and the Maylands foreshore.

'When did Pat get involved in your collection?'

'I suppose that sort of evolved over time. Initially, my main contact was Helen, and I just loved her enthusiasm and honesty. But, over time, I found that I also had lots in common with Pat – politics, attitudes towards the art market, attitudes towards other people, all sorts of things. He was a font of knowledge about the art world in this country, who had taught who to paint, deals that had been done over the years, who could be trusted and who could not.'

Mark had started to spend time taking advantage of an occasional quiet afternoon at work by catching up with Pat over a cup of tea at Pat's gallery or his storeroom. It was in those moments that Mark had realised that this is what he most liked to do. And it was while sitting with Pat, sad and confused after Sharon's death, that Mark had first mooted the idea of leaving his career as a surgeon.

They pulled up outside Olivia's home.

'Should we concentrate – with Olivia – on how you will be dealing with the article in the *West*?' Linda said.

'Good idea,' said Mark, taking the bottle of Mumm from the back seat and heading towards the front door, in happy anticipation of the rapturous greeting the two of them would receive from his grandchildren.

35. SATURDAY DECEMBER 7

James Devlin awoke after eight am Melbourne time, foggy-headed after having consumed too much wine the previous evening, and emerging from a series of vivid but rapidly dissipating dreams.

He opened his eyes, bridging the gap between dream and reality as he lifted his heavy head off the pillow. He was alone, as he had been for over a year now. Although there had been a number of serious relationships over the years, he had never married and did not have any children. For all his appeal to Melbourne's high society, he was most comfortable in his own company, most confident in his own judgement.

He heard his phone's SMS signal and grabbed at it. There were a couple of messages from Catherine Deehan but he felt too groggy to attend to them. He sat up on the edge of his bed, steadied himself and set off to shave and shower before facing the day ahead.

❖❖❖

Midmorning, James Devlin headed off for a walk around the Edinburgh Gardens; its oak and elm trees towering under the blue sky, the sounds of children playing and owners calling their dogs were a soothing background for thinking through his situation. He stopped at the park to read the messages from Catherine Deehan.

The first text was brief: *Looks like you were on the money again! A fake Dickerson in Perth.* The second was a screenshot of the article in the local Perth newspaper which he magnified as much as his screen would allow but which he could still only barely read. It was by someone named Jonathan Bolton.

'Recent and renewed speculation about a new wave of art fraud has been given added credibility by claims from an experienced Western Australian art collector that he has been sold a high-quality fake said to have been painted by revered Australian artist Robert Dickerson. The work was purchased from Mt Lawley gallerist Mark Lewis, a former surgeon whose Beaufort Street premises opened in 2017 ...'

Devlin read on, conscious that this was more or less what he had hoped would happen as a result of his conversation with Cathy Deehan; he knew that this would already be causing Mark Lewis great discomfort but that Lewis' reputation would ultimately be justly salvaged although badly bruised. Serves him right, he thought. Irrespective, this was a useful distraction that would deflect Lewis from pursuit of Devlin's past, and would buy James time to consider his best course of action.

He sent a return text: *Thanks. Had not seen that. It's a worry. J.*

Then he read on.

'... Nationally regarded art dealer James Devlin was recently quoted as being concerned about the emergence of highly sophisticated fakes of well-recognised and collectible artists, preying on collectors desperate to acquire their works. Meanwhile, aggrieved collector Tony Peterson says that he had spent a "six figure sum" in purchasing his work. "People need to be very careful. You cannot assume that every art gallerist knows what you think they should. There are good fakes out there and you cannot necessarily trust the gallery to protect you." Peterson is considering his next steps in an effort to reclaim his money ...'

Devlin appreciated that he did not really know exactly what Lewis knew about him. His rational, pessimistic self believed that Mark Lewis had stumbled upon a painting that he recognised as a Devlin, and had somehow solved the riddle of its provenance.

His more optimistic self wondered if this was a more speculative venture on Lewis'. behalf – that he had figured out the connection between Garth Barrett and himself and that he was probing that relationship more in the hope than the expectation of finding something of note. That, however, did not explain the involvement of Linda De Vries. Devlin needed to know whether or not there was a painting at the heart of this and, if there was, he needed to get that painting away from Mark Lewis, quickly – and secretly – into his own possession.

He slowed his pace and called Brad Collins from his mobile. This time, he knew, he was taking a much bigger risk, but he had to find out what was driving Mark Lewis' interest in him. Brad listened to the request. He retained a neutral tone as he responded.

'This will require a listening device. And that means someone to put the device in place and then to listen. There are significant legal and cost considerations.' He paused. 'But it is entirely possible, and I have colleagues who can attend to this expertly and discreetly.'

Devlin understood that he was about to cross a line, but he had to get to the bottom of what was going on in Perth. He authorised Collins to make things happen, emphasising the importance of speed. The Christmas–New Year break would soon see the gallery close or reduce its hours, and he wanted the surveillance in place immediately. Collins agreed to call back within hours with a plan and a quote, and the conversation came to an abrupt conclusion.

36. SATURDAY DECEMBER 7

Mark lay in bed next to Linda, her steady breathing – her very presence – soothing his turbulent thoughts. He had been very late to bed after crafting a robust defence and explanation of the Dickerson sale, and emailing the Dickerson family to advise them of the impending newspaper article. As agreed the previous evening at dinner, he had already sent the same article through to Olivia, who had the editing and IT skills he lacked to add material to the website.

Patrick had also penned an article about the recent history of forgery in Australian art which would be added to the website; Pat was a diligent student of the national art scene and knew, in person, almost all the relevant players – artists, dealers, collectors and fraudsters. And he had a way with words. The agreed approach had been to 'own' the Dickerson as an authentic, original work and defend that position staunchly, on the website and face to face in the gallery.

Despite having slept only briefly, Mark was keen to read what the newspapers had written about him and his gallery, and impatient for ten o'clock to come so that he could open the gallery and face whatever music might be coming. He and Linda had arranged to meet with Olivia, Helen and Pat for breakfast at nine – he still had hours to stew before then. He felt anxious but keen to get on with the day.

❖❖❖

'It's a pity that Jonathan Bolton didn't include any of his conversation with me in the article,' Mark said, annoyed. 'Not one word from my side.'

He and Linda were each reading the article, having reached The Old Laundry early precisely for that purpose.

'Actually, it's quite telling,' Linda said. 'He makes no effort to settle the issue about authorship. It's just a sellable story with a somewhat salacious theme and a very pretty picture.' There was a large photograph of Tony Peterson, glowering beside his painting. 'He gives the owner free rein to retaliate at a perceived injustice while the newspaper permits aspersions to be cast at you. The *West* doesn't commit itself to any particular belief about whether or not this work is a fake. Lazy, second-rate journalism in my opinion.'

Olivia arrived at that moment, a copy of the article in her hand and a look of righteous indignation on her face. 'It's awful, Dad!'

Mark rose to hug her and replied, 'Don't worry, darling. The truth will emerge. We'll all get over it. Did you manage to sort out the website?'

'Yes, it all looks good. And I've added Pat's piece in too. It's all really interesting – I didn't know much at all about art fraud in Australia.' At that moment, Helen and Pat arrived to join them for breakfast, the atmosphere easing, as if the group's shared conviction about the authenticity of the painting, the injustice of the article and the disloyalty of the collector would somehow protect the gallery from momentous injury.

❖❖❖

By midday, with a strange mixture of relief and disappointment, the group determined that this had all been a storm in a teacup. The gallery had been quiet, not a single phone call had been received, and a smattering only of potential customers had wandered mostly aimlessly around the current display. The neat stacks of the two articles added to the gallery's website overnight had not been disturbed.

Helen, Pat and Olivia left just after midday, and Linda headed off around twelve forty-five to buy some sandwiches for her and Mark. Just before one, the gallery door opened and a noisy entourage of people barged in. Mark looked up, startled. A striking woman brandishing a microphone approached him, while a cameraman followed, pointing his camera at Mark.

'Mark Lewis?' she demanded.

Mark stood up, immediately on the defensive. He hadn't anticipated the involvement of television – none of them had – and he scrambled to collect his thoughts. 'Yes, I'm Mark Lewis.'

Behind the TV team his eyes were drawn to the front door where Tony Peterson appeared, carrying his new painting, the news team moving aside to let him through in a transparently choreographed manoeuvre.

Mark's eyes narrowed as he appreciated the planned theatrics – this man was truly awful. He steadied himself, angry but determined to respond with dignity and professionalism, a counter to the gaudy spectacle that had just invaded his gallery.

The woman said: 'My name is Isha Patel from Seven News. Can you tell me if this painting is real or have you sold this man a fake?'

Peterson had commandeered an easel and was standing like a peacock beside the Dickerson. Mark felt momentary self-loathing and guilt at having sold this beautiful painting to this boorish man. It had spent over fifty years in the hands of just two different owners, both of whom had only ever admired it and appreciated it for its bold colours, characteristically stylised human figures, and deep pathos. And I, thought Mark Lewis, have sold it to a true philistine, happy to parade it on the streets and on television like a gold chain won by a thug in a bet.

'I am as certain as I believe anyone other than the artist himself can be that this magnificent painting is an original by Robert Dickerson.' Mark made his point and shut up. He knew that this was not live television, so that editing would inevitably be required. He suspected that the journalist was interested only in a good story and was indifferent to the authenticity of the painting. A media-friendly sound bite might survive that editing irrespective of whether it supported Tony Peterson or not. Short answers, newsworthy statements, never feel obliged to respond to the actual question – how grateful he was right then for the media training he had been given during a stint in the Western Australian Health Department a few years earlier.

When he said no more, the journalist countered: 'Aren't you aware of the recent increase in fake art in Australia? Shouldn't you have warned your client that this might be a fake?'

Mark estimated that the journalist was only twenty-five and wondered what research into this topic she had undertaken. 'Isha, this work is without doubt an original. Mr Peterson and I both considered the issue of whether or not this might be a fraudulent creation very carefully before completing the sale. Mr Peterson is well aware of the lengths to which my gallery has gone to establish authenticity and he was totally satisfied that it was an original when he purchased it.'

'But were you even aware that fakes have been flooding into the Australian art market over the last few months?'

Indeed, Mark had heard no such thing until the article the *Age* that had quoted James Devlin. And the journalist's reference to 'flooding' and 'the last few months' were undoubtedly of her own making; she would have hoped to have caught Mark off guard and off balance by now and was using exaggeration in an effort to maintain her position of control over their exchange. Mark repeated his mantra. 'This painting is an original by Robert Dickerson; it is not a fake. You should be examining the evidence that supports your claim that there's a sudden flood of fake art in Australia – who is your source? Why not ask him?'

Mark knew that he had veered off script, but he sensed that this was all linked to James Devlin and somehow to Charlie. He wanted to lure Devlin into the furore that, he was increasingly sure, Devlin had himself instigated.

Isha Patel pressed on. 'The source is James Devlin, and his views have been made very public just this week. Have you really not kept up with this topic?' She was evidently keen to confirm Tony Peterson's stated belief that Lewis was not sufficiently abreast of developments in Australian art.

'I have indeed read the newspaper article quoting Mr Devlin,' Mark said. 'Unless you have another source for your claims, I am sure you are misquoting him.' He knew that she had no other source – he doubted that there was, in any event, any real substance to Devlin's recent assertions – and he knew she would be anxious about the accusation of misquoting any source.

'Are you going to give Mr Peterson his money back?'

Mark had discussed this at length with Pat. Refunding the money would be unequivocally difficult for him and, just as bad, might give credence to the notion that this painting really was a fake and that Mark Lewis really did sell fakes. Moreover, it might open the floodgates to anyone who had ever purchased art from his gallery to turn up with the painting requesting an immediate refund.

'If Mr Peterson can provide an authoritative, independent opinion, in writing, that this painting is not by the hand of Robert Dickerson, I will gladly return his full purchase price in exchange for the painting. For the moment, this' – Mark pointed to the easel sporting the Dickerson – 'is his painting and he should take it home with him now. And he should take good care of it because it is both beautiful and valuable.'

'Whose opinion would you accept?' Patel fired back, battling to maintain momentum and to keep pressure on the gallerist. Right at this moment, Linda came in through the rear door of the gallery, sandwiches in a paper bag, alarmed at the unexpected spectacle in front of her, the camera suddenly turning towards her. Mark caught her eye, doing his best to convey a calm and controlled look, accompanied by a relieved smile that she had arrived.

Mark seized the moment to disrupt the rhythm and direction of the exchange. 'Linda – meet Isha Patel and the crew from Channel Seven.' The camera continued to roll. 'And this is Mr Tony Peterson. Isha, Tony. Please meet my partner, Linda De Vries.' Linda's introduction, digitally recorded for posterity, announced his confidence in Linda and in their relationship.

Before Isha could ask another question, Mark pounced. 'Would you let me show you and your team the painting in detail? Let me tell you all how we established that this was undeniably an original. And why Mr Peterson has actually made such an excellent purchase.' He was confident he could convince them that the painting was authentic if only they would let themselves be engaged in the story that underpinned its provenance.

But the journalist appeared to sense the story she had planned risked disappearing altogether. 'Whose authority would you accept as to the authenticity of this work?' she asked again. 'Or are you saying that you are that authority?'

Mark recognised the journalist's intent and searched for a suitable sound bite. 'There are dozens of suitable experts all over Australia including right here in Perth where this work was exhibited and bought for the very first time back in nineteen sixty-eight. But you need go no further than the artist's family who have also confirmed that this painting is a Dickerson original.'

Patel tried another angle. 'Do you have to check every painting that you sell by checking with the artist or their family?'

'That's a good question. And the truth is that I do have to check the veracity of every work of art that is brought into my gallery – I cannot sell something as an original if I'm not sure.' Mark would love to have added that this was true for every art gallery in Australia, but the fake Passmore just a few metres away upstairs told him that there were some of his colleagues who were less disciplined in their checking; and he didn't want to lead the conversation towards any discussion about fakes.

Another angle from the journalist. 'Is there a problem with fake art in Australia?' Mark could see how any direct answer to this question might rebound upon him – an inexperienced and naïve dealer if he said no, admitting possible guilt if he said yes.

He said steadily: 'I am totally certain that Mr Peterson's painting is an original, and an excellent one at that.'

'You haven't answered my question, Mr Lewis – is there a problem with high quality fake art in Australia right at this moment?'

'I am confident that I have never received, handled or sold anything other than what I have claimed it to be, whether a print or an original.' He believed that statement but didn't expect it would make the Channel Seven news that night.

Tony Peterson had clearly had enough of this measured exchange. 'You've sold me a fake and you know it! I want my money back now!' The camera focused in on him, happy to record his emotive outburst.

Linda had moved to Mark's side.

'Tony,' said Mark, 'you have bought a beautiful, original Robert Dickerson. Take it home and enjoy it.'

Peterson took a step towards Lewis, a hint of his temper and aggression flaring briefly before he backed away, evidently thinking better of that course of action. He snatched the painting up off the easel, turned around and stormed out through the gallery's front door, the camera recording it all.

Patel lowered her microphone, called the shoot to a halt and spoke directly to Mark Lewis. 'Thank you for allowing us to invade your gallery unannounced. You've been very patient. If I have any further questions, would you be happy for me to phone you or arrange a time to catch up?' Her tone was calm and friendly, the change in her approach disconcerting.

Mark accepted her handshake, took a business card from inside his phone case and handed it to her, thanking her – he didn't know why – and showing her and the crew out the front door. The entire episode had lasted barely fifteen minutes, but he felt drained and confused. Linda put her arm around his waist and he turned to face her and they hugged each other tightly.

'So, it's official, I'm your partner, am I?' Linda smiled at him and he replied with a loving kiss. 'You handled that incredibly well,' she said. 'She was trying really hard to provoke you, and then Tony Peterson started to become unhinged. I thought that he might get under your skin, but he didn't. You were great.'

❖❖❖

Mark and Linda watched the evening news on Channel Seven at Mark's place, with takeaway on their laps. It contained a brief, lame segment about the so-called fake artwork, and included a few well-rehearsed lines from Tony Peterson but not one second of Mark speaking, which omission conveyed the impression that he had been unwilling to contribute to the discussion, as if he was hiding something.

'That's as bad as the newspaper article – all assertion and no investigation!' Linda said.

'It could have been worse, I suppose.' Mark replied. 'We'll see what tomorrow brings. This summer break can't come soon enough.'

Their phones rang the instant the segment ended, Pat to ask how Mark had interpreted it and Olivia to ask Linda the same. The four remained in their respective, deep discussions for a few minutes, Pat signing off first while Olivia and Linda continued for several more minutes, their conversation veering off into unrelated subjects – children, plans for the evening and more.

'What did Pat think?' Linda asked once she'd said goodbye to Olivia.

'Not too much damage, he thinks. He suspects there might be some anxious former clients getting in touch over the next few days. And he's not sure that Devlin has finished with me yet.'

37. SUNDAY DECEMBER 8

Linda headed home after breakfast and Mark got to the gallery by eleven. True to Pat's predictions, he had, by midday, fielded several calls from clients, including the couple who had only recently purchased the small David Boyd, concerned about what they had seen on the evening news. Mark did his best to reassure them all and invited them to come into the gallery any time to discuss their concerns in person. Although none of the clients had asked to return their paintings, he thought that they were unlikely to be return customers; complete trust in the person selling expensive paintings was utterly essential to the prospect of repeat business. The potential for this episode to hurt his gallery – the damage that Tony Peterson and the media coverage might inflict – was becoming evident.

After about one pm, there was a steady trickle of visitors to the gallery, although Mark could tell that many of them were not interested in the art as much as they were checking out the stories they'd read about in the newspaper or had seen on television. It was a frustrating and annoying afternoon – 'character building', he thought to himself.

Just before three thirty, a woman came into the gallery. She was stylishly dressed: camel-coloured linen trousers with a short-sleeved cream blouse tucked in, a simple stone set in a gold ring on her right ring finger, no necklace that he could see, and an orange leather bag secured over her right shoulder by its strap. Her low-heeled sandals were also orange.

She didn't introduce herself in response to Mark's greeting but spoke in a clear voice. 'I'm looking for a gift for a very close friend who knows much more about art than I do, so I'm hoping you can help me.'

Mark smiled back at her. 'Do you have any idea what you think your friend would like? Do you know if he or she likes landscapes or still life paintings? Or possibly even abstract art?'

'She definitely likes abstract art, but I know nothing about it at all.'

Mark admired her bluntness. 'OK. From what you've seen at her place, does she like bright colours? Or maybe she has some darker, more sombre pieces. Or would you prefer to just buy something for her that you personally really like so that she will always know why you gave her that piece?' When giving Olivia and Becky art as presents, Mark had always preferred to choose works that he would be happy to hang in his own home; he had come to believe that this was the safest starting point for anyone giving art as a gift.

'Oh, she's dark and moody, that's for sure.'

'Last question, but it's an important one. What is your approximate budget? I don't want to show you works that don't make any sense to your budget.' Mark still didn't have a handle on this client. 'And you might be surprised to find out how much some pieces can cost.'

Her response was prompt. 'I'm hoping to spend around fifteen hundred, hopefully no more.'

'That's a very generous gift,' Mark said. 'I'm sure I can help you.'

He set to work immediately, leaving her to wander around the gallery's main display while heading for the storeroom to select a few works he had already imagined would fill the brief – a reasonable budget and a target composition right in his gallery's 'sweet spot'. And a few others that would add to the exercise of broadening her perspective; Mark enjoyed attempting to cultivate interest, appreciation and enjoyment of art among his clients, just as he never tired of others doing so for him.

The in-house security camera system allowed him to keep an eye on his gallery and whoever was in it while he was upstairs or in the kitchenette. He had no qualms about this woman but, as a matter of course, followed her movements from the upstairs storeroom monitor while he sorted through the racks of art held there. He caught glimpses of her walking all around the gallery and, when he returned, found her transfixed in front of an impressionist still life of hibiscus flowers by Sydney-born Sam Fullbrook, that hung next to the doorway through to the kitchenette and the rear door. The work was an exercise in simplicity and in brilliant, joyous colour. It was a favourite with gallery visitors, although its hefty price tag had, so far, discouraged all potential purchasers.

Mark set the various works he had selected on the floor and brought them up onto an easel one at a time. He explained to the woman – whose name he had yet found the opportunity to extract – a little about each of the artists, and about how and where the paintings fitted into their careers. Those that were outside her budget, he made clear at the outset but tried to make the connections that he, at least, believed existed between them and the works that were in her price range. They quickly settled on two modest-sized paintings, one by Ernest Philpot from around 1960, an exuberant abstraction of a challenging – Mark used the word 'sophisticated' – nature, and one by Miriam Stannage, a restrained impressionist landscape painting on paper, in muted green-brown-grey tones.

'These are both very well-known Western Australian artists, although much less celebrated interstate. But these are exactly in your price range and both represent genuinely good quality works.'

The woman looked at them closely and, with decisiveness, chose the Stannage. 'I wouldn't really hang that one at home,' she said, pointing to the Philpot, 'so I'll take your advice and go for the landscape. I really like it and it's been beautifully framed.' Mark was pleased to have the deal completed, and they headed to the desk to finalise the paperwork. Mark sat in his chair behind the computer screen and the woman sat down across from him and deposited her bag on the floor.

'I'd like to pay in cash,' she said.

Mark suppressed his surprise. He never felt comfortable holding on to large amounts of cash, although avoiding the irritating bank charges for credit card transactions was always a small bonus.

'To whom should I make out the receipt?'

'Cherie Dixon is my name. I'll give you my PO box.'

At that moment, the gallery door opened, and both Mark and Cherie jumped. Mark had been intensely focused on this sale and had imagined they were long past closing time. Cherie, he noticed, was just as startled.

An elderly couple, looking a little harried and out of breath, peered into the gallery.

'Are you still open?' the woman said.

'Yes, we are,' said Mark, smiling. 'Please come in and have a look around. I'll just be a few minutes and then I'll give you my full attention.'

The couple looked as if they were in unfamiliar territory and he wanted to put them at ease. 'We don't have to close at any particular time so you can just come in and relax, and I'll be able to help you shortly.'

'Sorry, Cherie,' Mark returned to his newest collector. Or so he hoped. 'That's fifteen forty, including GST. But fifteen hundred will be absolutely fine.'

Cherie drew a bundle of notes from her bag, which she handed to Mark. He counted the cash and completed the receipt. Then he stepped aside to wrap the landscape in bubble wrap, insert the brief precis of the work he routinely included with each sale, secured a business card to the outside with some additional sticky tape, and the two shook hands.

'I'm sure that your friend will love the painting. I'd love to know what she thinks of it.'

What a strange and unexpected encounter that had been, thought Mark, as Cherie left his gallery. But there was no time to dwell on it. He turned to face the elderly couple who had also stopped in front of the Fullbrook, and introduced himself.

Before he could offer any assistance, the woman – Mark estimated that she was in her mid-eighties – spoke up. 'This is a beautiful work. I remember when it was sold here at auction, maybe twenty years ago, and I have never forgotten it. What a treat to see it again.' Her husband remained silent, smiling at his wife's evident pleasure.

What a relief, Mark thought, that they weren't here to ogle the infamous gallery now thought to be trading in fakes.

'How can I help you?' he said.

'Actually,' said the woman, 'I think *I* can help *you*.' From her handbag she brought out a clear plastic envelope secured by a press-stud. She withdrew from it a card, folded down the centre, with print on one side, blank on the other. 'This is the invitation to attend the opening of an exhibition of Robert Dickerson paintings in nineteen sixty-eight. We went to that opening and we actually bought one of the paintings – a small charcoal which we've since given to our son. I think you'll be interested to see this.'

Mark took the folded card and read it.

You are invited to a private viewing
of recent paintings & drawings
And to meet the Artist
Robert Dickerson
To be opened by
John Birman
Director of the Festival of Perth
On Sunday 25th February 1968 at 11.00am
Raymond Bell Galleries
65 Hay Street Subiaco, Western Australia
Telephone 81 1863
Chicken & Champagne
Champagne by Kaiser Stuhl

This was, without doubt, the invitation to the exhibition at which Tony Peterson's painting had first been exhibited and sold. He opened out the card and turned it over to see that the image on its front page used to promote the sale was, in fact, that of Tony Peterson's painting. There it was – proof positive – Tony's painting had been displayed and sold at that exhibition, the original the family had said it was from the beginning, and exactly as Pat O'Beirne had called in an instant.

'Do you remember this work from the exhibition?' asked Mark.

'I've had this invitation for over fifty years, and I've looked at it countless times. I think that angry customer of yours will be well advised to shut up before he finds himself in hot water.' Her husband nodded, smiling again. With a doctor's reflexivity, Mark wondered if the man's reserve reflected a degree of cognitive dysfunction, the early stages of dementia perhaps.

Mark replaced the invitation in the envelope and handed it back to the woman. 'I'd love to scan a copy of the invitation. Would you both like a cup of tea?'

❖❖❖

Beth Ainsworth settled into her small rental vehicle, parked on Field Street, a bobbed brunette wig and an earpiece in position, a notepad on her lap, pen in hand and a Miriam Stannage landscape securely wrapped in the boot of her vehicle. She had been unnerved by the arrival of the elderly couple at almost the precise moment that, beneath Mark Lewis' desktop, she had securely planted a listening device as she had been instructed. It had been an elaborate, precisely choreographed and, to her mind, expensive ruse to enable placement of the device, but she was paid well to do what she did and the advice she had been given about the gallery and the gallerist had been accurate and effective. And she had been able to assess the interior set-up while she was there.

Moreover, she was fascinated by the art she'd been shown, and impressed by the gallerist's passion and knowledge. Despite looking carefully, she had not seen any piece of art on display that resembled the ones detailed in Brad Collins' briefing papers and she was now – officially – intrigued to find out what she could about Mark Lewis, his gallery and the specific painting or paintings he was presumed to have in his possession. She drew a simple floor plan of the gallery identifying the position of the security camera, the rear door, the stairway Lewis had ascended and the alarm system.

❖❖❖

Hazel and Fred Gilbert were Mark's favourite type of collectors. They had never had the means to acquire major pieces by major artists, but had spent their married lives together carefully accumulating works they could afford, fascinated by the paintings, the artists, the collectors and the whole world of fine art. Not only did they have admirable knowledge of Australian art, Hazel could recount specific exhibitions that they had attended that had left strong impressions, mostly good.

Their prized possession was a mid-career Guy Grey-Smith oil, but they had continued to collect well into their seventies, including works that they insisted were small by Western Australians Jeremy Kirwan-Ward and Joanna Lamb. Fred had suffered a small stroke a few years back which had impaired his speech but left him physically and cognitively intact and Mark felt a little ashamed at his initial presumption of dementia. The couple had left him feeling envious of their collection and impressed by their lifelong commitment to art – and very much looking forward to his next conversation with Tony Peterson.

38. MONDAY DECEMBER 9

Monday was Mark's day off. After a morning run, he ambled home, anticipating with pleasure advising the people at the *West* and Channel 7 about the exhibition invitation, and exposing Tony Peterson for the ill-tempered oaf that he was. He wouldn't be catching up with Linda this evening and would probably end up making himself a light dinner, a glass or two of wine rounding off what promised to be a good day.

After a shower and breakfast, Mark ventured out into the warm morning and sat at BOOtoo Café on Bulwer Street for an iced coffee and a quick read of the newspapers. There was no follow-up to Saturday's false art exposé and Mark knew that, even after he passed on the information to both Jonathan Bolton and Ray Clarke, no amplification let alone retraction would ever appear. The story was dead, the issue that underpinned it of no further interest to any of the journalists.

He made the call to the newspaper from his study after he returned home from the café, leaving a message on the senior editor's voicemail. He followed this by sending through an explanatory email to both Clarke and Bolton to which he attached an image of the invitation along with a picture of Hazel and Fred Gilbert.

Mark was not confident that he would hear from either man. He repeated the exercise for Isha Patel at Channel 7, also leaving a message on her voicemail and sending her through the same email. No response expected, but the issue put to rest.

Finally, he penned a more detailed and personal note to his contact in the Dickerson family attaching the image of the invitation, apologising to them for the fuss and distress, and assuring them that he expected no ongoing interest in the matter. Mark had sent the information and image through to Pat and Helen, Linda and Olivia on Sunday evening and he now savoured the moment as he deliberately delayed contacting Tony Peterson. That pleasure could wait a little longer.

For the first time in two days, Mark Lewis returned to the matter of Charlie's painting. He felt certain that Charlie was James Devlin's older brother and that Charlie was the artist James Devlin had pretended to be. It seemed inevitable to him that Charlie was no longer alive but still unfathomable that the pretence had never been exposed.

On the one hand, Mark was appalled at the sort of brazenness that might have enabled deceit on such scale. And he was no less offended at the likelihood that Devlin had likely been manipulating the art market with Garth Barrett's collusion; and that he had instigated or, at least, conspired in the creation of the recent fake art story. But he also wondered what possible good would come from exposing all of this. A righteous crusade that destroyed Devlin's reputation, along with the value of all the art sold in his name, would likely harm many more people than it would help.

The only concrete evidence that supported Mark's calculations about Devlin, however, was Charlie's painting itself – and the fact that it had been known to Jan Bilowski and in her uninterrupted line of sight for half a century. In the final analysis, Mark thought, it was Jan to whom he owed a professional duty; she had brought the painting to him for his advice and assistance. Charlie's painting was a fabulous work of art, and undeniably very valuable if included in Devlin's oeuvre. But it was almost certainly worthless if the probable truth about Devlin was made public. He knew that he had to speak to Jan, and he committed to do so that afternoon, even though he still wasn't sure about how much he should say.

❖❖❖

Beth Ainsworth had chosen a different spot in which to park her car and listen patiently to the sounds of the Beaufort Gallery, earpiece and wig in place, a pen and writing pad on her lap to take notes and to make sure that she recorded any important phone numbers, addresses or times for appointments. The gallery was closed on Mondays, but she had to consider the possibility of someone being there at any stage. She waited patiently, moving her car from time to time to seek out the shade. The morning had passed entirely without event, the gallery empty and silent. Beth listened and waited; a thermos of iced tea and a supply of sushi her only distractions.

Just after two, she drove to another parking spot, staying within five hundred metres of the gallery to maintain easy wireless contact, settling into a semi-shaded place on Roy Street close to Walcott Street. She sipped some more tea and waited. She was bored and her expectation of gaining anything from the day's surveillance was rapidly diminishing. But she prided herself on her discipline, and she continued to listen and wait.

The sounds of a door opening and movement within the gallery shook her alert. She did not imagine that Mark Lewis would suspect he was under surveillance, and all her experience told her that he was not knowingly involved in anything untoward. What she had been hired to do was to detect any connection between Lewis, his gallery and her client and, more specifically, to find out if there was anything to support the notion that Lewis was in possession of one or more paintings that were linked in some way to her client. She had her key words and her intuition to help her, although she had long ago realised that vigilance and patience were her most valuable allies.

❖❖❖

A little earlier, Mark arrived at his parking spot behind the gallery. He had driven in, first to do some banking from the previous day's sale and then to make the call to Jan Bilowski. He walked up the ramp and into the tiny shopping arcade that led to Beaufort Street, then turned off the arcade into the narrow alleyway from which he could access the rear door of his gallery's kitchenette. He unlocked the bolt and then the door, entered the gallery and tapped in the code to turn off the alarm.

The paintings from the previous afternoon's sale remained stacked around the walls of the main gallery area, the visit from the Gilberts having prevented him from tidying up. He disliked the mess and even more the appearance of a messy gallery that someone passing by might notice. Mark gathered the works and, in two trips, returned them to the upstairs gallery.

Then he settled in front of the computer screen and checked his inbox, planning with wicked satisfaction when he would call Tony Peterson. His mobile phone rang at that instant – it was Ray Clarke from the *West Australian*. They exchanged greetings a little guardedly before Clarke spoke up.

'I am pleased you've found definitive proof of the painting's origins. That should settle the issue for everyone.'

Mark accepted that the journalist was in no position to apologise, but he couldn't resist a pointed comment. 'The family's word was always sufficient proof and you know that, Ray. That invitation turning up was an unlikely stroke of good fortune. Honestly, when we undermine the established processes for confirming authenticity, we do so at everyone's peril. I think you were out of line to run that article with so little substance to support it. I don't expect you'll be following it up with a clarification?'

Mark knew full well he would not. From Clarke's boss' point of view, and probably from the wider public's as well, the story – such as it had ever been – was of no more interest. And Clarke clearly saw no point in denying or defending Jayne Lee's position.

'What was Tony Peterson's reaction?' Clarke asked.

'I really don't know. It's his painting and it's in his possession. Unless he chooses to pursue this matter further, as far as I am concerned, that deal is done and dusted.' On that terse note, their conversation concluded.

Mark was surprised at the hard edge to his own words, but he realised that he owed Peterson nothing and that Peterson had done nothing to deserve anything more from him.

It was time to call Jan Bilowski. Mark went to pull her number from his contacts – still unsure what he should tell her – but was interrupted once again by a call to his mobile. It was Tony Peterson.

He braced himself. 'Mark Lewis.'

'When were you going to tell me about the exhibition invitation?'

'I felt sure that your friends at the *West* or Channel Seven would do that, Tony.'

'I want that invitation, Mark. It'll be important if I ever try to sell the painting.'

'I don't have the original. It belongs to the people who brought it in to show me. All I've got is the same image Ray Clarke must have sent you. Or was it Ms Patel? I don't need the original.' He knew he was being provocative, but he truly didn't care one bit for Tony Peterson.

'I would like you to get the original for me, Mark. This hasn't been any fun for me, you know.'

Mark bit his tongue. 'Tony, I do not have the original. It does not belong to me. The couple who brought it in were very gracious to have done so, but I'm not going to ask them to hand it over. They collect these things – thank goodness.'

'Listen, Mark.' Mark could hear Peterson's temper bubbling up again, but then he managed to settle himself. 'The invitation will go really well with the painting. You understand that. It makes sense for them to be together.'

Mark could not disagree. Like many collectors, he shared a sense of the history and origins of the paintings in his collection. One of his prize pieces was a landscape by Guy Grey-Smith which, by complete serendipity, was still being painted back in 1963 when the work, far from completion but easily recognisable, and the artist were captured in a photograph. Mark had tracked down the photographer who had generously provided him with a signed and retrospectively dated copy of the photograph. Together – the photograph of the artist in front of the evolving work of art and the final version of the painting itself – portrayed more than just a moment in time.

'Tony, I get what you are saying, and I'd have loved that invitation as well. A sort of memento of this episode.' Though more like a medal of honour, or a war wound, Mark thought. 'But the owners want to keep the invitation. You and I both have to accept that we can't have it.'

'I don't think you're taking me seriously. You ask them again – please – and you let them know why I want it. I paid you one hundred thousand for that bloody painting and you owe me big time. Just get it for me.'

Tony's cork had well and truly popped, thought Mark.

'Tony, I think we can both be totally satisfied that your painting is an original. The media won't have anything more to do with this story. The whole issue is finished, you have your painting, and I'm simply not going to get that invitation for you. The matter is over.'

There was a moment's silence, the businessman seemingly immobilised by rage and frustration. Mark took the opportunity and hung up.

The time had come to speak to Jan Bilowski.

39. MONDAY DECEMBER 9

Beth had listened, intrigued, to Mark's side of the conversation first with Ray and then Tony. It was reasonable to assume, she thought, that Ray was associated with the newspaper; she googled the newspaper's website on her phone. It didn't take long to identify Ray Clarke as the senior arts editor and the likely caller. Still, she wondered about the invitation that elderly couple had brought in to the gallery the previous afternoon – how would that so decisively end the debate about a painting's authenticity?

When Beth Ainsworth had accepted this brief, she quickly found out about the ruckus that had engulfed Mark Lewis and his gallery surrounding the sale of a supposedly fake 'masterpiece'. She had read the newspaper article and had watched the brief television news segment and she had a clear mental picture of Tony Peterson. She continued listening with undiminished interest and focus.

'Hello, Jan. This is Mark Lewis from the gallery.'

'Hello Mark, I've been waiting to hear from you.'

Thank goodness for speakerphone.

'Jan, I think we have identified Charlie.'

Beth sat up. This was exactly what she needed to hear.

'His name is Charlie Templeman and he was a pupil at Katy's school until nineteen seventy-two. Does that surname ring a bell?'

'No, Mark, I never knew much at all about Charlie.'

'I am fairly sure that Charlie Templeman painted Katy's work, Jan. But I have not been able to locate him, and I cannot find any reference to any current Australian artist by that name, or anyone at all by that name who might have been your Charlie.'

Beth scribbled a few key words.

'So, you think the painting is worthless after all?'

'Not exactly,' said Mark. 'You will recall when you first showed me the painting that I reacted to it, as if I recognised it, you said.'

'Yes. You looked like you'd seen a ghost.'

'Well that was because Charlie's painting looks very much like it might have been painted by a very well-known Melbourne artist by the name of James Devlin. Of course, your story made it clear that it had been painted here in Perth in nineteen seventy-two by Charlie, while James Devlin's career started in the eighties and he was exclusively based in Melbourne. So, either it was a fluke that it looked like a Devlin, or there is a really important connection between Devlin and Charlie.'

There was a pause, both women waiting to hear what Mark would say next.

'I need to make it clear to you, Jan, that the style, the materials used, the size of the painting – everything about Charlie's painting – is consistent with the belief that Charlie's painting is one and the same as the works of James Devlin. Now, there's a very specific signature that Devlin used on all his paintings that your painting does not have, so that's a sort of a black mark against my theory. But I've checked out my conclusion with two of Perth's most knowledgeable art consultants and they agree with me one hundred percent.'

'What conclusion is that?'

'I haven't come to a final conclusion yet, Jan, but let me explain what I think is most likely.'

Beth held her pen away from her notebook, suddenly aware that she was holding her breath in anticipation.

'I've discovered that Charlie had a younger brother named John ... John Templeman, also born in Perth. And that this younger brother shares the exact birthdate with James Devlin. Day, month and year. Now, James Devlin had a very strange career as an artist – maybe spread over about five years, no more, before he threw in the towel, abandoned being an artist, disappeared to London for a couple of years and then returned to Melbourne to set up his own gallery. He never painted again.'

'I don't quite get what you're saying, Mark.'

'OK Jan. What I'm saying is that I have a strong feeling that James Devlin was John Templeman, that he was Charlie's brother. And that he moved to Victoria with Charlie and their family around about nineteen seventy-two. I think Charlie continued to paint after that as well. I'm not sure what happened to Charlie, but I'm fairly certain that Charlie is, after all, the painter of all these famous paintings and that his brother – James Devlin – pretended to be the artist.'

Beth continued to listen as she texted Brad Collins in Melbourne: *Lewis handling painting for local client that resembles work by Devlin painted by Charlie Templeman. Other experts have sighted and agreed. Lewis believes Devlin is Charlie's brother. Charlie likely painted all of Devlin's works. Whereabouts of Charlie unknown. Awaiting info about location of painting. Likely in Beaufort gallery. Stand by.*

The professional in Beth Ainsworth was pleased to be proving her worth; at a personal level, she was captivated by the emerging story.

'I'm still confused,' said Jan. 'Have you spoken to this James Devlin? He'd know for sure.'

Beth thought: if Mark Lewis is right, Devlin is a fraud; and his career as an artist and gallerist a proverbial house of cards.

'Jan, I haven't spoken to him. I think you can see why it might be a difficult conversation. I've been really frank with you, Jan, but I have to emphasise that, so far, this is all just a theory. To be honest, if it didn't concern your painting, and if I didn't genuinely believe that what I've told you is true, I wouldn't be sharing any of this with you. I suppose there are very few people who know the absolute truth and one of them is Charlie. And I'm not sure he's even still alive.'

'What do you plan on doing next?' asked Jan.

'To be honest, I've been a little distracted of late by other things happening in the gallery, so I've not progressed this as far as I'd wanted. It'll soon be Christmas and the gallery closes then for about two weeks. Can I hold on to the painting for a few weeks more? It'll be perfectly safe here.'

'Of course,' said Jan. 'It's all sounding rather complicated though. I don't want any trouble.'

As the call ended, Beth fired off another text to Brad. *Charlie's painting confirmed in Beaufort gallery. Advise if further action required.*

40. MONDAY DECEMBER 9

Brad Collins had arranged to meet with James Devlin in Devlin's Collingwood office. Collins had spoken to Beth Ainsworth at length and had read – and re-read – a transcript of Mark Lewis' conversation with the woman called Jan. He had the information for which his mentor had been looking but had also learned more than he had imagined – or wished – he would have.

Until receiving the text messages from Beth Ainsworth, he had not really understood why James Devlin had been prepared to take such a grave and expensive step as planting a listening device. But the prospect that Devlin might be shown to have misrepresented himself to the Australian public for over a quarter of a century, however inconsistent with the man he had come to know and admire, was clearly sufficient motivation for such extensive surveillance. Now, Collins found himself worrying about what the next step might entail.

It was after ten pm. The building was empty save for the two men who sat in Devlin's office, *Odyssey* looking down on them without judgement. Beyond the windows, Melbourne lay dark.

'We have identified a painting of interest,' Collins began, 'and we are confident that it is in Lewis' gallery. Lewis clearly believes that there is a connection between this painting and you – and your art.' Collins commenced with what he felt was the essence of the brief he had been given and which he had handed on to Beth Ainsworth. 'We have heard the full conversation Lewis had earlier today with the person who brought the painting into the gallery for Lewis to assess, quite recently we believe.' Collins observed James Devlin keenly as he continued. 'They refer to it as "Charlie's Painting" and they repeatedly refer to a person named Charlie.' Collins awaited Devlin's response and further instructions. He had withheld, for the time being, any reference to the Templeman family, or anything of Lewis' contention about whether or not Devlin was the artist.

Collins noted that Devlin's expression remained unchanged. But the unblinking stare with which he returned Collins' gaze exposed the significance to him of the mention of Charlie by name; Collins immediately understood that the contention – the entire scenario that Lewis had articulated in his conversation with Jan – could well be true. But Collins was first and foremost acting in a professional capacity and he remained committed to supporting James Devlin.

'OK,' said Devlin, 'this is what I need you to do. Every day counts now.' His voice was low and his instructions precise, and Collins nodded his assent.

41. TUESDAY DECEMBER 10

Mark spent over three hours upstairs in the gallery, undisturbed by any customers, sorting through the storage area. The grumpy disposition with which he had arrived at the gallery had mostly lifted. He had felt chastened and anxious after his conversation with Pat the previous evening, Pat having rebuked him for being so open about Charlie and James Devlin with Jan Bilowski.

Even still, Mark had done what Pat had recommended and he now completed the wrapping of numerous works of art, sealing them with tape and identifying them carefully for future reference. In the process of what Mark thought was an unnecessary, frankly paranoid, exercise in concealment of Charlie's painting, he had begun to settle into the routine of sorting out his stock. And he revelled in the rediscovery of works he hadn't seen and appreciated for many months. He retrieved a beautiful work from the 1930s, by Sydney-born, Western Australian artist Portia Bennett. Like many Australian women artists of that period, her art had not always been as critically or commercially acclaimed as that of her male counterparts. But her pictorial account of urban life in Perth represented an important, technically excellent and artistically significant contribution to the world of Australian art. This particular painting showed children in swimming costumes with a merry-go-round in the background, impressionist rather than realist, in oil on hard board, capturing the period, the sense of summertime and the simple joys of childhood.

It was a special work, having never been sold during Bennett's lifetime, hanging in her suburban home in Nedlands up until her death in 1989. Mark had bought the painting at auction a few years later – it was one of his earliest acquisitions and was, like so many, purchased on Helen's expert advice. It had hung in his and Sharon's bedroom for over twenty years. He had taken it down at the height of his grief after her death but now looked at it again with renewed pleasure; and he recognised in that pleasure that the pain of Sharon's loss was subsiding. He smiled to himself – he couldn't wait to take it back home.

Mark set the Bennett aside. He continued with his exploration of the stockroom, choosing paintings based on their size to wrap, obscure from view and note on the outside for later identification. By the time Mark had done as much as was prepared to do, his mood was fully restored, and he was now more amused than annoyed at having followed Pat's advice. He felt that his stockroom had been put in some sort of order, that he was leaving the gallery with many works now more soundly protected, and that he had, at least, rediscovered one small treasure of Western Australian art.

He went down to the kitchenette to put on the kettle and make himself some cereal and yoghurt for lunch. He demolished the meal while scanning his emails, anticipating catching up with Linda after work. They were meeting at his house and planned to go for a walk to the river foreshore. Mark had convinced her to try out a new Thai restaurant on Bulwer Street operated by two Thai sisters and notable for the freshness of their food, their warmth and their hospitality. He hoped that Linda had appreciated the private joke – she had insisted that she would reserve her judgement.

❖❖❖

Beth found a new spot to park, this time on the north side of Beaufort Street, looking on to the flat green lawn of the Mount Lawley Bowling Club, its Art Deco style clubroom evoking an era long passed. A game of bowls was underway, all four players following the passage of a bowl as it slowed and approached the pin.

She had been surprised to be asked to stay on by Brad Collins. His request had been for her to listen closely and provide him with real-time feedback about Mark Lewis' movements as he prepared to leave his gallery. Although Beth knew this would not be until close to five pm, she settled in to listen around two. Collins wanted to hear from her regularly and was very specific about the need for detail about Lewis' departure.

Beth's conclusion was this: Collins was planning to enter the gallery and retrieve Charlie's painting. It would likely be him in person, she thought. Waiting for the ideal time to force entry would likely be based upon what she told him. From what she knew of Collins, he would not be violent; but there were always unknown factors and random human responses that made this sort of action unpredictable and risky. Getting hold of that painting was clearly of great importance; the precision of her advice might prove critical not only to the success of the Collins' mission, but to Mark Lewis' safety.

Line of sight would have allowed her to provide Collins with more precise directions, but the gallery fronted onto a busy part of Beaufort Street and she could not reasonably observe the interior of the gallery without drawing attention to herself. Listening would have to do.

She recalled the layout of the gallery as she listened for Mark to close down his laptop, tidy up in the kitchenette, set the alarm and leave the gallery into the laneway behind. That would surely be when and from where Collins would make his move. For now, she had little to do – the gallery was exceptionally still, occasional rather heavy-fingered tapping on a keyboard and the odd sigh reassuring her that someone was still at work. There was a solitary phone call from a concerned friend or customer – she could not tell which – offering consolation after the fake art fiasco, she surmised. This time Lewis kept the speakerphone off. The few words he contributed to the conversation affirmed that it was Lewis who was in the gallery today. Beth sent Collins a brief text to that effect; a phone call would soon be required.

Collins responded: *OK. Will call later. Keep me informed.*

❖❖❖

Brad Collins walked past the gallery twice, relating the fleeting internal appearances as seen through the street front display window to the internal floor plan that Beth Ainsworth had sent him. He also walked down the arcade that led to the car park behind the small shopping complex, noting the short blind alley that led to the rear door of the gallery. Collins veered briefly into the alley to note how the door was secured.

He saw the CCTV cameras that would have tracked his entry into the arcade and his brief diversion to inspect the lock, but he felt comfortable with his simple disguise – false beard, spectacles with reflective lenses, and loose-fitting clothing – that he would discard afterwards. It was after three pm when he returned to his car which was parked, unbeknown to either of them, less than one hundred metres from where Beth Ainsworth was listening to what was happening in the gallery.

❖❖❖

Just before five pm, Mark sent his last email and closed down his computer, the sounds alerting Beth to his impending departure. Brad Collins' phone rang and he answered without delay.

'I've just heard the front door being locked and bolted,' said Beth. 'I'd say he is minutes away from leaving.'

'Thanks. You can leave it now. Close down and head home. I'll expect your invoice tomorrow.' And Collins hung up. He got out of his car and walked briskly to the rear entry of the arcade, knowing that he had to act with speed and precision. The last ten years of his police career had been in Special Operations and he felt confident and focused as he approached the rear door of the gallery.

He had visualised the scene inside and the action he needed to take; matters would be especially complicated if he could not enter before Lewis armed the alarm, so he had prioritised early entry into the building. He reached the rear door and listened intently. Lewis was washing a dish or a cup; then he heard them being returned to a cupboard; a series of light switches were flicked. Collins made his move. He removed his peak cap, pulled a stocking over his head with his gloved hands, replaced his cap, withdrew a mock handgun from his jacket pocket, picked the lock with ease, and swiftly entered the gallery.

Lewis was standing no more than a metre from the open door, empty-handed and utterly caught by surprise when Collins barged in. Before Lewis could say a word, Collins struck him across the chin and rushed forward to control the unconscious man's fall to the floor. Then he put the mock weapon back in his pocket and dragged Lewis into the kitchenette, away from the street view. He closed the rear door and returned to the inert man, taping his mouth and covering his head in a loose dark cloth bag. He secured Lewis' ankles very firmly, leaving him the ability to spread his legs by about thirty centimetres; the left ankle was further secured to the plumbing under the sink.

Collins noted Lewis' deep breathing and estimated that he would regain consciousness in a minute or two, but that his movements would be slow and ineffective for several minutes longer. Lewis' mobile phone had dropped onto the floor and Collins picked it up and placed it in his own coat pocket for now.

He secured Lewis' wrists in front of his torso and taped them in turn to his ankles so that, when he came to, he could not reach up and remove his head covering or his mouth tape. Collins imagined that the alarm would be raised soon enough by those waiting for Lewis so he knew he had little time to spare.

Lewis was already groaning softly by the time Collins had him securely confined. It was already just before ten minutes past five when Collins headed up the stairs to inspect the stockroom. He was confronted by an orderly scene – dozens of paintings wrapped and stacked, and still more hanging in a compactus arrangement. Devlin had shown him numerous images of his paintings so Collins might more easily identify Charlie's painting. He had been told that there were two likely sizes: small and rectangular – 90cm × 60cm – or larger and square – 100cm × 100cm. He noted numerous wrapped paintings of potentially appropriate size and was a little alarmed at the number of paintings that were so thoroughly wrapped but conscious of the need to work quickly. He decided to inspect the wrapped works first.

Then, in his pocket, Mark Lewis' phone rang. Collins tried to collect his thoughts. Whoever was calling Lewis would have expected him to answer; and now that he had not answered, to call back soon. He looked at the phone – the name Linda appeared on the screen.

Collins needed to be methodical. He noted what was written on the wrapped paintings, hoping for some identifying feature. As he proceeded, he set aside those that he estimated to be the right sizes. Each was identified on a white sticker by artist, year and painting title, but none made reference to 'Charlie'.

There were three separate rows of stacked paintings and the final painting in the third stack, positioned behind several larger paintings, the farthest away of them all, was unmarked and of suitable, square dimensions. He opened it without hesitation but was disappointed to find a work in pastel colours that was signed 'Stannage'. And he was confused. Why had Lewis not written the details of this particular painting on the outside, as for the others? Why had it been secreted away behind other works?

He quickly opened the next wrapped work and confirmed it was the work that Lewis' notation indicated it would be. The next work likewise was what its notation purported it to be. He paused and considered the time he would use up opening them all. Lewis' phone rang – again it was 'Linda'. Collins knew that he had to leave soon. It would be a defeat to leave without the painting, but it would be a disaster to be caught in the gallery, even by someone who posed him no physical threat. He looked at the compactus and decided that he should inspect those that could be easily seen in case Charlie's painting was hanging in full view. He started closest to the door and moved towards the far wall. There were varying numbers of paintings in each section depending upon their size, but none resembled the works that he had been shown by Devlin. The last section contained a series of small works, most no more than 30cm square. Charlie's painting would not be among these and Brad knew that he had very little time left to look for it. He had to leave. He considered opening one more of the wrapped works when he noticed some bubble wrap protruding from the space between the compactus and the wall.

He separated the compactus as widely as he could. He could see a wrapped painting wedged between the fixed section of the compactus and the wall, and he grasped the edge of the bubble wrap. He lifted the wrapped painting out. It was marked 'CP Untitled 1972'. That could be code for 'Charlie's Painting' thought Collins. It was about 90cm × 60cm and Collins knew that this was the right one. Lewis had hidden it and he had found it.

Lewis' phone rang again. Again it was from 'Linda' and he knew that his window of opportunity was rapidly disappearing. He tucked the painting under his left arm, turned off the light, skipped down the stairs and walked into the gallery proper. He placed Lewis' phone on the seat of the chair at the desk, then reached under the desk front where, in the place Beth had described, he found the listening device.

Collins pulled the device away from the undersurface of the desk and placed it in his pocket. He observed Lewis moving slowly on the floor of the kitchenette and stepped past him through the exit door and into the alleyway out of sight of the CCTV, where he removed his mask, closed the door and took off his gloves. The muffled sound of Lewis' phone ringing a fourth time inside the gallery caused him to draw breath. Collins gathered himself, replaced his cap and walked briskly but with composure down the arcade, back out into the late afternoon sunshine, down the walkway into the carpark, and then towards his car.

He placed Charlie's painting on the back seat, sat down in the driver's seat, and replayed the last fifteen minutes in his head, scanning his memory for possible lapses or errors. He was convinced that Lewis had not been seriously injured and, confident that he had completed his mission safely, he drove away. He would dispose of his gloves, mask, beard, cap, jacket and sunglasses as well as the listening device in a skip he had located at a building site well away from the gallery, before delivering the painting to the downtown hotel where Devlin was waiting for him.

❖❖❖

Beth Ainsworth had intentionally listened until the end. The unanswered phone calls and Lewis' moaning had made it clear to her that Collins had forcibly entered the gallery in search of Charlie's painting. She had heard the coarse sound of the device being removed from under the desk and the clear sound of the gallery door closing; the subsequent sound of footsteps indicated that she was now listening to Collins walking away from the gallery, the device in his pocket.

She pondered her culpability in this undoubted crime. Hopefully, Lewis was not seriously injured – she had the impression that Collins was a professional and that he would not have been comfortable with any serious collateral damage. The closing of a car door struck a stereophonic chord and she looked up and to her right – the sound was close. A small white sedan pulled out on Field Street, quickly turned left heading north onto Queens Crescent and drove directly towards Beth who was parked facing south. She removed her hearing piece and observed Collins' expressionless face as he drove past.

Beth removed her earpiece and collected her notes. It was time to step back, eliminate unwanted evidence and prepare to go home.

42. TUESDAY DECEMBER 10

The heat was stifling. Mark was finding it hard to breathe and a dark, searing fog limited his view. The merry-go-round was rotating to a familiar tune that made him wonder who was phoning him. Linda stepped off the merry-go-round and smiled at him. She was naked and very beautiful, the sun creating a golden haze around her head, but he worried that she would get sunburnt in this heat.

'What happened to Charlie?' she asked. Mark was confused. He had never met Charlie and had no idea where he was. Pat appeared, from nowhere, sweating profusely, and appeared to be pointing away to his left. Mark couldn't breathe and his face was hurting from the intense sun bearing down on it. He groaned, hoping that Linda or Pat would help him.

The music stopped and Linda was instantly gone, to put on some clothes, Mark thought. A dark cloud descended, hiding Pat from view, and then there was nothing but silence. Mark moved to touch his sunburnt face but couldn't make his hands reach. He tried again; his hands were stuck together; his jaw was painful, and he could feel a restriction over his mouth. He tried once more to reach up to his face, but he felt the attachment of his hands to his feet that stopped him. He opened his eyes and understood that his face was covered. He was flat on his back and, evidently, bound and gagged.

Mark attempted to piece the facts together, methodically, as if he was still in clinical practice and trying to sort out a baffling diagnostic dilemma. Where was he? Where had he been? What day of the week was it? He heard a door close and it sounded like the door of his gallery. He had been in the gallery, he recalled, packing things up. He wondered at first if he had fallen on to his face to make it ache so much. But his hands and feet were bound and, as his thoughts started to take clearer form, he realised that he must have been concussed, almost certainly assaulted. His phone rang – the merry-go-round music – sounding as if it was a few metres away, and he had no way of getting to it. He listened to it ring out. For a weird, muddled moment, he wondered if it had been Sharon calling him, but a clearer voice told him that it must have been Linda. A recent image of her naked body passed through his brain in another flash of confusion. He had to get himself free, his inability to breathe comfortably through his mouth adding to his growing claustrophobia.

Mark tried to think logically, to calm himself. He recalled now that he had he had been packing up works of art. He had been trying to hide Charlie's painting, and that Pat O'Beirne had told him to do so. He couldn't recall what time of day it had been. Someone – possibly more than one person – must have broken into his gallery, knocked him unconscious. He appreciated now the source of his aching jaw. They'd bound and gagged him; they were surely coming to steal Charlie's painting.

He rolled on to his right side to take the pressure off his back.

He hoped that they hadn't found the painting. He had wrapped it and placed it inside the wrapping of a much larger work – *Drying Sheds* by Nigel Hewitt. Hewitt's exposition of light and shade in this work was sublime; if the intruders had found Charlie's painting, Mark mused incongruously, they would at least have seen, along the way, a masterwork of Western Australian art.

Was there any other explanation for what had just happened? Had this been a less targeted, 'common or garden variety' art theft? For a brief moment, Lewis even imagined it might have been Tony Peterson acting out his anger and desire for retribution. Whatever else was true, Mark thought wryly, he had been dealt with by professionals. He could recall nothing of his assault, let alone of his assailants, was utterly unable to contact anyone to seek assistance, but was essentially unharmed.

He moved his jaw from side to side, appreciating the pain but suspecting that nothing had been broken. The taste of blood in his mouth and the irregularity his tongue could feel over the inner lining of his left cheek pointed to minor injury only, as well as to the likely site of the blow to his chin.

What if they had taken Charlie's painting, he wondered suddenly.

What would happen to it? Would it be destroyed? He knew that James Devlin would have been behind this and that he would be unlikely to ever display the work. But would he actually destroy it? That beautiful, brooding little picture.

Mark rolled onto his back again. But what if they hadn't found Charlie's painting? What if they had left empty-handed? Or if they had been tricked into taking the wrong work? Then Devlin would be stuck – he would not have control over Charlie's painting, and he would have declared his hand, knowing that Mark understood the essence of his lifelong deception. That Charlie Templeman had been the artist, that James Devlin had been a fraud on a monumental scale.

Groaning, Mark rolled to his left side. He knew that Linda and Olivia would figure things out in good time and he wasn't concerned that he would be left in the gallery overnight. These thoughts stirred a sudden and overwhelming surge of positive emotion – affection for his daughters and their families, a thrill at the simple prospect of seeing his grandchildren, a feeling of deep humility in the face of Linda's affection and intimacy, amazement at the shrewdness of Pat's advice, gratitude for the many wonderful people who enveloped him so generously with their love and support. He felt no anger towards those who had hurt and restrained him. Ridiculously, trussed and unable to see, he felt a powerful sense of optimism.

He had been right about Charlie's painting. He and Linda had been right about Charlie's connection to Devlin. The truth might never be proven, but they had solved much of the puzzle.

What, he thought through his aching face and painfully trapped limbs, would he do in any event, if the painting had not been found, if it was still hidden and wrapped within the Hewitt? What would be achieved by exposing James Devlin? What possible good would be accomplished by deleting the value of Devlin's works owned by so many collectors, let alone by the devastation that would be wrought on James Devlin and his reputation by these actions? He didn't know Devlin, didn't have any idea what reasons he might have had for pretending to be the maker of his brother's creations, but at his very core, at that moment, Mark felt absolutely no malice or anger towards this man.

Through the restraining tape, he smiled, content that he knew enough of the truth and that he needed to know no more. He lay and contemplated the situation at length. He realised what he wanted to do; but it would depend upon whether or not Pat's subterfuge had been successful.

The sound of the back door of the gallery opening and simultaneous shrieks alerted Mark to Olivia and Linda's entrance. He could sense the lights being turned on and their presence at his side.

'Are you OK, Dad?' Olivia's voice was tremulous.

Beneath the sack over his head, Mark grunted to at least indicate that he was conscious and to advise that his mouth had been taped. He even felt amused and relieved, his abiding sense of positivity reinforced by the arrival of these two wonderful people. Nothing, he felt sure, could shake his sense that the world was, at this moment, in weirdly perfect balance.

Linda wrestled the sack off Mark's head and he saw the alarm in her eyes. She grasped the tape covering his mouth which was wound around his head and Mark's return gaze and raised eyebrows indicated his consent for her to remove it; it had been secured well and it was apparent that it would be painful to remove. Linda proceeded with merciful determination and speed.

Mark exhaled forcefully, expressing a strange mixture of pain and relief. Olivia had started to cut away the tape binding her father's legs and wrists. 'Don't wriggle, Dad, or I'll end up cutting you. Just keep still!' In the sharpness of her tone, Mark understood that Olivia was also thinking of her mother, the pain of losing her, and the terrible moment, just passed, that would have brought back that memory of loss with alarming clarity.

'What happened, Mark?' said Linda.

He saw that her eyes, like his daughter's, were filled with tears.

'I've been attacked,' Mark said. 'I think I might have a broken jaw.' He would have smiled reassuringly if it hadn't hurt so much. 'Also: I think they were professionals. This has got to be about Charlie's painting.' He had risen to his feet but was still feeling a little unsteady. 'Can you check to see if they took it?'

'I'll check upstairs,' said Olivia.

'It's hidden in the big Hewitt,' said Mark.

Olivia stopped on the lower step and turned around. 'What do you mean it's hidden in the Hewitt?'

'It's wrapped inside the big Hewitt. If that's been unwrapped, they'll have found it for sure.' Mark could not get his jaw to do any more. Olivia stared at her father open-mouthed, as if she couldn't believe what the arrival of one small painting had done to the sanctuary of the gallery. She shook her head, then turned and bounded up the stairs.

'It's a huge mess here,' Olivia yelled back to them. 'There's bubble wrap everywhere and they've put paintings all over the place.' Mark could feel the indignation in Olivia's voice. 'I think I can see the Hewitt. It's still wrapped.'

Mark could hear the moving and unwrapping of a painting. He held his breath.

'Charlie's painting is still inside it! I don't think anything's been damaged.'

With difficulty, Mark called up to her: 'Can you look between the compactus and the wall? There was a painting there. They might have taken that.'

'Which painting was that?'

'That early Roger Kemp.'

'That's insane! That's more valuable than any Devlin.'

Mark was too sore and weary to explain his thinking. It had been the right size, for starters. And, imagining that Devlin would open this painting expecting to be seeing one of his own, Mark hoped Devlin would simultaneously appreciate that he had been tricked and that Lewis considered the two works of comparable standing.

In a minute, Olivia came down the stairs, Charlie's painting in her arms. 'Nothing in that space at all, Dad. And no sign of the Kemp anywhere else.'

'We should call the police,' Linda said.

'I'd rather not,' said Mark.

'Dad! You've been assaulted and tied up. They've tried to steal your property. They've taken at least one of your paintings. You can't just do nothing.'

'Olivia, darling, I had some time here on my own to think about this. I need to get my jaw checked first. For now, can we just set the alarm and lock up?'

Olivia and Linda stared at him but said nothing.

'I want to speak to Pat and Helen. And I need to figure out where Charlie's painting will be safe – they'll soon realise that they don't have the real thing, and that we still do.'

43. TUESDAY DECEMBER 10

James Devlin sat in front of the painting in his Northbridge hotel room. Downcast, Brad Collins somberly described the evening's events in detail. The manner in which so many paintings had been wrapped, and the way in which this one had been labled, made it appear to both of them that Lewis had anticipated the theft.

The painting was a simply framed board, 90cm × 60cm, just the size of the one for which they had been looking. The painting before him was an exquisite early oil by Roger Kemp, with geometric shapes in pale blue, red and white on a background of various shades of grey, an early style that presaged Kemp's later, larger works on canvas that would evoke the appearance of stained glass in a distinctly ecumenical theme.

Lewis shook his head, half in dejection, half in admiration. If the Kemp was indeed a decoy, then Lewis was sending him an unambiguous message: Charlie's painting was no less exquisite, no less valuable, no less important.

Devlin's sense of defeat was balanced by the respect for Charlie's painting that the gallerist evidently accorded it. He was intrigued by Lewis, and he desperately wanted to see Charlie's lost painting. Collins had reassured him that Lewis had regained consciousness and that he would recover fully. Equally importantly, Devlin was reassured that Collins would not be identified and that nothing could decisively link either of them to these events. They accepted that Beth Ainsworth would likely have figured out what had happened, and they had even considered the possibility that she might have tipped Lewis off. But Collins was insistent that she was a thorough professional and completely trustworthy; her reputation and livelihood would not survive any disloyalty to those who engaged her services.

'Brad, I've asked too much of you on this occasion, and you have done so well. I'll take it from here. Head home to your family, I'll sort you out on Monday. As far as you are concerned, this matter is now over.'

'Thank you, James. I'm sorry it has turned out the way it has.'

Collins left him alone with the Kemp and the knowledge that Mark Lewis had outsmarted him. And that he had landed him with a valuable painting that they both knew Devlin would never destroy, but the possession of which would connect Devlin to this theft and the underlying deception. But Devlin also realised that Lewis was no less stuck with Charlie's painting, unable to attach any value to it and, somehow, held hostage by the responsibility of taking matters further. The two gallerists were in a sort of limbo. And Devlin knew his half-a-century-long charade was close to its end.

❖❖❖

When Mark and Linda emerged from the clinic, it was after nine thirty pm. Olivia was home with her family, having been dismissed some time ago from the after-hours waiting room by her father. The GP on duty had been a former student of Lewis and had been both diligent and respectful. She hadn't known whether or not to believe his story about an unseen assailant and wasn't sure why the police hadn't been involved, but the absence of any obvious fracture on the OPG X-ray was reassuring and she figured that Dr Lewis could decide for himself whether the circumstances warranted further investigation.

Linda drove Mark to the late-night pharmacy where he filled his prescription for a strong analgesic and they headed back to Glendower Street. She'd made it clear to Mark that she wasn't comfortable leaving him alone for the night and, in any event, she had packed an overnight bag. 'I don't know about you, but I'm starving. As soon as I've put you to bed, I'm heating up the soup that's in your fridge.'

'I don't think I could eat a thing.'

Linda turned into William Street as they approached Mark's home. 'OK, Rocky, before you lose consciousness again, what's your next move going to be?'

Mark was desperate to get home to take his painkillers but still managed to appreciate Linda's resolute good humour. The evening must have presented her with a whole series of disturbing experiences; he wondered at what point she might conclude that this relationship was proving more trouble than he was worth. 'Thank you for taking me to the clinic.'

'You make it sound like I'm a workmate who has stayed with you after you'd had a few too many drinks.'

'I didn't mean it that way.' He touched the left side of his face, swelling now accompanying the throbbing pain. 'You know I am truly grateful for your ... for having you. But I feel like I've gotten all of us into a real mess. I'm really sorry.'

They pulled up on Glendower Street, and Linda turned off the engine. 'Let's face it, if it wasn't for that painting, we'd never have met at all. So, here we are, it is a bit of a mess, but we're in it together. And I'm very happy, so don't be sorry.' She removed the keys and asked again, 'What is your plan?'

Mark leaned his head back against the seat. 'While I was lying on the floor in the kitchenette, you know, I wasn't feeling particularly worried. I was sore, but I actually felt incredibly positive; grateful and humble; lots of love for you, the girls, my grandchildren.' He reached for Linda's hand. 'You know, it struck me so clearly – as if I truly knew what had happened to Charlie and James – that Devlin isn't a bad person.'

Linda looked sceptical.

'I know how ridiculous that must sound,' Mark said. 'My jaw is telling me exactly that. But there was this intense moment of clarity as I was coming around, that Devlin was somehow more the victim of his pretence than its beneficiary. And I realised that I do not want to punish him any further. I want to reach out to him. I want him to see Charlie's painting. I think there may be a good reason that Charlie hasn't been given credit for his paintings. For sure, I want Charlie to get the recognition he deserves. And I want Charlie's painting to be honoured for the great work that it is. But I wouldn't be shattered if that also meant that Devlin carried on with this façade.'

'What if it means that Jan misses out on a windfall?'

'I know. I'm trying to figure out how to protect them all. How to protect Pat and Helen's investment as well. None of them probably think that it's all that important, but I do.'

'What about Olivia, Pat and Helen? Are they also going to be happy to reach out to someone who has been a fraud? And someone who has directed such a violent attack at you?'

'Yes, yes, I get that too.' Mark squeezed her hand. 'I need to speak to them all. I'll call Pat and Helen tomorrow and maybe we can meet them in the gallery. The place will need to be cleaned up.' He sat back up abruptly. 'Where is Charlie's painting, by the way?'

'Safely in my boot,' Linda reassured him. 'Now let's get you both inside.'

The night was still, lights reflecting in Hyde Park's central lakes, highlighting a couple of ibis grazing on the park's south-western verge. Mark walked gingerly towards the front gate of his home, Linda carrying Charlie's painting beside him.

44. WEDNESDAY DECEMBER 11

In his Northbridge hotel, Devlin rewrapped the Kemp and decided that he would have it returned to Mark Lewis before he flew back to Melbourne. In his possession, it was the only living proof of the theft. He had desperately wanted to see and possess Charlie's lost painting but that had eluded him.

It was already well after one am, Melbourne time. He ordered room service and a bottle of red wine, a 2010 vintage of Cullen's Diana Madeline, offered at considerable cost by the hotel. Then he sat in darkness, sipping his wine and distractedly scanning the email inbox on his mobile. There was nothing urgent since he had last looked. In any event, he thought, what could now really be important? As for so much of his life, he found himself alone. And lonely.

He stared at the image on his home screen and then retrieved the original picture from his photos. It was of the painting entitled *Universe*, 120cm × 90cm, acrylic on board, that hung in his study. It was the only one of his paintings that he had hanging in his home and the one with which he would never part.

Universe was dominated by blocks of blue of different shades, each in its own way reminiscent of the Australian summer sky. In this work, there was equal weight given to a muddy pink, a colour rarely used to this extent in his other paintings. Centrally, there were glimpses of white and black as well as a brighter pink that gave the work a distinct sense of movement, of dynamic action. One solitary sweep of black paint pointed towards the right-hand edge of the work, like a bird in flight trying to escape the painting. It had been precisely these sorts of vibrant brushstrokes, the innate sense of balance and proportion seen in this work, the alluring though confined palette, that had alerted James

Devlin to his brother's ability and to the merit of Charlie's art.

And it was *Universe* that was standing, freshly painted, when he and Garth walked back to James' home early one afternoon, after footy training had been abandoned because their coach had cancelled, unwell, at the last minute. His parents were both at work, his father having secured a job at the local branch of the Bank of New South Wales, his mother having started, initially part-time, as a sales assistant for a new and – by local standards – upmarket women's clothing boutique. Since moving to Upwey, Charlie had spent almost his entire time in his bedroom studio, constantly – and occasionally ferociously – churning out paintings.

In Devlin's red-wine haze, memories of his parents swirled.

Long ago, he had come to understand how unhappy his mother had been, constantly dissatisfied with her social status and restless in her pursuit of approval and affirmation. Laura had told him how her own parents had separated when she was an infant. Her father – James' only living grandfather – left and never returned, and she had remained her single mother's lifelong 'project', and the object of her mostly misplaced adulation.

According to her own account, Laura had been attractive and generally sporty, but had no interest in studying and was only too pleased to leave school after year ten and look for a job. It was at work that she had met John Templeman, handsome but not ambitious, and who she married, hastily, in an effort to escape her mother's claustrophobic attention. She was – always had been, James conceded – embarrassed and ashamed at what she regarded as her lowly circumstances.

Laura's mother died of breast cancer when Laura was pregnant with Charlie. She made no effort to remain in contact with any other family members and willingly isolated herself from them all, on both her and her husband's sides. Charlie's cerebral palsy, although mild, was a bitter blow to her. Even though he was clearly of normal intellect, his physical appearance and disability were, for Laura, a source of pain and embitterment. She lamented what she saw as Charlie's limited prospects of experiencing a normal working or family life, and her own entrapment by circumstances not under her own control.

When Charlie was eight, his behavioural problems forced his parents to remove him from the state school and send him to the Sir James Mitchell School. James was never on the receiving end of his brother's tantrums and frustrated outbursts and, over time, he had come to recognise that Charlie's behaviour was the result – not the cause – of his mother's difficulty in accepting her imperfect child. His mother's shame was compounded by her rising awareness that her easygoing husband had limited prospects of economic and social advancement.

Laura's great consolation was her second son James, christened John Junior. As her own mother had done, Laura focused an excessive adulation on her handsome, athletic second son. And she grew to believe that, for his sake as much as hers, they needed to relocate and start afresh, somewhere they were unknown to their neighbours and where they would be able to forge for them a different and more prosperous identity.

As he cradled his fourth glass of wine, James recalled his mother's determination to reinvent them all. They had moved to Melbourne and found a sprawling block in Upwey where they had a large unkempt backyard with a small forest of gum trees, surrounded by empty backyards. It was the seclusion from neighbours this arrangement offered that had most appealed to Laura Templeton, now calling herself Vanessa Devlin. His father had reluctantly agreed to be renamed Stewart Devlin, acquiescing as had always done to his wife's determined ambitions, and anxious not to further disrupt his family's delicate balance. But he had always been unhappy about the move East and deeply so at the repudiation of his own identity.

James had observed these changes through a teenager's prism – he had found the whole notion of taking on a new identity with a hidden past, and the imperative of maintaining family secrecy, somehow thrilling. He didn't then appreciate, as he did now, his father's sense of disempowerment. James had accepted his new name with cool indifference and was unconcerned about whether he fitted in at school, his handsome face and sporting ability enabling him to be regarded as aloof and mysterious rather than arrogant. He got on well with another talented football player, Garth Barrett, and the two struck up an easy friendship.

In the new house, Charlie had declared his room off limits to other family members, part of his adolescent rejection of their move East. That he had been allowed to do so reflected Laura's willingness to let Charlie to remain invisible to the outside world for however long that might continue. Both James and their father tried to entice Charlie outside, but he rarely ventured out of his room let alone out of the house. Even now, James did not understand why Charlie had rejected their family's reinvention so totally. After all, Charlie did not have a single close friend back in Perth. In Upwey, isolated and dejected, Charlie had been handed board after board on which to paint. He had been as prolific with his production of art as he had been uncommunicative and angry.

In the quiet hotel room, James heard his own breath become deep and deliberate, as if he might stop breathing if not for his conscious decision to continue. He remembered how he and Charlie had always been very close. Charlie had been a person of few words, and James had learned early on to divine his brother's thoughts from his expressions and actions.

There was a stillness in the house that afternoon that James instantly recognised as foreign, and a sudden dreadful apprehension that his brother was missing.

It had been a risk to bring Garth Barrett home for a snack and a drink while never intending to let him know about Charlie, but it was precisely that risk that had appealed to James. Garth was unmoved when James asked him to wait in the kitchen while James disappeared deeper into the house to investigate the disturbed equilibrium.

In the cavernous back room that Charlie had used as both bedroom and studio, alongside the freshly finished painting, James found Charlie.

His brother's suspended body was utterly motionless, his face a swollen and discoloured version of itself, strangled by an electrical extension cord secured to an exposed wooden beam in the ceiling. There was the stain of a pool of urine on the floor beneath his feet. Decades after the event, James Devlin could easily summon the emptiness he felt at that moment. Not shock or sadness – they would come soon enough – but a void inside him, a sense of irreparable loss. Standing dazed beside his brother's body, James stared at the freshly painted board, its urgent slash of black paint signalling to him that Charlie had left, broken free; that he was gone.

He heard the front door open and close and knew that his mother had come home. She would soon arrive and see for herself exactly what had transpired.

James poured another glass and looked deep into the image of

Universe. Where, he wondered, had Charlie made his first brushstroke on that painting? Where had he placed his last? There was no suicide note, only this painting. What had Charlie been trying to tell them? Devlin drew another deep mouthful of the wine, and recalled the moment his mother had entered Charlie's room.

There was blankness in her eyes, rather than surprise. Behind her he saw Garth enter the room, looking for his friend.

'Get a ladder and the secateurs from the garage, James.' His mother had turned to face Garth Barrett with an odd formality. 'I am Mrs Devlin, James' mother. And Charlie's mother too.'

James recalled leaving the room, half-stumbling, to gather the objects as instructed. And the dawning comprehension, and then horror, on his new friend's face.

Once he had returned, he steadied his brother's body and took its weight, while Garth climbed the ladder and cut the cord; James could still feel the weight of his brother's body, and – now sitting in a hotel room thousands of kilometres from home – a wave of loss and regret, sadness and weariness overcame him. They had laid Charlie on his bed, covered him with a blanket and listened to his mother's instructions. Garth was to go home but they were not to say a word – neither of them, not to anyone, ever. Not for one minute did James doubt his friend's loyalty or that he would keep the dreadful secret. And, once their father returned from work, Charlie would be buried in the backyard.

Now James relived the foreboding he had experienced at the thought of explaining to his father what had happened; the distress with which his father had reacted, in such stark contrast to his own reaction or Laura's; and the sound of the shovel on the earth as, later that night, under his mother's soundless supervision, he had dug his brother's grave. It had been a deep, wide hole, possibly over two metres deep, and it had taken him many hours to dig and over an hour to refill. It had been James and his mother who had grappled with Charlie's body, still dressed in the clothes in which he had taken his own life and lowered him into the grave.

In the first few days and weeks after Charlie's suicide, once the numbness had worn off, James had felt that he was going to burst, that he needed to share his grief and his love for his brother with someone, with anyone. But, while his father had been inconsolable, his mother had been disciplined in the control of her emotions and he had chosen to follow her example. At football that first weekend, he had stayed close to Garth, not to bolster his friend's support for their conspiracy, but in the hope that by physical proximity, this trauma, shared but unspoken, might somehow be lessened.

As the weeks passed, James came to accept Charlie's loss. But his father had been paralysed by grief and guilt. He did not return to work, became progressively more listless, and refused to seek assistance. Vanessa continued working in the boutique and maintained her household duties. James remembered clearly her detached, mechanical demeanour as she observed her husband's devastation.

Fewer than five weeks after Charlie's burial, James' father took his own life by means of an overdose of opiate painkillers and alcohol. He did it on a Saturday night when James was staying the night at Garth's. James had always believed that his father did this so that his mother might discover his body rather than inflict this trauma on James for a second time. He had left a note apologising for his action and expressing his love for his family.

His mother had called the ambulance, accompanied the body to the hospital, handled the explanations and subsequent funeral arrangements and buried her husband – using his new identity – explaining the suicide on the basis of longstanding mental health issues compounded by their recent relocation. There was never any mention of their recent change of name and not a word about Charlie. Neither Vanessa nor James made any reference to Charlie in any forum; their neighbours had been supportive and kind in the face of Stewart's suicide but appeared not to know anything of Charlie.

Charlie's grave remained unmarked. That October, with dry weather predicted, James and Vanessa began to erect a shed overlying the gravesite. James dug a one-metre deep rectangular trench with retaining walls made from timber and filled it with concrete. He smoothed the surface to allow the subsequent building of a robust metal shed which he and Garth assembled and secured to the substantial slab over a weekend in December once the school year had finished. The location of the shed – Charlie's burial site – was close to the corner of the block so that it would not impact greatly upon the use of the backyard; along with the depth of the slab, it meant that Charlie would likely never be found.

If James had ever felt anger towards his mother, it had – along with many emotions – been hidden deep inside, and could no longer be retrieved.

45. WEDNESDAY DECEMBER 11

When James Devlin woke, it was five am, his body clock still on Melbourne time despite his heavy head. It was a cloudless morning and he set off from the hotel for a walk, south through the CBD to the riverfront where he turned left, heading into the rising sun. The steady pace he kept and the soothing sight of the Swan River were conducive to formulating a plan of action, but his thoughts were dominated by memories. By the time the new shed in Upwey had been erected, the only evidence of Charlie's life were the scores of paintings, many brought over from Perth – and many more produced in the short time they had been in Upwey – that were stacked in his room and in the old garage. Vanessa had brought them all inside to protect them from the fluctuating temperatures and the threat of heavy rain. It was all they had left of him, maybe a total of two hundred works of art.

As he paced along the walkway, James recalled how he had devised the plan to display Charlie's art. He had been working part-time in a Melbourne art gallery while studying at Monash, and had developed a love for his job and a good eye for fine art. The first exhibition and sale of Charlie's paintings in the guise of James as the artist – just twenty works which James reckoned Charlie had completed in Perth – had been, for James at least, an unequivocal act of love and pride which both James and Vanessa had expected would be the end of the exercise.

Neither of them had anticipated the brisk and positive response to that exhibition. James began to see how Charlie's talent offered them both the real prospect of short-term financial gain as well as a career pathway for him into the world of art, and he formulated a clear-headed strategy to patiently exhibit and sell the remaining works in sequence, submit them for prestigious art prizes, build a brand and then find an exit strategy as the pieces ran out.

Vanessa was diagnosed with advanced ovarian cancer in her mid-fifties, when James was just twenty-seven. James could still recall the shock of that diagnosis and his unrealistic expectations of treatment. Extensive surgery and devastating chemotherapy failed to contain it and she had died the following year. Despite his grief, he had persisted with his plan, contrived a credible departure from his career as an artist and, after a choreographed stint in London, re-entered the world of art as a gallerist.

Deep in thought, Devlin turned left again, heading north past the restored and repurposed old Treasury building on his way back to his hotel. He crossed the inconspicuous Barrack Street bridge and, recalling the view from this point, made a point of turning to face south down Barrack and take in the view of the bridge with the Perth Town Hall clock tower in the background. It was this scene that had been captured so beautifully back in 1954 in Ernest Philpot's nostalgic painting entitled *The Sleeping Bridge*, which Devlin had admired on display at the nearby Art Gallery of Western Australia on more than one visit to Perth.

It was only after his mother's death that James had come to appreciate how strong his mother had been, although he had asked himself more than once if, in truth, she had been incapable of feeling normally. And he also appreciated that he had been no less calculating in plotting his career and that he was more like her than he cared to admit.

❖❖❖

The left side of Mark's face was swollen and still painful but less so than he had imagined it would be. He had risen early, stepping gently out of the bedroom in an effort not to disturb Linda. He closed the door behind him and sat in the lounge area appreciating the brightness of the morning light and the gathering warmth; a persistent breeze blew through the open windows but it would soon be time to close them and put the air conditioner on.

Messages were already waiting for him on his phone. The first was from Olivia asking him to call at any time to let her know how he was;

and the second from Pat O'Beirne saying much the same. Olivia must have let Pat and Helen know what had transpired.

He texted Olivia: *No fracture. Feeling much better. Thanks for rescuing me. Will call later xxx*

To Pat he typed: *Can you speak? You were 100% right.*

His phone rang immediately.

'How are you feeling?' asked O'Beirne.

Mark gave him a brief account of what had happened, as far as he could piece together, and assured his friend there had been no serious injury. He described the process he had followed to confuse and delay the thieves, as Pat had advised, and the theft of the Kemp which he had successfully misrepresented as Charlie's painting. 'I have no idea how you knew he would attempt to steal the painting. How did he even know for sure that there *was* a painting or that it was necessarily in the gallery? It was a high-risk strategy, if you ask me.'

'That just tells us he was desperate to get hold of it and that he engaged professionals to do the job. And, let's face it, Mark, you told more or less all of Melbourne that you had a painting by Devlin. He'd have been watching you, for sure. Some sort of surveillance. I don't know. Maybe that guy who came in last week. He sounded suspicious to me. He could've planted a device and they'd have been listening to you.'

'I suppose you're right,' said Mark, lightly touching his cheek. 'If he had been listening in, he'd have heard everything I'd said – actually, everything we all said. I find it hard to believe that anyone would've gone to such extremes – to such expense – to get that painting. I'll look in the office for a listening device when I go in this morning.' Not that Mark had any idea what one would look like.

'There'll be nothing to find, Mark. They'd have cleaned up when they left last night. They won't have left a trace.'

How Pat O'Beirne knew all this, Mark could not fathom. But he had been right about so many things so far. Even so, Mark thought, he would still have a look for the bug.

Linda approached, placing her hand on his shoulder. He turned his head down to his right shoulder to kiss her hand, and continued speaking to Pat. 'I want to tell you what I'm planning to do. It might sound strange to you, but I have decided that I want to meet with Devlin and show him Charlie's painting. I want to know what really happened to him and Charlie, and I don't want to make this thing public. Not yet, at least. There's got to be another way to sort this out.'

Mark knew that his friend's silence meant he was thinking, not necessarily that he disapproved. At length, Pat said, 'Do you think Devlin's here in Perth?'

'I think so. Devlin would have wanted to see the painting – to confirm that it was the right painting – as soon as possible,' Mark said. 'If that is true, he will have come to Perth. And if he did, he might still be here. And if he *is* here, he'll now have the added problem of what to do with the Kemp.'

'I'm sure he won't hold on to it,' said Pat. 'He knows that you've figured out a large part of his fraud. But I can't imagine he would destroy a beautiful painting. I reckon he'll get it back to you. He knows he can't let anyone else see it. What's more, he knows that it's you who has to decide what to do next, not him. Basically, Mark, it's up to you now. I agree. Go call him.'

'Any idea how to get hold of him?'

'I've got his gallery's details – I'll send them through. They're probably open for business already. That's a start.'

A text from Pat with Devlin's gallery's phone number pinged in his phone. 'I don't know how to thank you, Pat. Honestly, I thought you were being totally paranoid telling me to hide Charlie's painting. I didn't appreciate how dangerous this whole thing could get.'

'Let me know what happens,' said Pat.

'I will,' said Mark, and smiled. His friend was not one to say 'I told you so.'

Mark put the phone down and reached up to squeeze Linda's hand. 'How'd you sleep?'

'Like a log,' she said. 'Have you let Olivia know you're OK?'

'I've sent her a text message and I've told her I'll call her later. I think I need to locate James Devlin first of all.'

Mark rang the gallery in Melbourne and was greeted by a recorded message that told him that the gallery opened at eleven am, meaning that they had more than an hour to wait.

'We've got plenty of time.' He paused. 'To get an early coffee.' He smiled at her. 'I'm not shaving this poor swollen face this morning.'

'Yes, plenty of time,' Linda answered, shaking her head and grinning back at him. 'Your face isn't too sore then, is it?'

'Consider this a sort of clinical experiment. The effect of vigorous exercise on post-traumatic facial pain. It might even be worth publishing.'

'A short abstract, at best, I'd suggest.' She took him by the hand.

❖❖❖

Breakfast at The Alex was most agreeable. Devlin devoured the newspaper as well as his poached eggs on sourdough and enjoyed his coffee enough to order a second. Then he retrieved Richard Barclay's contact details from his phone.

He sent Barclay a text using his second phone, the one usually reserved for communication with Garth Barrett: *I require a package to be delivered anonymously to Beaufort Gallery in Mt Lawley this morning. Collect from reception at Alex Hotel Northbridge. Invoice to Brad Collins in Melbourne. Confirm with him if required. Urgent and confidential.*

Next he sent a text to Brad Collins: *Have arranged return of decoy painting to Beaufort Gallery using Richard Barclay. Please authorise if he checks with you. Expect his invoice and forward to me directly. No need for you to contact RB. All is good here in Perth.*

Collins responded immediately with a thumbs-up emoji.

Devlin briefly immersed himself in the opinion pieces and letters to the editor, sipping his second coffee and waiting for Barclay to respond. Despite the hour, his reply was prompt: *Understood. Can collect at 10am. Approximate size and nature of package?*

Painting. Wrapped. 90cm × 60cm. Ask at reception for package in name of Kemp. Many thanks.

All good. Discretion assured.

❖❖❖

Devlin had just finished his second coffee when he received a text message from his gallery director, Roberta: *Just took a call from a Perth Gallerist, Mark Lewis, about possible acquisition of work by Roger Kemp. Does this sound right? He's the guy that got bad PR last weekend about a possible fake Dickerson. Will send his number separately. Be careful! All good here. Robbi*

Devlin smiled at her solicitous tone. He replied: *Thanks. Saw that story too. Will let you know what it's about. I'll be fine.* Another text message with Lewis' contact details arrived and Devlin returned to his room to make the call to Mark Lewis in complete privacy.

❖❖❖

Mark was in his car, already on his way to his gallery, when his phone rang with a No Caller ID. He answered in trepidation.

'Mark Lewis speaking.'

'Hello Mark. This is James Devlin. Roberta Conte from my gallery just let me know that you had called and you wanted to speak to me.'

Devlin's choice of words was careful, thought Mark. Not making mention of the Kemp and not letting on that he was in Perth. But the immediacy of his response was an unambiguous sign that he wanted to speak. 'Yes, I have something that I think you will love to see, and I was hoping that you might, by chance, be in Perth at the moment so I can show it to you.'

'As it turns out, I am in Perth. I'm staying at the Alex in Northbridge, but I'd be happy to meet you wherever you'd like. I've not got anything else planned.'

Mark pulled into his parking spot behind Beaufort Gallery. 'It's a wonderful piece by a wonderful artist, James. Can you make it to my gallery by ten? We're only a twenty-minute walk from the Alex.'

'Nine thirty is perfect. I've got your address. I'll see you soon.'

Mark sat in his car, his heart beating fast. It wasn't even a quarter to nine. He stepped out of the car, took Charlie's painting from the back seat and headed into the gallery. He unlocked the bolt on the rear door with his key and entered the gallery feeling oddly like an intruder. But there was surprisingly little disturbance in the main gallery, shreds of tape on the floor in the kitchenette and a little streak of blood – his blood – on the wall and the floor between kitchenette and gallery. There was no sign of forced entry from the front entrance. He headed back and climbed the steps to the storeroom. Bubble wrap and masking tape were strewn around the floor, but all the paintings had been stacked against walls: here at least the thief had taken great care.

Mark hated paintings being stacked directly on each other – they were always safest when they were hanging on walls – and he moved them back into good order, covering them this time with cotton sheets to keep dust off during the summer break and reusing the bubble wrap to protect them from pressing against each other and from direct contact with the floor. He stacked the works with the smallest ones against the wall, placing progressively larger works moving out, again to minimise painting touching painting. It was an act of reverence, undertaken in silence, acknowledgement of the innate dignity he accorded each work and out of respect for each artist.

Downstairs, he swallowed some more paracetamol to damp down the ache in his face, cleaned the tape and the blood stains and put on the kettle. He had not yet removed the 'Closed' sign, wanting time alone with Devlin. He sent messages to Linda, Olivia and Pat advising them that Devlin would be meeting him at ten and inviting them to come to the gallery to meet him – assuming things had gone well – around eleven. Finally, he unwrapped Charlie's painting and placed it on an easel in optimal light, admiring its depth and intensity one more time before turning it around to display Charlie's message to Katy and covering it with a sheet.

Spot on ten, Mark saw someone approach the front door, knock and peer in.

For the briefest of instants, the two men observed each other through the closed door. For a month, they had been watching each other's moves intently from across the country. Now they saw each other plain, and in the flesh, separated by just a few millimetres of glass. Mark reached for the handle.

46. WEDNESDAY DECEMBER 11

By the time James Devlin had returned from London, he had plotted a plausible and authentic course for his life as the owner of an art gallery. He knew the commercial art scene better than many people appreciated, having actively stage-managed his own career as an artist and having composed each exhibition from the finite pool of Charlie's works at his disposal with great critical and commercial success. And he understood more than anything else that perception and appearances carried weight among collectors even more so than among critics, and that he would need to control and even manipulate those perceptions if he was to succeed as a gallerist.

He had reached out to Garth Barrett in London, knowing that members of the medical profession represented a sizeable proportion of art investors and that Barrett would be a credible collector and an ideal partner in his plan to boost prices for the artists whose works he would come to handle and sell. And that their unbreakable connection forged out of their shared deceit about Charlie had created a powerful mutual trust.

Their ploy would, of course, have to be discrete, carefully planned and mutually beneficial. Although Devlin had remained in only limited contact with Garth after they left school, Garth's silence during Devlin's short but high-profile career as an artist vouched for his loyalty and his capacity for confidentiality. For Devlin, Garth embodied the ties of friendship and trust, and occupied part of the space that had been left void by Charlie's death. For Barrett, James exemplified courage and resilience in the face of the most intense grief imaginable, grief that he had witnessed first-hand.

Devlin's judgement had subsequently proven correct on all counts and his scheme had played out to good effect. The two men had been willing and trusting partners in their distinct but contained manipulation of the art market which had continued well beyond the need for either of them to do so. They had remained fierce friends and the only surviving holders of the truth about Charlie.

Until now, thought James Devlin, as Mark Lewis opened the door.

❖❖❖

The two men greeted each other with a firm handshake and a tentative smile. Devlin observed Mark's swollen face but made no comment. Over Mark's right shoulder, he spotted a covered painting on an easel; he knew that was what he had come to see. Lewis started: 'I've just boiled the kettle. Can I make you a cup of tea before we look at the painting?'

'Yes please,' said Devlin, looking about with curiosity. 'I love that Fullbrook. I've not seen one like that in a while.'

'I bought it twenty years ago or more. I believe it came from a Queensland collection.'

That would be hard to let go, thought Devlin. But that, he long ago discovered, turned out to be the name of this game – forever handling things of beauty, scarcity and value even if for just a short while, before letting them continue their unique journey in the possession of someone else. Lewis retreated to the kitchenette, while Devlin cast his eye around. A work by Western Australian artist Brian McKay caught his eye – a patchwork of blocks of colour from the early 1960s, much like the more well-known Western Australian Guy Grey-Smith, both inspired by Russian-born French artist Nicolas de Staël. It was a beautifully balanced abstract work, a wonderful example of its type and a distinct insight into the Australian art scene of that era.

Lewis returned with steaming mugs of tea. He placed his on a small table he had positioned close to the easel and invited Devlin to do so too. 'A local brought this in one month ago,' said Lewis. 'It had been the property of her sister, Katy, who was once a pupil at the local school for children with cerebral palsy, which Charlie had also attended.'

Devlin winced at the mention of his brother. He held his breath as Lewis removed the covering sheet.

To Katy
Love Charlie
November 1972

A silent cry reverberated within his chest at the sight of his brother's handwriting. He wracked his brain for any memory of Katy. Was it possible that Charlie had been in love when his mother took them both away to Victoria?

'Apparently Charlie gifted her this work just before he graduated, and, I presume, moved away from Perth. I'm guessing you and your family went to Victoria around that time, changed your names and made new lives for yourselves.'

Devlin felt Lewis watching him. Not trusting his voice, he nodded slowly.

Lewis moved back to his desk and retrieved the photograph of Katy watching a partly obscured Charlie at his easel that Linda had found in the archives at the Sir David Brand School. 'This is Katy – her sister has confirmed that for us – and I'm pretty sure she is looking at your brother.'

At the sight of Katy's open, laughing face, and his brother, Devlin let out a strangled shout, then burst into tears. Decades of suppressed sadness and shame emerged in a tumultuous eruption, mixed with relief and even joy at the sight of his brother at what must have truly been a happy point in his brief life.

'I'm sorry,' said Mark, 'it must be a shock.'

Devlin tensed as the other man approached him and held him in a firm hug, then he felt his whole body relax and give way to its sobbing.

What a strange sight we would be for anyone looking through the gallery window right now, Devlin thought, reaching at last for his handkerchief.

'Are you OK?' Mark said, stepping back.

'Yes, I think I am.'

'I met my current partner, Linda, in the search for Charlie's identity and she has been a huge help in finding out about it all. She also made the connection between your date of birth and that of John Junior. Are you ready to see the painting?'

'Yes,' said Devlin, 'I am.'

Mark turned the work around. The style, palette, size, materials and the sheer energy of the painting were unmistakably Charlie's. The manner in which the viewer's eye was torn upwards, heavenwards, above the blue sky and into dark, outer space was, Devlin felt, overwhelmingly the work of a genius. His brother.

'I think it is a masterpiece,' Lewis said. 'It's something about which you can be proud. Truly. We've been referring to it as *Charlie's Painting* although I've named it *Turmoil*, if you don't mind, in keeping with the naming of your other works. It really is so full of dark energy.'

Devlin approached the painting. He came within thirty centimetres, inspecting it in detail. In every brushstroke, his brother was there, speaking to him, transmitting inspiration and hope to him through his furious gestures.

Then he looked up at Mark. 'You can appreciate, I think, that I know every square centimetre of every painting Charlie ever painted. As if I'd painted them myself.' Devlin raised his eyes to look at Mark Lewis, aware of the irony in his admission. 'Or *knew* until now. I'm looking at this painting and … it's like opening an old letter that I didn't know existed that he might have written to a close friend or a family member. And now I'm reading that letter – I'm learning something new about him, I can literally hear his voice telling me something … small, maybe … something about him that I never knew, that no-one ever knew.' He looked directly at Mark Lewis. 'I never knew anything about Katy.' And he began to weep again.

'I don't know what happened to Charlie or why you took on his work, James. I can see how sad you are, but right now, to be honest, knowing that I have reunited you with this painting, and with your brother … that makes me feel glad.'

'I realise that my world is about to … tumble around me,' said Devlin, 'but I am grateful that you did recognise this for what it is and have allowed me to see it.'

'James, you should know that I've been looking at all this with the help of a few other people. And they are due to meet me here very soon.'

'I know. The O'Beirnes are involved and your friend – Linda – and your daughter are also both wrapped up in this.' He felt another pang, looking at Lewis' swollen face. 'I am so sorry you've been hurt –' He checked his words mid-sentence to avoid overtly incriminating himself but felt he did not want to avoid the matter entirely. He had no idea what Mark Lewis intended to say or do about the gallery invasion or the assault.

'My chin is going to be OK,' said Mark. 'Nothing's broken and the swelling should go down over the next few days. Pat and the others will be here soon. I think we all have some questions. But I want to put a proposition to you. Can I tell you what I'm thinking now, before they all get here?'

'Please,' said Devlin.

'Charlie's body of work is truly wonderful and the recognition it is beginning to receive as well as the prices they are beginning to bring are well deserved. It really doesn't matter – well not to me, anyway – whether they are in your name or in his.'

Lewis turned to inspect Charlie's painting again and continued. 'My involvement in this was at the request of a true innocent, Katy's sister Jan. Don't get me wrong, Jan is a smart and delightful person. But it was my services that she engaged, and I feel a strong duty to her to act in her best interests. Likewise, in Pat and Helen's interests, as they also have an early Devlin.'

It felt odd to hear them called that, now that his subterfuge had been exposed.

'This has been deception on a grand scale, as I'm sure you know, James. But I think that exposing it right now will not only devalue Charlie's painting for Jan but will devalue every other painting attributed to you. Pat and Helen will lose, collectors and investors all around Australia will lose, major institutions will be embarrassed, the whole Australian art scene will be diminished. And – much, much worse – Charlie's talent will be irretrievably denied.'

A stillness had gathered inside the gallery, the two men oblivious to the day outside, pedestrians regularly passing the gallery on the footpath, the midmorning traffic in full sun on Beaufort Street.

'Here is what I propose,' said Mark. 'I'd like you to formally identify *Turmoil* as a legitimate work within James Devlin's oeuvre. If you agree, I'd like us all to place a current value on it, as if it had always been in your suite of works. That is what I will pay Jan Bilowski for the painting, which I will own. That way, Charlie's writing on the back of it will not be exposed, at least not for now.'

Devlin nodded, his mind whirring. 'I mean, yes, that's OK. That's incredibly generous of you. But, isn't that just kicking the same can down the road? And, even if you are comfortable maintaining the deception, how will the others feel about it? How will either of us know that they will keep this to themselves? It's not just you and me who know what has taken place.'

At that moment, Devlin was jolted by the sound of knocking on the front door of the gallery. A tall man holding a wrapped painting under his left arm was peering in at them. Lewis opened the door and accepted the painting as the man spoke.

'Nice to see you again, Mark. I've been asked to deliver this to you, and I'm assured that you'll understand what it is all about.'

Lewis stepped back with the painting, nodding slowly. Devlin caught the eye of the delivery man, who he knew would be Richard Barclay, suspecting that Barclay, in return, knew that he was James Devlin.

'Thank you,' said Lewis, 'I'm very happy to receive it. Mr Jones, isn't it?' Lewis took the painting from Barclay but made no move to open it.

'That's right, Mr Lewis, Robert Jones.' Barclay smiled broadly but offered no further explanation, just lifted a brief hand in farewell.

The silence inside the O'Beirnes' Mazda was icy as Pat pulled into a parking spot near Beaufort Gallery. Not for the first time, Helen and Pat did not see eye to eye about matters in the realm of art. In particular, Helen was in no mood to play nice with James Devlin. Where she was generous, excitable and passionate, Pat was measured, analytical and factual; where he was prone to pessimism coloured by fatalism, Helen was optimistic but uncompromisingly unforgiving. As Pat turned off the ignition, Helen broke the silence.

'I am prepared to hear what that man has to say about that painting. I am prepared to see what Mark wants to do about all this. I'll bite my tongue about Mark's plan, whatever it is. But I will not pretend that Devlin is some sort of saint when I now know for sure he is a fraud.' She was struggling to keep her rage under control, her voice trembling in the face of her disapproval. 'And *he* would lecture the rest of us about fakes? It's … disgraceful!'

Pat raised his eyes heavenward, grateful for Helen's fleeting concession. But he knew that she was right – as so often she had been over the years, about people and art alike – and he shared her distaste for the likes of James Devlin. Decades of disciplined professionalism and customer-focused advice, endeavouring to direct clients to the best works for their collections, trying to weed out dishonest and corrupt practitioners, yet being regarded as perennial 'amateurs' by so many collectors and dealers, had formed a deep vein of frustration running through their careers in art. And here they were about to meet the golden boy of the Australian art scene, artist turned gallerist, socialite and benefactor. A fraud of the first degree.

But they had both come to trust Mark Lewis, not only for his judgement about art, but for his generous nature, his preparedness to stick his neck out for others in need and his unerring faith in their own advice and judgement. If Mark was planning – somehow – not to expose James Devlin, they knew they owed it to him to hear what was being proposed.

They walked up Walcott Street and turned left into Beaufort, only just avoiding a collision with a tall man momentarily distracted by his mobile phone within metres of the front door. The man looked up and apologised, his involuntary flash of recognition returned only by Helen's searing gaze of displeasure. She caught Pat's eye and, with the thinnest smile, extended him her reassurance that she would behave. Pat smiled, equally faintly but no less sincerely, in appreciation.

❖❖❖

'Thanks for looking after this,' said Mark, holding up the wrapped Kemp. 'I love this painting and I'd have hated for it to have to be hidden away somewhere.'

The back door opened, and Olivia entered. Mark saw her taking in the scene; she marched towards her father and he made the introduction.

Devlin shook her hand firmly. 'I am pleased to meet you, Olivia.'

Olivia looked at him coolly but her tone was courteous. 'I am pleased to meet you, too.'

'As I told your father, I've learned quite a bit about you two over the last few weeks. I've already told him how grateful I am that you recognised this painting for what it is. And how moved I am that you regard it so highly.'

Now the front door of the gallery opened again and Helen and Pat entered. Mark spoke as they approached warily.

'Pat. You've met James Devlin before. And Helen, I'd like to introduce you to James. We've been admiring Charlie's painting together,' he added, in an effort to thaw the icy atmosphere that the O'Beirnes had brought with them. He wished Linda had been able to get away from work a little sooner, to be here to help ease them through.

But then James Devlin spoke. 'I'm delighted to meet you, Helen. You are well known in Melbourne for your knowledge and your honesty. And I personally hold you and Pat in high regard. When I first learned of Mark's interest in me and when I pieced together what was happening – and I mean no disrespect to Mark – I was confident that he was being advised by you. There are many people in the East who trust and respect what you do here in Perth.'

Mark smiled to himself. Helen and Pat hated the arrogance of those big city gallerists and collectors who dismissed their deep understanding and knowledge of the Australian art scene just because they weren't based on the east coast. He could see Olivia and the O'Beirnes struggling to balance their preconception of this man with the comments he had just made; and with the evident ease between him and Mark.

'Helen, what do you make of the painting?' Devlin added.

Helen looked discomfited. Was he referring to its provenance, its authorship or its appearance? 'Mark has already shown us the painting. Several times,' she said evasively.

Now Linda entered through the front door, bringing in a gust of warmth and good humour. Unexpectedly, Helen – perhaps more relieved than any of them at Linda's timely interruption – stepped towards Linda and gave her a hug. With a brief smile at Mark, Linda extended her hand to James Devlin. 'I'm Linda De Vries from the Ability Centre. It's James Devlin, I presume?'

James and Linda shook hands and exchanged brief and courteous greetings.

'James has just posed Helen a curly question, Linda,' said Mark. 'He asked her what she thought of Charlie's painting. But I think, James, that we all have a few questions for you first, if you don't mind. Can I bring out the table and some chairs so we can sit down, and I'll make us all some tea?'

'Let me do that, Dad. You stay here and conduct the inquisition.'

Pat gave a short bark of laughter.

'I love the painting,' Helen said suddenly, as if she was keen not to be seen to have resiled from Devlin's challenge. 'It is such a dark and unsettling picture.'

Mark loved the way Helen used that word – picture – to describe a painting. It recalled for him his first ever contact with Helen – the beginning of his journey into art as an investment and then art as the inspiration for a career.

'There are so many elements to it, competing for attention,' Helen said, 'but at the same time all brought together by the central aspect, that dark rectangle, that both joins and separates them.'

They all stood before the work together.

'There is earth, sky and outer space,' Helen said. 'There is turmoil, but there is peace as well.'

'What I find more surprising than anything else,' said Pat, 'is that it was painted by a teenager. Charlie was barely seventeen when he painted this work.'

Then they each took up a chair and sat forward, as James began, for the first time, to recount Charlie's story.

48. WEDNESDAY DECEMBER 11

It was well after lunchtime but Mark wasn't hungry. Linda had returned to work, Olivia had happily accepted the rest of the day off, and Devlin had returned to his hotel to catch the six thirty pm flight back to Melbourne. The O'Beirnes had stayed for a little longer than the others, just to check that Mark was OK.

It had been an emotional and confronting exchange with James Devlin, and indescribably sad. True to her word, Helen had remained firm with Devlin, holding him in a fierce stare as he swore to cease his manipulation of art prices and the people reporting on them. They had then unanimously resolved what should now take place and Mark was printing off some documents in anticipation of Jan Bilowski's arrival, which visit he had arranged only after James Devlin had departed the still-closed gallery.

Mark let her in as soon as she appeared. Mark saw her gaze drawn to Charlie's painting to Katy which was still displayed on the easel and in good light. He could not detect any particular reaction to the painting and noted again her dowdy attire, a short, brown, woollen jacket despite the warm weather and her beret; yet, he thought, she seemed remarkably cool and composed.

'Welcome, Jan, I'm really pleased that you were able to come in this afternoon. It's been a bit crazy around here this past week or so.'

Jan looked at Mark. 'Looks like you've been in the wars,' she said.

Mark had forgotten what his bruised and swollen face must look like. 'Oh yes. I should have warned you – I was attacked in the gallery last night but, amazingly, that has all helped to sort out this painting.' He knew that he shouldn't lie to Jan – and he suspected that she'd see straight through him anyway if he did.

'Before I explain what I would like to propose to you about this painting, I want to show you a painting from a recent exhibition in Melbourne.' Mark showed Jan a printout of *Paradise* which had recently set the record price paid for a work by James Devlin at the Sotheby's auction. 'I hope you can see that there is a strong resemblance between this painting and Charlie's.'

'I see the likeness. I wouldn't want that one in my house either.'

'This painting is bigger than Charlie's,' Mark said, 'which means that you'd expect it to be more expensive.'

'Really? That sounds too simple.'

Mark could still recall his own surprise, many years earlier, at finding out that the value of a painting was often connected to its size. He had found it easier to understand that works on paper, especially watercolours, might not be as valuable as those painted in more durable materials such as oil or acrylic, and on more sturdy surfaces such as canvas or wooden board, because the watercolours and the paper were inherently more fragile, more prone to deteriorate over time.

'I know what you're thinking, Jan, but size does matter. At the very least, if you consider the simple cost of materials – a bigger sheet of canvas and the expense of the oil or acrylic used to make the painting. More costly materials mean a more expensive painting.' Mark didn't sense any great conviction in Jan's nod and smile – he could tell that she just wanted him to get on with it.

'Anyway, someone paid around seventy-five thousand dollars at auction for this painting last month. If we do nothing more than halve the price for Charlie's painting, which is exactly half the size, the price of Charlie's would be somewhere in the vicinity of forty thousand dollars.'

Jan took off her beret, looking perplexed. 'But this is Charlie's painting. And the one from the auction is by that man Devlin. How can you use the price for that painting as a guide to Charlie's?'

Mark – together with Devlin – had thought long and hard how to broach this with Jan. 'Before I explain exactly how I've come to this proposal, I'm going to put the proposal to you first. I also want to tell you that my proposal has been developed with the advice of the very best people in art here in Perth, and with the advice and the approval of James Devlin himself. He was in the gallery this morning and he agrees one hundred percent with what I am about to propose.'

'I want to offer you fifty thousand dollars for this painting.'

'Fifty thousand dollars!' said Jan.

'You need to know that I will be buying it for myself, for my own collection, because it is a wonderful painting, and because the story that it tells – which I will explain to you shortly – is the saddest, most amazing story I've ever heard about any painting.'

She looked at him as if she was not really listening at all.

'I would understand if you were thinking that, maybe, I'm hoping you will be so surprised at this big offer that you will accept it straight away only to find out later the painting was worth even more and that you'd have been better off selling it at auction.'

'Well you're right about me being surprised. But I still don't understand. Fifty thousand is a fortune.'

'I truly believe it is a fair and accurate price for this painting. Although, to be honest, that value depends totally on how James Devlin and I manage the process of exposing the truth about Charlie. You see, what I told you on the phone on Monday was correct – Charlie was the person who painted all of Devlin's paintings. Charlie Templeman and James Devlin were brothers after all.'

Jan blinked but said nothing.

'Charlie loved painting but died young, and their father died soon after. After a few years, when he realised that Charlie's paintings might be received well in art circles, Devlin devised a plan to raise money – for him and his mother – by promoting himself as the artist. He doesn't deny that it was a grand deception, but at the time it allowed him to support himself and his mother, and he has always been proud of his brother's talent and gratified that others have agreed.

'If we were to try to sell this painting with Charlie as its artist, on its own, it would have little or no value. Exposing the truth about Charlie and about James Devlin right now would ruin Devlin's reputation, destroy his art gallery and wipe out the value of every work he ever claimed to paint. Including Charlie's painting.'

Jan pondered this proposal. 'Are you offering me fifty grand for Charlie's painting, or for a painting that you and Devlin might later say is one of Devlin's? I mean, it doesn't sound quite right.'

'You're absolutely right, Jan. I know it sounds as if I am trying to buy your silence so I can later sell the painting as a Devlin. What we know – what Devlin has openly admitted to me – is that all the paintings attributed to him were actually painted by his brother Charlie. So, this painting is and always will be by Charlie. But the challenge for me and for James Devlin is to find a way and a time to explain to the Australian art world how he came to claim credit for his brother's paintings, without creating a scandal that will cause untold damage, and from which no-one at all will benefit. For now, exposing James Devlin and all his paintings as fraudulent will harm Charlie's work.'

'So, will you be claiming Charlie's painting as a Devlin? And will that rebound on me somehow? I don't want to end up in trouble.'

'I understand. And I don't want you – or me or anyone – to end up in any trouble. For now, Jan, if you accept my offer, Charlie's painting will come to my home and be hung there. It will not be displayed in public and its story will not be repeated to anyone who doesn't already know it. It will only ever be exposed for what it is when Devlin has revealed his own story. And he and I have agreed how this will be done and when.'

'Which is how?'

'The only time it makes any sense to reveal the truth is after Devlin's death. He is going to prepare a detailed confession to be published after his death. I will help him craft that confession and my family will be aware so that, if I die before James Devlin, the confession will still proceed when *he* dies. In truth, since Devlin and I are about the same age, any benefit that follows from this plan will likely be for my family, not for me. And this plan means that it will be for future generations to decide whether Charlie's paintings are, after all, of any commercial value.'

'What if that plan doesn't work, Mark? You'll have lost fifty thousand dollars. If you ask me, you're taking a big risk.'

Mark knew that Jan was right – he had already had to work hard to convince Linda and Olivia, Helen and Pat of the merit of spending such a large sum on such an uncertain quantity. Devlin too. But all had agreed that this was the best route to pursue. How they would construct the necessary confession would be critical if there was to be any chance of redemption for any of the actors in this strange performance; success depended on his and Devlin's plan working. They had already begun the planning of what they hoped would be as much a celebration of Charlie's talent as a declaration of James' guilt.

'OK, Jan. You can leave it with me to try to sell in Charlie's name, if you prefer. In my opinion, it will attract very little at all. Or you can take it back home and hold on to it for later. Either approach will save me money right now.' Mark pressed his hands together and brought his fingertips to his lips and continued with added emphasis. 'You are my client and I want to do the right thing by you. I'm offering you full market value for a genuine Devlin, but you are free to wait and see whether there is another way you'd like to handle the matter. For what it is worth, the bill of sale will make it clear that this painting is by Charlie Templeman. If I am asked – and I hope I'm not – I will state confidently that it is by Charlie. I cannot claim that it is by Devlin. Even Devlin has agreed to verify, in time, that it is, like all of his works, by his late brother. But I will not be actively exposing the truth about Devlin right now. That admission will have to be made in due course.'

Jan stared blankly at Mark. He continued. 'But there is also an upside for me in buying it from you, Jan. If this plan works well, Devlin's paintings will become known as Charlie's. And Katy's painting will ultimately be the central work of Charlie's short and tragic career, something special among an already very special set of paintings. If we can do that, not only will Charlie's painting be unique and meaningful for me and my family, it will also become very valuable. It's just that it's very unlikely that it will be me who benefits directly. This will hopefully be a legacy for my children and grandchildren.'

There was silence in the gallery as they both dwelt upon the proposal. At length, Jan spoke: 'I suppose the deal also includes me saying nothing about Charlie or Devlin to anyone?'

'And no mention of the sale price, either,' said Mark. 'You will have to sign a confidentiality agreement that guarantees me that you will not.'

Jan nodded in acceptance.

'You know,' Mark said, 'I can survive losing my fifty thousand dollars. Although it is a lot of money for me too. But James Devlin would be destroyed if this story became public without him getting to tell it from the beginning.'

'Of course, I will accept your offer, Mark, and the conditions. It is a huge sum of money for me. And you needn't worry about confidentiality. Not for a minute. I'll sign whatever you want. But, can I ask what exactly happened with Charlie and James Devlin?'

Over tea, Mark recounted the full story to Jan, as Devlin had told him, save for the involvement of Garth Barrett which, he had promised James, he would not divulge. Only Mark's inner group would be party to knowledge of that association, for which assurance Devlin had readily agreed to suspend that and all other similar commercial arrangements. His days of manipulating the prices of art with the help of Garth Barrett and others would come to an end.

In her impassive way, Jan Bilowski listened to the account of Charlie's tragic life and that of the Templeman-Devlin family. When Mark had finished, Jan spoke. 'I don't think many people understand the impact having a disabled child has on their families.' She clasped her hands in her lap and continued. 'My own family suffered awfully. My parents were university educated but were never shown respect in this country. Their Polish accents always had them labelled as immigrants, as if they were second-class citizens. And when Katy was born, they had to come to grips with her disability and we all had to adjust our lives around her.' Tears welled in Jan's eyes. 'I grew up ashamed of my parents and my sister. But I was the one who had to look after Katy when Mum and Dad died. I could never leave Katy and I couldn't think about marriage or having my own family.' She shook her head. 'What James Devlin did was wrong. But I think maybe I can relate to what he went through, what he did for his mother. He has been a fraud, but he was also clever and courageous.'

It was close to five o'clock when Jan stood to go, returning her beret to her head.

'Thank you, Mark. I had no idea I would get you into all this when I brought Charlie's painting in here. You know that I am very happy to accept your proposal. But I want to thank you for more than just the money. I am so happy that you found that photo of Katy for me. You have treated me so nicely, from the beginning. Lots of people would not have bothered or might have tried to rip me off. I think you are a very good person.'

They finalised payment arrangements and bid each other farewell. The gallery was calm and quiet as Mark locked the front door behind Jan. For the first time, he left Charlie's painting in full view on its easel, absorbing once again its youthful turmoil, his spirit moved and lifted by the threads of love, family duty, tragedy and redemption playing out on its surface. Then he headed for the back door, set the alarm, exited and secured the lock. He couldn't wait to tell Linda how it had all turned out.

EPILOGUE

Epilogue from the biography of Charlie Templeman, *Masquerade. The complete works of Charles Kevin 'Charlie' Templeman* written by James Harold Devlin AM (published and released upon Devlin's death).

❖❖❖

This, then, is the true and complete record of my brother's brief life and prodigious talent. I openly admit that I engaged in a serious deception. I apologise without reservation to the many people – friends, colleagues and collectors alike – who I will have disappointed and whose attitude towards me will, I must accept, be impaired now that the detail of my actions is known. I apologise most especially for doing so posthumously, through this publication, and for that I beg particular forgiveness and understanding.

My motivation in assuming authorship of my brother's paintings was threefold. Firstly, my mother and I were struggling financially, and this venture seemed like a potential source of much needed revenue. Indeed, I have profited handsomely from this deception, although I believe that I have done my best to return the good fortune Charlie's paintings afforded me to others who have been less fortunate.

Secondly, I was at that time already convinced that I wanted to fashion a career in art, and – in my youth – confident enough to believe that I recognised the commercial appeal of Charlie's work and fearless enough to conduct this fraud in full public view. In part, I wanted to prove to myself and to my mother that I was both a good judge of art and a good judge of how things worked in the Australian art world. For what it is now worth, I believe that my subsequent success proved me correct on both of those counts.

In truth, despite my conceit, I never anticipated the rapturous extent of the response that Charlie's paintings – and I – went on to provoke. That much was not predictable. Such is the precarious nature of fate.

Much of the gain and the ongoing misrepresentation that followed this initial success proceeded at a pace and with such enticing personal benefit that I was, it seemed to me at that time, unable to bail out. I hope that people who are disappointed or upset by my deceit, or financially injured by any adverse price adjustment in the art market, will at least acknowledge that Charlie himself was never injured, diminished or denied by my actions.

In fact, my third motivation for initiating this protracted charade was to honour Charlie and his extraordinary talent. It was through living alongside him and in the presence of his paintings that art's grace and beauty were revealed to me, and the notion of a career revelling in that beauty was first conceived. My brief 'career' as an artist was a form of devotion to my gifted brother, and my much longer career as a gallerist was in large part homage to his skill – and to the skill of artists more widely.

My most impassioned request, then, is that Charlie be rightly acknowledged as the maker of all his paintings, and that Charlie's artistic genius be hailed by all those who are moved and inspired by abstract art. I was not the artist: that is now laid bare. It was my brother who painted these works but who, in despair, took his own life. He lost everything, yet I went on to triumph and fame.

I plead with everyone connected to or interested in art that Charlie's paintings are not diminished in stature as a result my dishonesty. It is within this plea that the explanation for the posthumous nature of my admission is contained. For it was not my lack of courage to face up to the truth, or to confront the art world's inevitable approbation, that accounts for the timing of this declaration. It was only that, had I admitted that truth while still alive, the public recrimination rightly directed at me would have obscured the much more important truth – that Charlie Templeman was a true master of Australian fine art.

In my absence, I sincerely hope that all due attention is directed towards Charlie. It is now, and was always, Charlie's legacy that most deserves recognition and celebration.

And it is to his genius, and with the most profound love, that this complete record of his works is dedicated.

ACKNOWLEDGEMENTS

It is one thing to concoct a story that might be of some interest to others. It turns out to be an altogether more complex task to then convey that in writing. Only through Georgia Richter's vision, patience and skill, has this story been crafted into a novel. I am both humbled and grateful beyond description for her guidance and her care. Many thanks, also, to the entire team at Fremantle Press whose combined talents and shared mission have been inspirational.

It became apparent to me very early on in the process of writing this book that I would not be able to progress without a concrete image of Charlie's painting, literally a hook upon which to hang a hat. Likewise, it was soon evident to me that the credibility of the story depended upon the existence of a whole series of Charlie's paintings to create a deeper sense of the artist's oeuvre.

I have long admired the work of Perth artist Teelah George. Her facility with pure abstraction and her distinctive and unique style made her my first choice for the task of producing Charlie's paintings. I provided Teelah with only the scantiest description of the book's storyline and of Charlie's specific circumstances, but she agreed to work on the project without hesitation. My only guidelines were that the works should be pure abstraction, and be painted in acrylic on masonite boards. The subsequent paintings proved both visually arresting and of great assistance in progressing the writing of the book; I am indebted to Teelah for her extraordinary creative talent.

Whereas the materials and dimensions of each of Charlie's paintings are accurately described in the book's text, their designated locations are entirely fictitious. Many – but not all – of the paintings, galleries and artists, newspapers and television stations, coffee shops and restaurants named in the manuscript are real but the events in which they feature are pure fiction. The specific descriptions of fraudulent activity related to works of art by Ray Crooke and John Passmore are fictitious. The Wynne Prize for 1985 was awarded to renowned Australian artist John Olsen. The characters of Charlie and Katy – and all the other characters in this book – are entirely fictitious. Any resemblance to real persons, living or dead, is coincidental.

Growing up in a household with paintings on the walls undoubtedly contributed to my lifelong fascination with and love of fine art. For this (and much more) I am indebted to my parents.

My first real introduction to the world of collecting fine art was through Patricia and Ian Flanagan of GFL Fine Art. Their encouragement, guidance, honesty and good company over more than twenty years have been every bit as enjoyable as the art they have shown me along the way and have been fundamental to my appreciation of art's 'grace and beauty'.

I am grateful to Jessica Bridgfoot, curator at the Bendigo Art Gallery, for providing me with details of its collection of 1980s paintings, and for (unwittingly or possibly telepathically) providing me with an unexpected display of some of their wonderful 1980s works when I visited Bendigo, incognito, to help me better describe Mark and Linda's visit to the gallery.

Many thanks also to Anne-Maree Sulley at the Sir David Brand School in Coolbinia, whose patient explanations helped me construct events surrounding Charlie's school experience.

Thanks to Ben for stoically driving me from inner Melbourne to Mount Martha so I could better appreciate James Devlin's journey; and to Carolyn, with much love, for allowing me the time to write, notwithstanding the fact that we were supposed to be on holiday or that there was plenty to be done around the house.

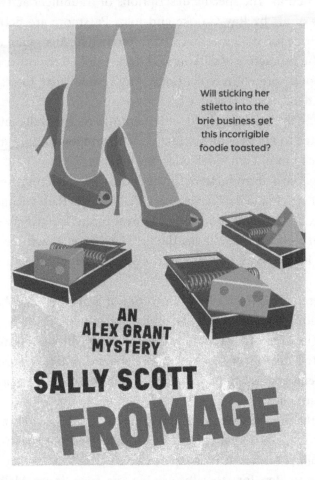

Will sticking her stiletto into the brie business get this incorrigible foodie toasted?

AN
ALEX GRANT
MYSTERY

SALLY SCOTT
FROMAGE

Journalist Alex Grant is enjoying the last days of her summer holiday in Croatia when she is accosted by an old school friend, Marie Puharich, and her odious brother, Brian, both there to attend the funeral of their fearsome grandfather's two loyal retainers. The only plus in the whole business is meeting Marco, the family's resident adonis. An incorrigible foodie, Alex is unable to resist visiting the Puharich creamery in Australia's south-west to snoop for stories and eat her body weight in brie. But trouble has a way of finding Alex. What begins as a country jaunt in search of a juicy story will end in death, disaster and the destruction of multiple pairs of shoes.

FROM WWW.FREMANTLEPRESS.COM.AU

'a brilliant new voice in Australian crime fiction'
DAVID WHISH-WILSON

Fifteen-year-old Darren Davies is found facedown in the Weymouth River with a gunshot wound to his chest. The killer is never found. Ten years later, his mother, Sandra, receives a visit from the local police. Sandra's best friend has been found dead on a remote Pilbara road, and Barbara's DNA is a match for the DNA found under Darren's fingernails. When the investigation into her son's murder is reopened, Sandra begins to question what she knew about her best friend. As she digs, she discovers that there are many secrets in her small town, and that her murdered son had secrets too.

First published 2022 by
FREMANTLE PRESS

Fremantle Press Inc. trading as Fremantle Press
25 Quarry Street, Fremantle WA 6160
(PO Box 158, North Fremantle WA 6159)
www.fremantlepress.com.au

Cover design Nada Backovic, www.nadabackovic.com
Cover image www.stocksy.com/192822/art
Printed by McPherson's Printing, Victoria, Australia

 A catalogue record for this
book is available from the
National Library of Australia

9781760991272 (paperback)
9781760991855 (ebook)

 Department of
Local Government, Sport
and Cultural Industries

Fremantle Press is supported by the State Government through the Department of
Local Government, Sport and Cultural Industries.

 MIX
Paper from
responsible sources
FSC® C001695

Fremantle Press respectfully acknowledges the Whadjuk people of the Noongar nation
as the traditional owners and custodians of the land where we work in Walyalup.